JAN 2015

EMERGENT

EMERGENT

RACHEL COHN

HYPERION
LOS ANGELES NEW YORK

First Edition
1 3 5 7 9 10 8 6 4 2
G475-5664-5-14196
Printed in the United States of America

This book is set in Adobe Caslon Pro.
Designed by Marci Senders

Library of Congress Cataloging-in-Publication Data
Cohn, Rachel.
Emergent / Rachel Cohn.
pages cm—(Beta series ; 2)
Summary: Elysia, has finally learned that she has a soul, and although she
knows it hurts Zhara, her First, that Alexander has chosen her as his life mate,
Elysia, cannot give him up and instead takes her place fighting by his side in the
revolution of clones and humans against Demesne's twisted regime.
ISBN 978-1-4231-5720-5 (hardback)
[1. Cloning—Fiction. 2. Family life—Fiction. 3. Love—Fiction.
4. Resorts—Fiction. 5. Islands—Fiction. 6. Science fiction.] I. Title.
PZ7.C6665Eme 2014
[Fic]—dc23   2014015069

Reinforced binding

Visit www.hyperionteens.com

SUSTAINABLE FORESTRY INITIATIVE Certified Sourcing
www.sfiprogram.org
SFI-00993

THIS LABEL APPLIES TO TEXT STOCK

For Emily (the Saint)

ZHARA
PROLOGUE

"DEATH PAR-TY! DEATH PAR-TY!"

We chant these words while drumming our fists on the sailboat's floor as we sunbathe on the deck, waiting for some weather to happen. I've known my fellow runaways for less than a day, but we're already tight enough to summon a suicide pact.

Reggie, Holly, and I are big fakes. Our death party is not really a suicide pact. It's a romp, a dare, the name we've given our adventure to reach the legendary Demesne—where only the dead are allowed entry without prior invitation, so they can be recycled into clone slaves. The richest people in the world, who own the hideaway of Demesne, restrict human access to their hallowed island to only their invited guests. Three runaway juvenile delinquents with a crazy dream to see Demesne would never reach that destination as invited guests. But we'll risk high seas and whatever else happens to try gaining access. Fun!

"Death par-ty!"

In Cerulea, where we come from, the sun and heat are relentless. The only interesting "weather" we get there is when yet another brush fire in the hills sends plumes of black smoke over our town, and our water supply is turned off for a day or two to redirect the scarce resource toward the fires. The fires happen so often, they're not even catastrophes. They're just more destruction—but less hardship, we're constantly reminded by our parents, than what their generation experienced.

As the sun blazes down from a cloudless blue sky over our idle spot, somewhere in the ocean within the Demesne archipelago, my fellow runaways and I chant, we taunt, we beg: *"Death par-ty!"*

We're baked, we're bored, and we're high on 'raxia.

"What'd you guys get sent to the camp for?" Reggie asks Holly and me. Recounting crimes and misdemeanors: always a great conversation starter.

"Vandalizing a desalinization plant," says Holly. "It was just some cool-looking graffiti. I still don't see what the big deal was. It's not like I blew the place up."

Reggie says, "Old people who grew up during the Water Wars get way too possessive and freaked out over their precious liquid resource."

"Their trauma," I sigh. "Get over it already."

Holly says, "I didn't realize the building was so high-security and whatever. It was ugly and sterile. I thought it needed some color. And some artfully painted penis clown faces."

Reggie busts out laughing. "That was you? I saw it from the other side of the fence as the security team was cleaning it up. Great work!"

"Thanks," Holly says. "Sadly, the judge didn't appreciate my creative vision. He sent me to the camp for rehabilitation. What about you guys?"

Reggie says, "I stole a dune rider and went joyriding."

"Big deal," Holly says, unimpressed.

Reggie adds, "I stole it off the grounds of the Base."

"Whoa," Holly and I both say.

"My dad's a drill sergeant on the Base," I say. *He cares way more about the Universal Military than he does about me,* I don't say. "You're lucky you only got sent to troubled-teen wilderness camp. It could have been prison."

"It should have been," says Reggie. "But my mom's a lieutenant colonel in the Uni-Mil. How'd ya think I got on the Base, anyway? She begged the judge for leniency. What was your crime, Zhara?"

"'Raxia addiction!" I say, and we all laugh. For the ancient Greeks, *ataraxia* was a word meaning sublime tranquility, freedom from stress and worry. 'Raxia is the modern word for the pill that provides that same feeling. Tingles of sweet, calm awesome.

My reply is funny, but also true. My dad's solution to dealing with a teenage daughter with a drug problem was to send her away rather than deal with her. He knew I couldn't resist the offer: either be kicked out of the house, or kick the habit at the wilderness camp. *It's near Demesne.* Dad knew if he dangled that word, I'd go without resistance. Even though the camp's island location was pretty far from the paradise island of Demesne, it was the closest I could probably ever hope to get.

When I was little, my mother used to put me to sleep with a lullaby she made up about Demesne.

> *I dream of Deh-mez-nay, the harsh world so far away.*
> *I dream of Deh-mez-nay, the heaven where Zhara and*
> *I will stay.*

Our home back then was strewn with pictures and paintings of Demesne: its violet sea, its emerald mountains, its luxury homes built for the richest people in the world. The images were so prominently displayed throughout the house, I think I was four before I realized we didn't actually live on Demesne. *Our starved world needs to be reminded of beauty,* Mom would say every time Dad protested a new Demesne-themed house decoration: violet-painted bedroom walls, fake palm trees in the living room, a secondhand oxygen machine to pump her tiny craft room with a knock-off version of the premium air experienced everywhere on the real island of Demesne. *Why shouldn't paradise be for everyone?* Mom always asked.

I guess Mom got tired of waiting for Dad to share her enthusiasm for escaping to paradise. Mom left us when I was eight and died a year later, but I never stopped hoping to get to Demesne, for her.

Only yesterday, I met Reggie and Holly for the first

time at camp orientation, and I invited them to run away with me. I suggested we steal a sailboat in the dead of night and set sail for Demesne. The 'raxia I had secreted away in my duffel bag was all the incentive they needed. We knew we'd never be allowed into Demesne even if by some miracle we did get there. But why not have fun trying to crash that island's exclusive rich-people party?

"Death party incoming!" Reggie exclaims with excitement.

"For serious," says Holly, pointing upward to the sky.

"Pretty!" I sigh.

The change in the sky is so sudden, it's like day has immediately turned to night. Gone are the cloudless blue sky and blazing sun, replaced by a dark gray sky peppered with billowing purple clouds swirled in magenta tones. None of the pictures I've seen do them justice. These clouds are the signature runoff from Demesne's protected sphere. The private island of the world's wealthiest people is bio-engineered for perfection, offering its residents supreme luxury and tranquility. The side effect is that the wider area of the Demesne archipelago is cursed with the accumulated bad weather that is diverted away from the exclusive island. The volatile weather systems that are pushed back from Demesne to keep it safe and serene bind together outside the island's "ring" to create monster storms that wreak havoc across the rest of the archipelago. The magical-looking toxic clouds are the picturesque bonus.

"Those clouds are freaking insane with the amazing," Holly whispers.

A light rain starts to shower our bodies, and it's weird—the rain is warm, and feels almost sweet, like drops of lavender candy.

"Best death party ever," I murmur, loving the rich purple-magenta swirls in the sky and the soothing, warm wetness on my skin. This is what toxic-magic rain feels like! Gorgeous.

Then the sea below us begins to angrily churn, quickly turning to a roar, and we fall silent. No more small talk. We're too stunned, and too baked, to react. We barely know how to sail a boat, much less in a storm. There's no time to panic, because immediately the wind picks up, and the rain turns to sharp hail that pellets our skin like knife blades. This is not nice rain anymore.

We scream, but there's no way for us to take cover. Within seconds, the boat lists so violently that we can barely hold on to the rails. A wave several stories tall approaches, raising the boat up like a roller coaster, then crashing it back down. The boat tilts over, throwing our bodies into the bitter, violent sea.

I see nothing but gray, churning ocean as I tumble below the surface, desperately trying to hold my breath in before my lungs rapidly fill with water. I need light from the surface to guide my way up, but there is none, probably because I don't deserve the help. I didn't earn it, as Dad used to remind me after failed dives. But not for nothing am I an Olympic-diving-training dropout; somehow, my body goes on autopilot, and I manage to swim up to the surface even without light to guide me. I grab on to the rope ladder at the side of the boat, gasping for air. I climb back onto the boat, hoping to find Reggie and Holly there. I see them in the water on the other side of the boat. The current thrashes them, and their arms flail as they try not to drown. I look around frantically for life vests. I see them on the other side of the boat and race across to grab them. Just as I toss the vests overboard to Reggie and Holly, another wave breaks across the boat.

This time, the water's assault is enough to kill me.

I don't know how I know, but I know.

I am dead.

Even in death, I feel cheated. Where's *my* freaking white light? My heartbeat has slowed to a near stop. I should be on my way to the sweet afterlife. But all I get is pitch-black darkness, an unending abyss I try to swim through, dive through, cajole into light, and beg for clarity.

This netherworld must be my punishment for the death party. It's my punishment for being such a terrible daughter. It's vengeance on the hellbeast—my dad's name for me, announcing his disappointment that my headstrong nature continually gets in the way of his hopes for me. I've shamed myself and shamed my father. I can never go home after what I've done. I've died—and taken two other runaways with me, at my invitation.

I've been sent neither to heaven or hell, but to limbo. It's some horrible halfway house of black space and blank space. I fight it. I can't help myself. I scream even though no one can hear me. I kick. I wail. I rage. Resisting being told what to do—*die, already*—is what I do best.

My mind feels awake, but I can't move, I can't *see*

anything, and I can barely breathe. I know my body lies on the soaked boat's deck, which I feel being pushed up and down by the rise and fall of the ocean. The movement is calmer now—the worst of the storm is over—but the dial-down of the storm's fury can't save me. I'm already dead, just like Reggie and Holly.

Aren't I?

I hear a loud, gruff male voice call out, "Yo, there's a body in the boat below! Looks like a real Tasty." I'm doubting this is God's voice announcing my passage through the pearly gates. I'm pretty sure S/He'd word it better.

Another voice, also male, says, "Two other bodies floating by, starboard side."

"Tasty?" asks the other man.

"Not Demesne-level aesthetic."

I'm dead, but flattered. *Tasty* is the slang term often used to describe Demesne "workers," because they're ridiculously good-looking. Demesne is serviced by clones replicated from recently deceased human bodies called Firsts. The Firsts are twentysomethings chosen specifically for their superior looks—hot bodies and gorgeous faces. Personality not required: the Firsts' souls are extracted so that the clones can be functioning workers on Demesne without the complications of human emotion. Rich people want their servants to have a pleasing aesthetic—and not be troubled with free will.

"Pulse?"

I feel a hand press a finger against my wrist. "Negative." It's the 'raxia, I realize. Before the storm hit, I took too much, then baked in the sun too long. That has to be what's caused my heart to seem like it's not beating. I've felt this before when taking too much 'raxia—the slowing down of the heart that's taken many 'raxia users to their premature deaths. But my heart has never slowed this much—never enough to be mistaken for dead.

"Bring this one on board, then. Didn't expect such a good haul today."

I'd always heard that the bodies of Demesne clones came from pirates who stormed and pillaged naval carriers that were repurposed into refugee camps after the Water Wars, but I assumed that was a myth. Now's a sucky time to find out the myth is true.

My body is completely numb, and my heart is only a faint whisper of a beat that only I can feel—and just barely. I can't move, I can't speak, I can't protest.

I hear Mom's voice in my head: *I dream of Deh mez nay.*

Guess I'll make it there after all, Mom. I just never thought it would be this way. As a First.

Please let me be all the way dead when it finally happens, when my soul is extracted and a clone is replicated from my body.

I'm sorry, Reggie. I'm sorry, Holly.

Xander, I'll never stop loving you.

I feel my body being hoisted through the air, and my mind goes empty, mercifully returned to darkness.

And then, like a sudden jolt of electricity, I wake up.

This time I can move. I touch my index fingers to my thumbs and stretch my toes long and wide. I can feel. This might be real. My eyes flutter open, and I can see! This *is* real.

I'M NOT DEAD!

I'm in a white room that looks like a medical laboratory.

I breathe in, tasting the air. Yes, I can actually *taste* it. The air tastes of honeysuckle and jasmine, of a sweetness so beautiful I am immediately soothed. I made it to Demesne!

I couldn't have been cloned. My soul is intact. I feel it now, raging in confusion and panic mixed with a sudden and profound sense of gratitude. Somehow, I cheated death. I make a silent vow: *If I have truly been given this gift, I will never, ever do 'raxia again. I will appreciate this second chance, and not screw it up this time.*

I bite down hard on my tongue, to make sure this is real, relieved and joyful when I taste blood. This isn't a dream. I really am alive.

So now what am I supposed to do?

I don't know where to go. I don't think I'm capable of even standing up yet.

Then I realize I'm not alone. A male figure stands over me, dressed in a white lab coat. I can tell he is a Demesne clone, for he's branded with a black rose aestheticized on his left temple. I've seen images of these couture clones in news stories—who hasn't?—but I've never seen a real one before. The human age of this guy's First would have probably been early twenties. He has olive-toned skin, jet-black hair, and a hard face softened by a Demesne clone's signature fuchsia eyes. He's very tall and obscenely buff, with a body that looks like a professional bodybuilder's—sturdy in its mass, yet strangely vulnerable.

"Who are you?" I ask him.

"I'm called the Mortician," he says. His face mimics the human expression *curious.* "And I just resurrected you."

PART ONE: HEATHEN

ZHARA

1

A FUNNEL OF ORANGE AND YELLOW FLAME clouds spins over the ocean in the distance, easily sending off enough heat to thaw the pink frost on the ledge of our tree house in the jungle, hundreds of yards away.

"Looking good," I tell Aidan, who stands next to me, his arm raised so that his hand points toward the funnel cloud.

"Getting stronger each time," says Aidan, his face set to *pleased*. He crooks his pinkie finger, which temporarily shines in blue light, powered by the customized weather chip beneath his skin. He beams a red current from his finger directly into the middle of the funnel cloud. Lightning cracks through the middle of it, which erupts into a final explosion. The cloud expires into gray and black smoke, and its debris falls down into the sea, extinguishing within seconds.

I would never admit it to Aidan, but his weather terror skills kind of turn me on.

But it's creepy to be hot for a clone. I need to be better than that. I can't let my libido be directed by some clone's weird abilities with weather.

Before I came to live on this feral island that the clones call Heathen, the only weather I'd experienced was the monotony of Cerulea, where there were long days of scorching heat followed by hot, dry nights filled with the smoke of distant fires. A simple white cloud in the sky was enough to cause excitement, but those clouds were anomalies. In the short time since I was expelled from Cerulea by my own father, I've witnessed amazing purple-magenta swirl clouds, pitch-black thunderclouds, and orange-red funnel clouds, just to name a few. I'm still getting used to the jungle weather that's mercilessly hot and humid one day, then brutally cold and icy the next. No big deal. Soon enough, Aidan will lead the escaped clones to Insurrection, and I'll be back on Demesne with them, where the weather is perfect and soothing all the time. Since I'm Aidan's favored companion, obviously that means I'll even become Queen of Demesne. Not bad for a penniless drill sergeant's runaway daughter from Cerulea.

I can be patient. Paradise will be mine, next time I get there.

"You've perfected the flame funnel," I praise Aidan. "It'll just be a short matter of time until you use it to bring the Insurrection back to Demesne, right?"

"Ideally," says Aidan. "We can't hide out here too much longer, playing such visible war games."

"Don't destroy all of Demesne," I request. "Leave the good parts. So we can have fun playing there."

Aidan is a clone with no understanding of the concept called "fun." He says, "Destruction is a certainty. Unless the humans surrender quickly."

I'll teach him about fun. I'll just miss our feral homestead a little bit once we abandon it to return to Demesne.

I've lost track of time since I've been camped out in the middle of nowhere with these escaped clones. On Demesne, their human owners called these clones Defects, because they dared to feel. They call themselves Emergents. It's been several months since I woke up on Demesne and was promptly escorted away to live with the Emergents. The only real clue to the length of my stay here is the length of my hair, now almost white-blond from the sun, the black and blue tips growing longer and more brittle with each passing day. Some of the Emergents were trained as expert beauty stylists back on Demesne, but I don't dare ask them to interrupt their warfare training on Heathen to give me a haircut or pluck my eyebrows. There will be plenty of time for beautifying after Insurrection comes. Then, luxury skills will be utilized for their own purposes, if the clones choose—and not for servitude, which they didn't choose.

My stomach grumbles and I wish one of the Emergents would bring lunch up to the unofficial office I share with Aidan. The weather fluctuates too wildly to live and sleep in this tree house, so Aidan and I use it as the ideal lookout and planning point for various training exercises across the island. I like the tree house because it allows some privacy away from the constant stream of activity in the Rave Caves, where the Emergents keep their quarters and I share a cave habitat with Aidan.

Typically for a clone, Aidan doesn't care much one way or the other about privacy; that's my human desire. Our tree house "office" hang-floats from a branch rising at least twice the height of a ten-meter Olympic diving platform. It's built to resemble birds' nests, with a pyramid roof woven with thorns and bamboo, over a base made of plumed reeds, moss, and twigs. Ten years of free-falling from platforms the height of a three-story building for sport more than prepared me for this altitude. I guess the draw of extreme heights is in my blood; I can't escape it. My bed back in Cerulea was a hammock attached to my bedroom ceiling. Dad thought the added height would prepare me better for high-diving. People pay millions of Uni-dollars for views like mine—green trees! blue ocean! endless sky!—but those people usually require indoor plumbing and entry via elevator or stairs instead of climbing a webbed rope, and more interior space. Who needs more space? I don't own anything, except myself. Belongings don't belong here.

A tree house has been a great place for a lost girl outlaw. I am a natural fit here, on this land born of disaster. I court disaster.

A few generations ago, an enormous volcano erupted beneath the ocean. After the chaos of that eruption, after the tsunamis and land quakes that devastated continents in its wake, only one in the archipelago of tropical islands in the volcano's perimeter was considered habitable by humans.

That island became Demesne, and within a decade it was the world's most exclusive real estate. The other islands in the archipelago, teeming with wild jungle and dangerous caves, were considered useless. Only the savage could survive on those other islands.

We are those savages: me, plus the small militia of Emergents. Here, time and space are meaningless. Only survival matters. And the war to come. Insurrection, the Emergents call it.

I tease Aidan. "Will you keep me as a trophy when Insurrection happens?"

"Yes," says Aidan, straight-faced. Clones have learned how to survive on this savage island, how to manipulate weather, how to think and even start to feel like humans. But they totally don't get sarcasm. The bottom of Aidan's mouth loops up into a half smile, but I know the sexy look is a mimicked flirtation. I'm essentially his consort here, but that means his companion and his assistant—nothing more. Luckily, it also means I'll be the one human he allows to survive and thrive on Demesne, once Insurrection happens.

The Emergents plan to eliminate the human population on Demesne—the beautiful paradise created with the clones' hard labor. They consider Demesne their native land, and they want it back. It's not even revenge they seek. Revenge will just be a bonus.

The Emergents on Heathen number about fifty. They've utilized the skills the humans gave them—engineering, architecture, cooking, construction, etc.—for themselves. They've built tree houses and labyrinth underground dwellings. They've created irrigation tunnels in the subterranean caves to supply drinking water and to fertilize their crops. The clones who formerly engineered the sublime atmosphere on Demesne now use their skills to control the environment around Heathen. They've created a weather force field, so that any unwanted planes or boats that try to reach Heathen quickly become enshrouded in sudden storms that cause them to crash and sink. Eventually, the Emergents' weather-force-field experiments will be used to take back Demesne—and to shut it off from the rest of the world, so it can be theirs and theirs alone.

Aidan turns around to look out over the treetops toward the middle of the island, where Emergent workers are cultivating the fields of produce and plants that support the island. "The field laborers are wrapping up the morning's chores," says Aidan. "Must be lunchtime. Your stomach is like a clock. Shall we go?"

I turn around, too, see the rows of bright red torchflowers, and remind myself that I am hungry for food, and not the empty kind of nourishing those flowers could potentially offer me. The cuvée seeds that 'raxia is made from come from those plants. I could have as much 'raxia as I want on Heathen. The bright red cuvée torchflowers are a constant reminder of my failures, but also of my willpower. If I were strung out on 'raxia, I would never survive here. One must be constantly alert and able to adapt on Heathen. Sheer willpower—the same willpower I could never conjure to reach the Olympic diving team—keeps me from indulging. I need to rebuild that willpower reserve. Heathen is my test.

It's not such a bad life, actually. I *have* a life. I try to remember that and appreciate it, always. Every breath is precious after you've died and not gone to heaven.

Reggie and Holly weren't so lucky. I try to remember that also. I might be stranded in the middle of nowhere, but at least I got a second chance. Will the guilt and grief of their loss ever go away?

"Let's go eat. Unless you want to do some 'raxia first," I jokingly say to Aidan.

"I don't," he says, taking my comment literally, as he always does. "Once was enough."

Like me, the Emergents experimented with 'raxia pills when they were clone workers on Demesne. In Cerulea, I used 'raxia to numb the pain of the guy who broke my heart. 'Raxia was my way to give up on living. For the Emergents, 'raxia was their way to come alive. For humans, 'raxia induces a sweet elation followed by a beautiful calm. (I try not to think of that beautiful calm so I don't miss it.) For clones, 'raxia unblocks the brain inhibitors that were supposed to make them emotionless worker bees. One hit of 'raxia was all it took, and the Demesne clones were instantly changed. Those who took it then dared to question their involuntary servitude. They discovered they were clever— by choice, not by design. Once these clones were labeled Defects on Demesne, they were returned to the laboratory to be expired. No refunds or exchanges on these purchases were given, but no worries, the Defects would be put out of commission—permanently. Or so the humans thought. The Mortician back in the lab was marking the Defects' cases as expired, but he was actually sending the very much alive Defects to Heathen, to start new lives as Emergents and to prepare for Insurrection.

"Let's eat," I tell Aidan. I walk over to the rope ladder that leads down to the ground, and Aidan extends his hand to help me hold steady as I step onto it for the climb down. His pinkie finger, flesh-colored once again, is still warm from the surge of electricity he sent to the flame cloud, sending my body a pleasant jolt, the kind I used to feel only when Xander was near me.

The same finger touch that Aidan, who was known as the Mortician on Demesne, once used to bring me back to life sometimes has the added effect of making me feel weak in the knees now.

"What happened?" I asked the clone called the Mortician.

His pinkie finger was blue, as if there was a light beneath the skin, but within seconds, his finger returned to flesh color.

The Mortician regarded his finger with surprise. "It was just an experiment. I didn't think it would actually work."

"I wasn't all the way dead," I whispered. "I did too much 'raxia. I think that's what made it seem like my heart stopped beating."

"Maybe that's why it worked."

"What worked?"

His face turned to concerned. "The electric current in my finger. There's no time to explain. If the chip beneath my finger works, I won't be able to conceal the blue light from the humans. I'll have to join the others ahead of schedule. Like, now."

I had no idea what he was talking about and didn't care.

There was only one important question I wanted answered. "Was I cloned?"

It wasn't the time to be boastful, but I knew I had the right aesthetic for Demesne's couture clone class. As an athlete, I had narrow hips rounding out a tiny waist, with long, muscled legs, and perfect breasts. My sunflower-blond hair, tipped in blue and black at the ends, fell in waves past my shoulders and had been the envy of the other girls at school, along with my peach-toned skin and smooth, acne-free face. I knew I had the desirable aesthetic, because I could see the Mortician blatantly admiring it as I lay naked beneath a white sheet on the metal slab table.

He said, "Dr. Lusardi tried to clone you. It didn't work. You must be a teenager."

Usually, adults say the word teenager *likes it's an accusation, but the Mortician said it as an observation, perhaps because his human age didn't appear to be that much past teenage years himself.*

"I'm almost seventeen," I said, realizing the gift the Mortician had just given me: I'd reach my next birthday, probably.

"Dr. Lusardi hasn't mastered replicating teenagers yet," he said. "Your clone was a Fail."

"Good," I said, almost as relieved by that as I was just to be alive again.

Before I could ask him What next? *the Mortician lifted me from the table and into his strong arms, making sure to wrap the sheet tightly to cover my body. I felt protected. I breathed in the succulent air again. I wanted more of it. "Where will you take me?" I asked him. I didn't want to leave Demesne—I'd only just gotten there. But I knew the only way I could stay was if I voluntarily decided to die for real.*

The Mortician said, "There's a hidden beach in the coves nearby. Pirates who deliver bodies take shelter from outer ring storms there, and sometimes help those of us seeking Insurrection to escape."

Insurr-WHAT? Was he programmed to speak Nonsense? I had no idea what he was talking about besides the word "pirates."

I said, "Pirates sold our bodies here. They won't help us escape!"

"They will in exchange for the cuvée torchflower seeds that the escaped clones give them to sell on the open market back on the Mainland."

"So, the pirates make money delivering First bodies, then again by helping the cloned bodies escape? That's crazy. I refuse to go. I won't—"

The Mortician cut me off. "You have no choice." He walked toward a window that looked out to a mass of jungle. I peeked at the ground beneath the tangle of trees and saw that wherever we were, we were several stories in the air.

The Mortician looked like he was about to jump out of the window while holding me. So I was going to wake up from death just to commit double suicide with this cloned muscle man? Not so fast, pal. I started to kick free, but the Mortician was quicker than me, and in a flash, he grabbed a syringe from an exam table next to the window. He plunged it into my arm.

When I woke up, I was on Heathen.

2

I WAS NEVER VERY GOOD AT SCHOOL, EXCEPT IN history, which Dad relentlessly drilled me in, but in human behavior class I learned about the syndrome I probably have now, when prisoners or hostages start to sympathize with their captors. I'm not exactly a prisoner or hostage here, but I was brought here when a syringe into my arm knocked me out and eliminated my ability to make the choice to come to Heathen. Law enforcement officials would term that kidnapping.

Still, I stay. I've gotten used to it here. Plus, I have nowhere else to go—at least, nowhere better, besides Demesne, which is the ultimate better. I ache to go back to Demesne, but next time as a winner, with the Emergents. The rich people on Demesne claim their couture clones were created to be servants, but that's just a polite word for "slaves." I never cared much about clones' rights before—the clones I saw back on the Mainland were manufactured in labs and seemed like generic drones—but these Emergent clones were copied from actual people who lost their lives way too young. They look like people I knew. They look like me: real. It's hard not to feel like these duplicates deserve a better second chance than their Firsts' premature fates.

On a weirder level, I might also stay on Heathen because my personal captor is not at all hard to look at. At first glance, he appears threatening, but Aidan's stern jaw-line and buff muscles are softened by the black rose branded into his temple and the sweetness of his fuchsia eyes rising above his full, ruby-colored lips.

The Mortician on Demesne evolved instantly into a natural leader on Heathen. And I like power.

I follow Aidan back to the Rave Caves for lunch, feeling content to serve in his small militia. I also can't stop admiring the movement of his tight glutes, or imagine what it would feel like to trace my hand up the line of his olive-skinned spine, stopping to pull down at the black hair at the nape of his neck so I could kiss it like I'm a vampire. I almost let out a laugh, thinking how lucky it is that clones aren't able to procreate, because I'm trying to imagine explaining to our kids how Mommy met Daddy.

Aidan and I reach the mess hall inside the Rave Caves, where the kitchen team has laid out today's lunch: wild turkey gizzards cooked in mango juice, with chard greens stir-fried in garlic. I want to complain—*Gizzards, again?*

Healthy green vegetables, do we have to? But any lunch here is still better than the meals served at my school in Cerulea—that is, no meals at all. School lunch in Cerulea was strictly BYO, which meant students ate whatever left-over scraps the Base donated to Uni-Mil members from its own cafeterias, or whatever brittle fruits the parched trees in our family gardens cared to let loose. Any meal on Heathen is an improvement. The fact that there's even juice to sauce the meat, or chopped garlic in the greens, is a hopeful sign for the Emergents, who emerged without taste buds—or so they were told. Their sense of taste is still new to them, unlocked by the 'raxia that once turned them into Defects.

It's like the sea parts as Aidan and I walk through the dining area, bringing our lunch to the communal table. Two Emergents immediately vacate their seats at the head of the table in deference to the island's unofficial king and queen. I like this deference. I like these Emergents. They're way cooler than the cheerlords at school I associated with back in Cerulea—"friends" who didn't like each other, and especially didn't like me because I was "too pretty" and therefore "distracting." I didn't care much about hav-ing friends then—I was so fixated on Xander that I didn't bother much with social politics. Maybe that's what death cured me of—being disaffected. I care now that these Emergents, while not necessarily being my friends, at least appreciate my company.

Generally, the Emergents don't like humans—but they don't consider me human in the same threatening way as their former owners on Demesne. I'm a teenager, powerless—and allied with the most powerful Emergent on Heathen. His consort—but the celibate kind. So far.

Aidan and I take our seats at the head of the table, and as always, the Emergents begin peppering me with questions about the outside world. They never bother with small talk, and I for one am glad that was never part of their programming. I like people who get directly to a point. I'm the only source of education about the outside world that the Emergents have. They were born, or "emerged" as the clones say, as fully grown adult clones in a laboratory on Demesne. Their primary sources of information are data chips implanted in their heads, which contain only the data the humans thought the clones needed to know—the data useful only to the clones' service to humans.

Next to us sits Catra, an Emergent who was a chef back on Demesne but now has discovered her real niche: storyteller. She seeks to document the Emergents and their struggle. To that end, she constantly pumps me for information not contained on her knowledge chip. As usual, she dives right in. "If there were so many lab-grown clones already available in the world, why did the property owners on Demesne have their own line of clones, made from Firsts?"

I answer, "My dad always said Demesne clones were different because rich people are so vain. They always want something new, different, so they can always feel superior. Regular clones all look the same, genderless—like an average twenty-five-year-old she-male. The rich people wanted a superior aesthetic to accentuate their little paradise. And also they thought they were being eco, recycling dead people."

Until they met me, the Emergents didn't even know they were a rare strain of clones. Regular clones back in the world are grown in labs from cryogenic embryos. They're not replicated from Firsts, who each have distinctive appearances. Regular clones were designed to be functional but aesthetically boring, except for the blue-green mosaic skin patterns that distinguish them from humans. They were created to help end the war. I never paid attention to clone history at school, but at home, Dad drilled me on the subject any chance he got. He said I could never have a future until I understood the past. As if my long, exhausting days that started with early mornings of swimming followed by boring school and then hours of diving training weren't enough, Dad capped off my nights by quizzing me on history. Funnily enough, History was the only class I ever aced in school. At least there was one payoff to my nightly dinnertime torture ritual, courtesy of Dad.

Why do we have clones, Zhara?

Here's why, Dad: Climate change and global austerity measures sent the world into chaos. Rising sea levels caused major cities to sink, and prolonged drought severely drained water supplies. Fossil fuels became extinct. Modes of transportation suffered, severely disrupting the distribution of utilities, particularly water. This caused massive political and civil strife around the world. Billions of people died. Major cities were ruined by environmental and political destruction.

The chaotic era termed the Water Wars ended as environmental engineers devised ways to create energy and resources within the changed world. Some of the old cities were rebuilt on smaller scales, and new cities, like Biome City, were built on previously uninhabitable desert terrain. These new cities were built using cloud technology to modulate weather systems and bring rain.

How come we don't have these cloud technologies in Cerulea, Zhara?

Because Cerulea's primary employer, the Uni-Mil, prefers the harsh climate for training exercises at the Base, Dad. The Uni-Mil built an aquatics club in our town instead of letting us have rain. Yes, I know, Dad, the rest of the world gets the cool weather—but we got the only nice pool in the region, and because of the Uni-Mil's generosity, I get to train to maybe one day dive in the Olympics, the human race's one consistent connection to its ancient history. Whatever.

Having mastered how to modulate weather systems so that humankind could survive on Earth's revised terrain, the humans next manufactured clones to usher in the post–Water Wars age, a time of hope and growth that—yes, Dad, I get it—my spoiled generation is too lazy to appreciate. We don't know the suffering that came before. We grew up with clones to do our work. Clones were the primary labor force for reconstruction after the Water Wars.

"So we are a superior caste of clone?" Catra asks. She doesn't sound vain—just curious.

"That's a matter of opinion, not fact. Certainly you all

are better-looking," I acknowledge. "And way more feisty."

There are so many questions I, in turn, want to ask the Emergents. Aidan was confined to the laboratory compound on Demesne and didn't see anything else of the island paradise, so he's useless—and completely lacks enthusiasm—when it comes to learning about how the rich people live on Demesne. But oh, how I want to know. *Tell me about the luxury on Demesne! Tell me about the decadent meals, the amazing homes, the soothing sea, everything taken care of by an elite cadre of servants, and . . .* Yeah, maybe these queries are not so appropriate questions to ask of liberated slaves.

A female Emergent who acts as one of the messengers from the mountaintop base the Emergents built on the tallest tip of the island arrives in the mess hall, looking for Aidan. She runs to Aidan's side. "We've received a communication from M-X. The Uni-Mil soldier has been located."

Aidan stands up to leave. "This is the sign we've been waiting for."

"Will Insurrection be soon?" Catra asks, stabbing at the gizzard on her plate with a knife.

"I hope so," says Aidan.

"Should I come with?" I ask him.

We both know he doesn't need me. We both know he wants my companionship any time I offer it.

"Your choice," says Aidan.

I stand up. "Let's go. What's the mission?"

"Race me to find out."

* * *

When I run, there is no one on this island faster than me.

Aidan and I race through the jungle, then past the fields of cuvées, beacons that impel me to run even faster, reminding me: I must be stronger. To run wild—fast, hard, strong—is to be reminded of the privilege of being alive. When I was strung out on 'raxia, I could not run. I was listless, mute, bored. I'll never allow myself to be that person again. I'll never let my 'raxia problem cause someone else's death. Deaths, plural. Never again.

Aidan tries to keep up with me, but the bulk of all his muscles works against him. He's fast, but I'm more agile. I'm only five or six paces ahead of him, but I relish even that short distance.

I love being chased.

In my previous life, so centered on water sports, I used to let Xander chase me in the pool until I caught him. There's no race I can't win when there's a hot guy in the game with me. But in my need for speed, I don't notice the fallen tree branch in my path. I trip, and fall—hard—to the ground. Aidan doesn't proceed with the race as Xander would have, whose genetic imperative was to win any physical challenge, at any cost. Aidan stops and stands over me. "Are you all right?"

"Fine," I grunt. I'll have a big bruise. Not a big deal. "Give me a second and I'll get up. That was a hard hit."

"You should return to the Rave Caves. You don't need to be part of this mission."

"I'll at least go as far as the training camp with you. I'll rest in the tree house after. So what is the mission?"

"We were led to believe a sympathizer from within the Uni-Mil would be coming to assist us. I'm going to round up some of the Emergents to retrieve him with me."

"Why are you so sure the sympathizer is a he? Maybe it's me. A she."

Aidan extends his hand to me. I grab on to it and he pulls me up so I stand next to him, almost pressing against him. I look up into his fuchsia eyes, so pretty next to the black rose aestheticized at his temple. I avert my eyes from the fleur-de-lis burned into the temple on the other side of his face, the symbol of a Demesne clone's servitude.

The knee I just slammed into the ground hurts like hell, but my heart feels like it's swelling in another kind of hurt from Aidan's nearness. The hurt of wanting. Longing, I think it's called. I remember this knot in my heart so well, too well. It's what I felt whenever Xander was near.

"You were in the Uni-Mil?" Aidan asks me. I almost think there's a glint of *flirtation* in his fuchsia eyes.

It's so long—close to a year, maybe—since Xander. I want to kiss a guy again. Hold and be held. So much has happened since, but I'll remember how to do it. Surely kissing a clone is the same as kissing a regular guy. Oh, wait. I've never kissed a regular guy. Xander was the only guy I've ever been with, and he was a superhuman. Literally. He was an Aquine, genetically engineered for perfection. Xander's unseen strings of master DNA manifested in physical form through his intoxicating height, sandy blond hair layered by the sun with streaks of white gold, a rock-hard body, and turquoise eyes so deep and pure it was hard to believe they belonged to a mortal man. He was like the living definition of the word *swoon*.

But I've died and been resurrected since Xander. I've developed whole new skill sets since then. If I can nab an Aquine, how hard could it be to seduce a freaking clone? Tonight, I decide, after Aidan's mission—tonight is the night I get back into action. Indoor-sport variety.

"Race you to the training ground," I say to Aidan and take off, forgetting all about my bruised knee and wounded heart.

The Emergents' war games are being played in a swamp. Alerted to their location by the sounds of their grunts, Aidan and I find the group of male Emergents covered in mud. They are former construction workers from Demesne, a group of large, imposing men who speak little and fight hard in training. It's like they live for combat and nothing else. As four men crawl through the swamp, they hoist the body of the fifth member of their mock infantry unit on their shoulders. Their mission: to practice removing a dead or wounded soldier from the battlefield.

I seriously doubt that if an Insurrection happens on the paradise of Demesne—so tranquil it doesn't even have its own security forces—it would require swamp combat. But these Emergents like to play their games. All they knew on Demesne was the discipline of work, so it's natural that now that their time is their own, they should transfer that programmed work ethic from construction to sport.

If my drill instructor father were here, he'd throw an

obstacle into the soldiers' path, to make them fall out of formation and drop their uplifted soldier. The distraction would create chaos, forcing them to foster teamwork, to reassemble and solve the problem. Dad used those same obstacle tricks during my diving training. But the sound of an empty-shelled gun blast did not actually train me to keep my composure during a dive; it taught me to lose it, to never trust—myself, or him.

Aidan pulls aside Cesar, the drill leader. "The Uni-Mil officer we've been waiting for is on Mine."

Mine is an island further down the archipelago. An Emergent who is a healer lives there, alone. In exchange for having the island all to herself, she provides care to escaped clones. On the condition that they leave as soon as they are healed.

"What's the plan?" asks Cesar.

Aidan says, "We'll take a boat there to retrieve the officer. All I know about him is that he was serving on Demesne as the Uni-Mil's representative to the Replicant Rights Commission."

Cesar says, "*He's* helping us? I met him on Demesne. He came to interview us about our working conditions. What was his name . . . Blackburn, I think? Alexander Blackburn?"

WHAT?

"I'm coming with," I inform Aidan and Cesar.

One thing I learned from Dad: when you want a mission, truly want it, don't ask permission.

Just go.

Alexander Blackburn—Xander—is the man who broke my heart back in Cerulea. *How the hell did he get to this god-forsaken corner of the world?*

There can only be one reason.

Xander must have realized the huge mistake he made.

Xander's come for me!

3

WHAT'S PAST IS PAST, RIGHT?

Wrong.

My pounding, nervous heart lets me know: I cannot forget the past. I can't forgive it, either.

This always happens to me. I think I want an epic dare, and then I do it and immediately regret the choice.

Why did I have to volunteer for this retrieval mission?

I should have waited on Heathen for Xander, given myself some time to prepare for seeing him again.

"You're very quiet," Aidan says.

"Seasickness," I lie. *Heartsickness.* "How much farther?"

"The wind is good," says Cesar. "We should sight M-X's island soon."

I forgot, spending my days in the jungle and my nights in caves, how open the ocean looks and feels. There's nothing and no one else to be seen, for miles and miles. It's exhilarating and horrifying. Too much possibility. I know what this ocean can do to stranded travelers, to fools. I know how it can turn on you. *I'm so sorry, Reggie and Holly. Will the sadness and terror I feel every time I remember you ever go away?*

In the distance, an island comes into view, a small landmass swathed in a forest of trees, giving me an idea of how secluded and remote Heathen must appear from the outside. A speck on a map that no one back in the world cares about.

As our boat approaches the small island, we see a lone figure waving to us from the shore. "There's M-X," says Aidan.

"What's her story?" I ask, desperate for distraction.

Aidan answers, "She was a Demesne clone who had gifts for healing. She was labeled a Defect and subjected to torture instead of expiration. She escaped and chose to remain here. Mine is hers, alone. Her choice."

"She tended the Uni-Mil officer?" asks Cesar.

"I assume," says Aidan.

"What happened to him?" I ask. "Was he hurt?" My journey to this reunion—from wilderness camp to the death party, from Demesne to Heathen—has been *insane*. I can only imagine what could have happened to Xander to land him here, now. He's been aiding and abetting the clones? He deserted the Uni-Mil? What the hell?

I send a wish across the water: *Please let Xander be okay.*

Aidan asks, "I don't know. Why? Were you hoping the human would rescue you from Heathen?" He raises a black eyebrow at me.

"I don't need rescuing," I say.

"Of course you do," says Aidan. His fuchsia eyes assess my frown and he adds, "Not because you can't care take of yourself. But because when you are wild and impetuous, you allow yourself to end up dead."

We never land on Mine. From the shore as we approach, the woman called M-X shouts to us, "They're on the atoll on the other side of this island. You can find them there."

"They?" Cesar says to Aidan. My question exactly.

Aidan shrugs. "Maybe the officer has more escaped clones with him. We'll find out when we retrieve him. We don't have enough daylight hours left to ask M-X more questions now."

To M-X, Cesar calls back, "We'll go there now. Are you in need of supplies?"

"I'm in need of not being bothered unless necessary," M-X calls back. She turns around and walks away, quickly disappearing into the thicket of trees behind the shore.

It's another half hour sail to the atoll island on the other side of Mine. We know we've reached the right place when we see a canoe berthed on the shoreline of a perfect little microparadise of a tropical island: pristine white sand, swaying palm trees in the distance, smooth and relaxing waters.

I feel immediately relieved. Xander's not wounded. He came here to swim! I know it. The place is too perfect for him to resist.

My hurting heart feels suddenly brighter, happier, pounding with excitement. I hate him, but I'll never stop loving him, and now he's here. After all I've been through.

After all he's been through. We have so much to discuss, to figure out. Our lives are completely different from the last time we saw each other, but surely our hearts are the same: joined.

I can't believe I ever entertained the idea of seducing a clone tonight, when my superhuman is about to be returned to me today.

The sailboat approaches the atoll shore and I can't even wait for Aidan and Cesar to pull the boat onto the sand. XANDER! I SEE HIM! This is not a dream! He's emerging through the trees, lean and gorgeous, just as I knew he would be. I could not miss that tall, beautiful, genetically perfect man anywhere. I leap out of the boat into the shallow water and run as if my life depended on it, run toward the man who took my heart away once but now is going to give me my heart—and life—back.

"Xander!" I call out.

Wait.

What?

I'm too late. He's found someone else. He's holding the hand of another girl.

I run until I meet them at the shore, and then I stop, dead cold, in front of Xander and the girl.

I stare at her.

The girl is me.

The girl whose hand Xander is holding is my clone.

4

I HAVE TO KILL HER.

That's my first thought. She's *exactly* me, only not me. A fake, an imposter. An outrage I want to see destroyed, *immediately*.

By the symbols aestheticized on her face—a violet fleur-de-lis on her right temple and a plumed, purple-blue flower vined onto the left side of her face—she's clearly a Demesne-brand clone. My human emotion right now, boiling in every cell of my still very much alive soul:

RAGE.

MURDEROUS RAGE.

I didn't die! The 'raxia-induced death party caused my heart to stop, but I woke up! My body was retrieved by pirates and sold as a First, but the attempt to clone me on

Demesne failed because I'm a teenager and they don't make teen clones. Aidan told me so!

So why is my clone standing right here? Her fuchsia eyes—the primary physical distinction between a First and a clone—reflect the anguish I feel. Shock. Confusion.

"Zhara!" Xander exclaims. He drops the girl's hand and stares at me, equally joyful and horrified. "You're alive! How is this even possible?" He tries to pull me to him, to hug me, I think, but I recoil from his touch.

I'm not sure whom I want to kill more—him or her.

I can't even say anything to him, I'm so stunned by the sight of her. My clone has nothing to say, either. The sight of me must be equally as shocking.

"You look so different, Zhara," says Xander. "What happened? Are you all right?"

I barely hear him because I can't stop staring at her. The worst part of my clone's face? It's so pretty, so soft in comparison to the horror show I know I must look like by now. Since the last time I've seen Xander, I've been to hell and back. We made love and then he left me, and I retaliated by becoming a hellbeast to everyone except the one who'd hurt me and gone away. I failed at Olympic trials, got kicked off the cheerlords, and then my own father sent me away when my 'raxia problem got out of hand. I had a death party, was resurrected, and escaped a mad scientist's compound, taking refuge with escaped clones on an island so feral even the outlaws call it Heathen.

Sorry if I look like crap now. *Different.* I've been busy.

I've had no mirror to see myself, but I can feel the

leatheriness of my overexposed skin and the brittleness of my overgrown hair, matted and wild from sun and wind. I must look more like a monster than a seventeen-year-old girl by now. Hey! I had a birthday sometime in the last few months. Did anyone back in Cerulea even celebrate? Remember me?

The instinct to murder my clone, who looks so much sweeter and more innocent than I could ever be, temporarily fades as a bizarre thought occurs: *My clone and I could make the freakiest synchronized diving pair ever. At last, the gold could be mine.*

A sense of appropriateness at times of crisis has never been my strength.

What is the appropriate thing to say to the worst nightmare you didn't even know you had?

Hi. You seem prettier than me. I hate you already.

You cut my hair. I never thought I'd look good with short hair, but your little pixie-punk style actually looks good on my face.

(Yeah, I get it. This situation is literally life and death, and I should be thinking about other things besides my hair right now. I can't help myself. Good hair is so important, and I've let mine become an entangled monster.)

Really, the shock is too great. There's nothing to say to her. So that's what I say, my mouth agape, my jaw clenched into stunned submission, my heart pounding in horror. I say nothing.

Instead, I run.

* * *

I run down the beach and into the trees, past a sapphire-blue lagoon lodged in the middle of this island atoll. My clone just came from swimming in this lagoon with him. I know it; I *feel* it. The lagoon looks like a perfect little paradise and I hate her for sharing it with him. It should have been *me* there with him.

I run and run until my breath finally gives out and I slump down under the shade of a palm tree. I am: Exhausted. Confused. Horrified. My heart might give out right now and I wouldn't begrudge it doing so.

I wish I could die.

But I already have.

All death got me the first time was a clone who stole the man who stole my heart.

Xander follows me to my resting spot in the palm-tree shade. At least he has the decency not to bring her along.

So much has happened since the last time I saw Xander. There's too much to say to him. The best that comes out of my mouth is, "What's her name?"

"Elysia." Hearing Xander's familiar gravelly voice, I want to die again, but this time from unbearable pain in my heart—beating too hard for someone I loved, and who loved me back, just not enough.

Faithfulness is supposed to be Xander's genetic imperative. He's an Aquine. When they mate, it's supposed to be for life. I counted on that when I gave myself to him—mind, body, and soul. Even more than Aquines value their superior looks and bodies, they value loyalty. They have a divorce rate of zero, because they cultivate their people to choose forever mates over casual dalliances. Why was I the exception? Or is his relationship with Elysia a really sick extension of the "loyalty" he was supposed to feel exclusively for me?

Elysia. Even her name is better than mine.

I can't look at him. Sitting beneath the tree, I cover my head with my arms. I don't want him to see me, either. I don't want him to know I'm crying, even though I can't stop the shake of my body or the sound of sobs coming from my mouth. I won't share the sight of my tears.

"Zhara." He says my name gently. Xander places his hand on my back to comfort me, but his touch feels like poison. I flinch, and he removes his hand. "I thought you were dead. Then I discovered Elysia on Demesne, and I realized the mistake I'd made when things ended between us. I still had the same feelings for you—and they transferred to her. She was like a second chance with you." His voice is filled with pain and compassion, and not the mimicked kind I've gotten used to from clones. It's real.

My sobs abate, but not my fury. "You've got a strange way of acting out your grief. Did anyone even come looking for me?"

"I was training on the Base at the time, not allowed contact with the outside world. Your father sent a search party after your disappearance. I offered to go, but he wouldn't allow it. You were presumed dead. Your father was devastated. *I* was devastated."

I'm too dumbfounded to speak. Gently, Xander says, "The bodies of your two friends washed ashore. I'm so sorry. Did you know they died?"

"Of course I knew that. And they weren't my friends," I snap. Why am I being mean even to the dead now? What's *wrong* with me? "I disappeared so close to Demesne. Didn't anyone even worry that I'd been cloned if they never found a body?"

"The pirates who harvest Firsts could have taken the other two bodies to Dr. Lusardi, but they didn't, so no one made that assumption about you. The investigators assumed you drowned."

"But pirates *did* find my body. They sold it to Dr. Lusardi's laboratory on Demesne. Only I wasn't dead. I woke up."

"Indeed. I can see that you're very much alive."

"Why did no one search for me on Demesne?"

"Come on, Z. You know that practically nobody can get on that island except the people who own property there. And nobody thought Dr. Lusardi was working on teenagers. She publicly stated before the Replicant Rights Commission that she'd never attempt to clone teenagers, because their hormones would screw up her science. She said it was impossible to transition teen clones to adulthood so they were therefore invalid as subjects for her work. I know. I had to study all her statements before I took the Uni-Mil assignment on Demesne."

"Guess Dr. Lusardi lied."

Aidan lied. That galls me more. Dr. Lusardi's lie resulted in my clone. That sucks. Hard. But I have no relationship invested with Dr. Lusardi; I never met her. Aidan's lie feels so much more personal. Unforgivable.

"Your hair is different," Xander comments.

My head lifts up from hiding beneath my arms to stare at him in shock. "*That's* what you have to say to me after all this? 'Your hair is different'?" I shouldn't feel a small measure of satisfaction, but I do. He noticed my hair.

"There's too much to say. I don't know where to begin."

We both laugh softly, and for a moment, the tension is relieved. "Yeah. Feeling that too." My fingers wrap strands of wild blond hair, streaked now in blue and black. "After you left, I cut off the pink tips. I was feeling pretty beat up, so I got black and blue streaks. The roots have grown out, but the streaks remain. They remind me of how I feel. Damaged."

"Glad you haven't lost your sense of melodrama, Z-Dev." He's teasing, trying to keep the moment light, using his old nickname for me, short for Zhara-Daredevil. But I'm not laughing anymore. Instead, I glare at him. He averts his turquoise eyes from my face to look at the late afternoon sun. "Let's go. We need to get off this atoll before it gets dark. Elysia and I will return to the Rave Caves with you and the other Defects."

"They don't like to be called that. They've chosen the name *Emergents* for themselves."

"Excellent. That's what we hope for them. That they choose their own identities."

"Who is *we*?"

"Those of us in the military who have been secretly supporting the Defects'—rather, Emergents'—quest for Insurrection. For freedom."

It's just too much to take in. Last year, at the urging of my father, Xander joined the elite wing of the Universal Military, which Xander's peaceful Aquine people traditionally shun. His people also don't believe in cloning, because it's not "natural." But now Xander has gone AWOL from the Uni-Mil in order to aid and abet Demesne clones? My head's going to explode from confusion.

"Get up," says Xander.

"Don't rush me," I snap again. "I'll get up when I'm ready, not when you tell me to." I actually do want to stand up, but I won't do it now, because he demanded it.

"The sun will set soon. You know that's the most important time of day to an Aquine, because you always begged me to forego that sacred time so we could swim longer."

"So, wait. You can have sex with me and then decide after that we're not ready to be mates—completely against the basic philosophy of Aquines: valuing loyalty above all else. Yet you can't let go of your stupid Aquine twilight meditation ritual? You are the ultimate hypocrite!" It's my curse that in the many months since I've last seen Xander, between his military training and whatever has happened to him since, his body has filled out into unholy appeal. His bronzed legs and arms are more muscular, his torso fuller, his face harder and more rugged, his turquoise eyes deeper and more intense. I've been to hell and back. Maybe he has too.

Softly, Xander repeats, "I'm so sorry. I'll never be able to convey to you how deeply sorry I am. I was wrong. But what's done is done. All we can do is move forward." He looks above to the setting sun. "*Now, Zhara.*"

I will reject him as he's rejected me. I vow it.

"I'll leave when I'm ready," I repeat.

"We don't have time for a Z-Dev temper tantrum," says Xander. Instead of arguing with me, he simply lifts me into his arms and slings me over his shoulder. I beat his back with my fists and his chest with my feet. I try to squirm from beneath his arm holding me down. But I am nothing against the big man's strength. He does not waver as he walks through the trees with me over his shoulder, as if he didn't even notice that his clone girlfriend's First is clawing her fingernails down his rock-hard back, drawing blood but not causing his stride to slow down one bit.

Finally, I give up and just let him carry me.

I'm so tired.

Into his shoulder, I murmur, "Why does she have to come back to the Rave Caves, too? She's not even a real person. She's a fake. She's a—"

At last, I've drawn a response. Xander throws me from his shoulder to land me standing opposite him, so close I can feel the hiss of his breath on my neck. "She's not a fake. Elysia is very real. Be kind to her."

Is this the biggest joke I've ever not laughed at? "You're kidding me, right?"

"I'm not. Elysia will need your compassion, and your strength."

"Excuse me, I'm the one who was left for dead, cloned against my will, and forced to escape to the Rave Caves with a posse of Defects."

"Emergents. And she's had it harder."

"I don't even believe you."

"Believe me. Your clone is pregnant."

I die again.

"Is it yours?" I ask him.

"No."

Scientists say they don't make clones from teenage Firsts. They say they only make clones that can't replicate.

Adults lie and lie and lie.

"Why should I believe you?"

"If you know me at all," says Xander, "you believe me."

I do believe him. If Xander had murdered someone, he'd straight-up admit: *Yes, I did it.* He'd hold out his wrists to be cuffed and taken away, ready to accept his judgment. Did he knock up my clone? *No.* He said it; he means it.

If he didn't do it, who did? Is my clone not just my worst nightmare, but also a slut?

ELYSIA
5

"SLUT!" MOTHER SCREAMS FROM THE WITNESS stand. I should be concentrating on more important matters—like my imminent sentencing—but I can't help let out a little laugh at how funny Mother sounds, the shrillness of her exclamation completely at odds with her breathy, childlike voice. I was supposed to be an emotionless clone. Instead, I'm a victim of a terrible human oddity—a funny bone. Further enraged by my laughter, Mother points her bejeweled, burgundy-painted fingertip at me, and repeats her shrill accusation. "SLUT SLUT SLUT!"

The judge raps her gavel. "Order! Order! There's no need for such shouting here. Such ugly words. Tsk, tsk. Compose yourself, Mrs. Bratton."

Mother wipes her brow and takes a deep breath. "Sorry, Your Honor," Mother says quietly in her babyish voice. It's so obvious she's not sorry. The only thing she's sorry about is that rash purchase she made: me.

By Demesne standards, Mother's family is poor. Mother's husband, Governor Bratton, is the CEO of Demesne, the hired help to the rich property owners. Mother wanted to make a lavish, frivolous purchase like her richer friends, who looked down on her. She wanted to impress them by being the first to own a Beta—a teen test clone. Her older daughter, Astrid, had just left home for college, so Mother thought she could purchase a replacement companion to her other children, Ivan and Liesel.

Mother's not sorry that she treated her Beta like dirt, or that her son violated and impregnated her Beta. I'm not even sure she's sorry that her Beta killed her son before her son could kill her Beta. The only thing she's really sorry about is that all her fancy friends know what a fool she was to impulsively purchase a Beta.

The judge turns to me. "How do you plead, Beta?"

"To which charge?" I ask, my voice filled with *teenage disdain*. The crowd in the courtroom audibly gasps.

Alexander, sitting in the front row, turns around and proudly tells the crowd, "They breed these Betas to be extra insouciant nowadays."

I datacheck the unfamiliar word.

In·sou·ci·ant [in-SOO-see-uhnt]: Free from concern, worry, or anxiety; carefree; nonchalant.

Insouciant. Good word. I like it. That's what I want to be, free from concern, no worries about my judgment day coming sooner rather than later, not a care in the world.

I look directly at Mother, pointing at her as she did me, and I insouciantly accuse her of the word that's my hope for her future: "INDIGENT INDIGENT INDIGENT!"

> **In·di·gent** [IN-di-juhnt]: Needy; poor; impoverished.

Mother faints from the harsh accusation and has to be carried away by the Governor's clone henchmen. The crowd roars its disapproval—"Silence the Beta! Death to the Beta!"—in my direction as the judge struggles to get the room back under control.

"Order! Order!" the judge admonishes. The crowd quiets, and she turns to me again. "The murder charge! How do you plead? Don't dare with further insouciance."

"Guilty," I admit. "But it was self-defense."

"Don't be absurd," says the judge. "Clones have no rights to defend themselves." She bangs down her gavel. "Guilty as charged. Next charge: inciting insurrection. How do you plead?"

"I didn't start it," I say, as if I'm stating the obvious, because I am. Why do these people have to pin *everything* on me? "I just picked up where the other Emergents left off."

"Guilty!" says the judge. "Next charge: stealing my boyfriend. How do you plead?"

I look at Alexander, who shrugs, and then I look to the judge, who looks exactly like me, only with honey-colored human eyes, and unruly matted hair. *Seriously, get a brush already.* "I didn't steal him," I tell Judge Zhara. "I just borrowed him to help me get through a rough time. It's Tahir I love. Tahir, who is a Beta clone like me; Tahir, who—"

Judge Zhara cuts me off, sounding as shrill as Mother. "GUILTY GUILTY GUILTY!" Zhara shrieks. The crowd goes wild, jumping to their feet, hooting and hollering as they clap their hands in approval.

The Governor, standing at the door, exults with joy. "SLUT SLUT SLUT!" he yells at me.

The bailiff—a clone, aestheticized with a black rose on the side of his face—comes to the stand to handcuff me. "Her sentence?" he asks Judge Zhara.

"Kill her, already!" Judge Zhara tells the bailiff. Then she turns to face me. "Once you die, I can finally get my soul back."

It's so dark here in the Rave Caves. I can't stop sleeping. Maybe when I wake up, this nightmare will be over. Maybe when I wake up, I won't be pregnant, I won't be a fugitive, and I won't be pretending to care for the Aquine who considers himself my protector.

I wanted to escape with Tahir, my true-love Beta, not with Alexander and the Emergents. That I managed to escape Demesne was itself a miracle, but Tahir faced the most formidable obstacle of all—his parents. After Tahir's

First died in a surfing accident, his parents' grief was so great that they used their wealth and power to have his dead body cloned. My Tahir is a Beta like me. Unfortunately, his parents cling even harder to their First's clone; I don't know why. All they are doing is stalling their next wave of grief, when Beta Tahir finally escapes from them—or dies from Awfuls—or both.

In my sweetest fantasy for the future, I spend every moment of however many months I have left with my Tahir, before the Awfuls that Dr. Lusardi programmed into us cause us to burn out and die. I suppose if it's my fantasy, I can be greedier. Hope for better. I wish for a future where Tahir and I don't have to live our lives on the run, forced into being outlaws by the sins of our humans. Tahir and I live freely, wherever we want, however long we want. We won't live in paradise, and we won't live in dark caves. We blend in like regular people, with no need to hide in remote corners of the world. We roam city streets and climb cathedrals and thrash through rivers, living our lives to the fullest, appreciating those lives more than the humans because we appreciate how precious each breath of freedom is.

When Tahir and I do finally die, we're old, shriveled-up Betas, clasping our hands in one last clench of shared joy before we succumb to deaths earned by old age, and not violence or cruel programming.

Zhara, my First, lives. She died and then got a do-over. May I please have one, too?

*   *   *

"How long have I been asleep?" I ask Alexander, who's lying next to me on a surprisingly cozy bed made of sticks and boughs. Thousands of tiny pink crystals glimmer from the cave walls, highlighting the sharp angle of his cheekbones. "It's so dark in here. I feel like I could have been asleep for days and not known the difference."

He removes a piece of hair covering my brow and places a soft kiss on my forehead. "You've been asleep for maybe fourteen hours. You needed the rest after everything that happened yesterday. It was a lot. For me too. Wish I could sleep it off as well as you do. I've barely slept since we got to the Rave Caves."

"Everything is different now," I say, acknowledging the invisible third party in the cave: Zhara.

"Everything is weird now," says Alex. He pauses, and then adds, "Weird*er*. It was already pretty strange. But nothing is different in terms of my commitment to you and the baby." His hand touches my belly, and I know, even if he doesn't, that what he really cherishes is the unborn thing inside me. I will never cherish it. For some reason only he can understand, he's chosen to love and protect the thing for me. That's why I can't return him to Zhara. Yet. The baby needs someone on its side. That someone won't be its birth mother. As soon as it is emerged, I plan on giving it to Alex and letting him figure out what to do with it. I can give it life, but he can give it values. Loyalty. Strength. Kindness.

For a second, I think I feel the baby's first kick; then I realize it's not the baby shoving me, it's the ground below my bed. The ground shakes for a good twenty seconds as the sound of rumbling reverberates across the cave walls. Startled, I grab on to Alex, tucking my head against his neck and hanging on to his firm chest. "What was that?" I ask.

But he laughs instead of fears. "I think that was an earthquake! Incredible!" He presses his hands together and . . . applauds?

"I'm terrified! Why do you clap?"

"Because if that's what I think it was, it was the Emergents practicing to build a tsunami."

I datacheck *tsunami* and do not like the result.

"A tsunami could wipe out this island," I say to Alex.

"Or it could be used to take the Insurrection directly to the Demesne property owners."

"Oh," I say. That's a good idea, maybe. "Nice earthquake, then." The tremor was not so nice to my queasy stomach, which churns in anxiety or morning sickness, I'm not sure which. I grab on to my belly, thinking I'm about to throw up, but the moment passes. "Do they know?" I ask Alex.

"Who? Know what?"

"The Emergents. About the baby."

"They know. You're their hero."

"That's absurd. I've done nothing to deserve their admiration."

"You took justice on a human," he says soothingly. "You represent their potential future."

"Their future? I may turn Awful before they can even

achieve Insurrection. How could I possibly represent their future, if I've been programmed to die by eighteen or nineteen?" The Awfuls, the curse of the Beta clone. Thanks, Dr. Lusardi. May you rest in peace—*never*.

Alex reminds me, "We don't know your expiration date for sure. If you can get pregnant against all odds, maybe there's a cure for the Awfuls. Maybe you're the cure to the Emergents' sterility." Demesne adult clones are programmed to expire at the human equivalent of age forty, once their usefulness is complete and before their superior physical aesthetic turns displeasing. That gives these Emergents ten to fifteen years at most to enjoy their reclaimed land and newly independent lives, should they achieve Insurrection, unless they can figure out how to undo their genetic programming and make babies. "You're their hope."

I don't want to be the Emergents' hope. I want to be free of their struggles. I just want to be a regular girl, allowed to live in peace with the boy she loves. Tahir. Not Alexander Blackburn. I want to have that peace not attached to a premature death sentence.

I roll over on my side, turning away from Alex. "They don't need me. Let the Insurrection bring their souls back instead. Then the Emergents can finally be happy—and hopeful." And miserable, just like the humans.

Alex says, "I thought you already realized you have a soul."

"I suspected. When I saw that Zhara was still alive, I realized why."

"That's not why. Soul extraction is a myth. The Demesne clones have always had souls."

Instantly I am alert and awake. "Explain!"

"The answers are outside this room. The Emergents have their own way to explain it to you."

I jump to my feet, more than ready to face this new day unraveling yet another ball of human lies. Excited + Angry = Awful. That's the equation for the new Elysia—whose soul is no lie, apparently.

6

A LIGHT FLASHES ON AND OFF BENEATH THE boulder separating our "room" from the rest of the Rave Caves.

"They're ready for you," says Alex. "Are you ready for them?"

"Ready for what?"

"The Emergents have an orientation for you. I saw the program earlier this morning, while you were still sleeping. It's how I learned about the soul extraction."

"Ready!" My whole body has felt assaulted by heaviness and fatigue, but now I feel a palpable rush of energy. I want answers, already. I can't believe answers even exist in this nothing place.

Alex pushes aside the boulder. An Emergent stands on the other side, holding up her hand, which is illuminated like a flashlight.

"How are you able to do that?" I ask her.

"We've taken the locator chips that used to be under our wrists and reprogrammed the chips for different needs. And to turn off the humans' ability to find us, of course." I can barely see her face, but she clearly recognizes mine. "It's good to see you again, Elysia."

"Do I know you?"

"I was the pastry chef at the Governor's house."

I still can't see her face, but I know exactly who she is. "Catra! You made the chocolate soufflés and the lushberry pies!" The other primary want I have, should I ever achieve a free life where I'm not trapped by a dying clone race's need for Insurrection: chocolate. Every day, every meal, maybe. Chocolate scramble for breakfast, chocolate sandwich for lunch, chocolate casserole for dinner. I'm *hungry*. Now I remember: Catra and her delicious concoctions disappeared suddenly from my previous home. I say, "I was loaned for a week to the Fortesquieu compound. When I returned to the Governor's house, the desserts were not as good. Was it because you escaped?"

"Indeed," Catra says. "But I don't handle culinary tasks here. I've discovered my real talents are in drama production." That's a waste, *I* think. And, how is drama production even a valid or necessary role in a stranded environment of outlaws? "You'll see!" Catra chirps.

These Emergents are very, very different from the clones

they were on Demesne, I see. They express their feelings freely.

Catra uses her illuminated hand to guide our path across the caves. We follow what appears to be a stream built into the ground, a long and narrow water channel alongside our otherwise barren path of rock walls. "What's that?" I ask, pointing to the stream.

"Irrigation tunnels for the water supply," says Alexander.

The redirected technology chips. The irrigation tunnels. Creating these things requires resources. I'm confused. I ask, "I thought these islands in the archipelago were empty. Hostile for life. How is this possible?"

Catra says, "When we were Defects, we were stock-piling supplies, little by little, and transporting them when we escaped to become Emergents. We had some help on the inside."

"Who?" I ask, and Catra and Alexander both laugh.

"Yours truly," says Alex. "My job on Demesne was to serve as a Uni-Mil liaison between Demesne and the Replicant Rights Commission, to make sure the clones were treated 'humanely,' which meant nothing in terms of what the property owners could be held accountable for. It was my duty to interview the clones about their working conditions. There were some whom I could tell had become Defects. So I made sure there was no trace of the supplies they were stealing. I helped reprogram the island's requisition and accounting systems, you could say."

We reach an opening to a large area, lit with torchlights in each corner of the cave. "This is our dining hall and communal area," says Catra. A group of Emergents who have been sitting at tables in the room suddenly rise as we enter. I turn around, wondering what's so interesting behind me that could cause these people to rise so suddenly.

"They rise to honor you," says Catra.

The Emergents break out into shy applause, the sound barely discernible as they almost politely tap their hands together. Then I walk past the first table, and the shyness is gone. A female Emergent lunges toward me, and I recoil slightly, surprised. But she just wants to touch my arm. "Thank you," she says. The male Emergent standing next to her salutes me.

None of them look me in the eyes. I feel like they're all looking at my belly, to see if their hope is showing yet. I pull my shirt down and out, not wanting to offer a further view.

The Emergent called Aidan, who I guess is their unofficial leader, steps forward to greet me. He, too, touches my arm, but to lead me to a lectern built at the head of the room. I feel a slight *sizzle* when his hand touches me, then look down and see that the tip of his pinkie finger is a light blue color.

"We have the training orientation ready for you to see," Aidan says. "If you're ready to begin now."

Now I understand why so many are gathered. "The other Emergents here are also new arrivals?"

Aidan says, "No, they've seen this already. They just wanted to be near you." How flattering, especially since I have no real desire to be near them. I don't hate them, of course, and I hope they will achieve their Insurrection. I want them to have good lives. Free lives. But the only person I want to be near—ever—is Tahir. "Be seated and we will begin."

I sit down, and Aidan points his finger toward the empty wall behind the lectern. The wall suddenly illuminates like a holographic screen. "I have a customized chip beneath my skin," Aidan explains. "The file is saved there."

A holographic video, like the one I saw when I first emerged in Dr. Lusardi's compound, begins. A hologram of Catra appears. She has smooth, ebony skin, dreadlocked black hair interspersed with strands of bronze, and perfect facial features—high cheekbones, almond-shaped eyes with high arched eyebrows. Her fuchsia eyes seem to shine with *delight*.

Holo-Catra raises both her illuminated hands in a welcoming wave. "Hello, Emergents!" she says. "Great job making it here to Heathen. I'm here to tell you a little bit about the environment and explain how things work here. As you've probably noticed by now, Heathen is quite different from Demesne." An image of Demesne and its violet sea, called Io, appears behind holo-Catra, who moves her hands to direct the earth images north, moving the setting from the tranquil sea to the towering waters called the *gigantes*, then past the *gigantes* to the rough ocean and up, up, up, past little atoll islands, past Mine (here the audience behind me applauds again—I guess many of them, like me, took refuge with M-X after escaping Demesne).

Holo-Catra's hand stops on Heathen. I let out a gasp as beautiful purple-magenta clouds swirl over the island. "Yes, these clouds look beautiful," says holo-Catra. "But here's what those clouds mean on Heathen. Danger." The background transforms into Heathen's jungle, where lush green trees sway and tropical birds sing. What's so dangerous about that? I wonder. The purple-magenta clouds hover over the jungle and send a light rain over the landscape, producing beautiful rainbows in the mist. *How beautiful!* I think. Then the rain turns to hail the size of human fingers—with blades at the tips. It's like an icy avalanche of dagger pellets. The landscape shifts, taking shelter inside the Rave Caves. "And that," says holo-Catra, "is one of the many reasons we choose to live in caves." Images of clone quarters and the communal dining hall we're in now flash behind her.

Next, she takes a bite out of a piece of raw fish. My stomach revolts at the sight, and I swallow a sudden surge of bile. She says, "Fortify, my friends. Just as on Demesne, you'll have a role here. The difference is: your role here is your choice. You can fish for food, cultivate the fields of produce, serve as a lookout, become an environmental engineer. No matter what your role, you will spend your remaining time training." Artillery fields and military-worthy obstacle courses—in lagoons, in the caves, in the jungle—appear behind her. "Insurrection is coming, comrades. We *will* be ready!"

The orientation video ends. It was good, I guess—certainly an improvement over the last one I saw, on Demesne, which instructed newly emerged clones on their new lives of slavery. But it failed to address the fundamental question I want answered.

"But what about the souls?" I ask Aidan.

Aidan points his blue finger at the blank wall again to cue another video. "This is the second part of orientation. This was taken with a stealth surveillance monitor we hid inside Dr. Lusardi's private office."

My heart sinks as I see Dr. Lusardi, with her corkscrew of long orange hair, sitting at her desk, wearing a white lab coat. She's the reason I emerged. She's the reason I'll barely have a chance to live. Then my heart sings in surprise, because sitting on the other side of her desk is the next best thing to Tahir—his father, Tariq Fortesquieu.

"Where is First Tahir's soul?" Tariq demands. "I want it back. This Beta Tahir is so rote. He's breaking his mother's heart. He's incapable of affection."

"'Raxia will unblock that," advises Dr. Lusardi.

"No 'raxia," says Tariq. "That's what contributed to First Tahir's death. We tried so hard to discipline him, but Tahir was a playboy. We loved him too much. We looked the other way when he indulged in alcohol and 'raxia. We thought he was just a young man sowing his wild oats. 'Raxia was what led to his death. No. I demand the soul you extracted when you made Beta Tahir. Return it to him."

Dr. Lusardi pauses, then leans in to Tariq. "First Tahir's soul is there."

Tariq looks around the office. "Where?"

Dr. Lusardi touches her head, then her mouth, and then her heart. "Here. Everywhere. Mind, body, soul."

"Don't be oblique. I won't tolerate it!"

Sounding *fearful*, Dr. Lusardi confesses, "There's no such thing as soul extraction. It's a myth my First developed in order to sell the Demesne clone product line. Souls die when Firsts die, of course. But when their clones emerge, souls emerge too."

"The same souls?" Tariq asks, looking confused.

"Not the same. New souls. They form organically. Clones do have them, but don't know it. So my First developed brain inhibitors to block the clones' feelings, to make them emotionless, so they seem soulless." As if trying to justify herself, Dr. Lusardi amends, "The clones *are* soulless. Because they don't know their souls exist. And they wouldn't know what to do with the souls if they did."

"This is an outrage," says Tariq slowly. But I can see by the look on his face: he's trapped by the lie. He and his wife have tried so hard to pass off clone Tahir as their actual son, First Tahir. To acknowledge the lie of the soulless clones and spread it would dismantle the entire haven of Demesne. "What does 'raxia have to do with it?"

Dr. Lusardi says, "'Raxia has the unintended side effect of unblocking those brain inhibitors. But no Demesne clone should experience *want*. They should never desire 'raxia to begin with. It shouldn't be a problem. Let this be our little secret."

Tariq, normally so calm, uncharacteristically raises his voice. "You're saying the entire workforce on Demesne could be compromised if they simply took 'raxia?"

"Sorry," says Dr. Lusardi, who herself is a clone. According to M-X, who'd worked in Dr. Lusardi's laboratory, the real Dr. Larissa Lusardi was murdered. She objected to her clones being used as slaves. ReplicaPharm, the corporation that financed her work and most served to profit from it, decided her righteous sense of ethics was all wrong. They killed her, and then cloned her to finish her First's work.

So it's no surprise that her apology sounds *insincere*. This Dr. Lusardi's not sorry.

I have a soul.

It wasn't my imagination.

It's my own, not borrowed from my First.

I feel . . . *joyful*.

"Where's Zhara?" I ask Aidan, realizing she's been gone through this whole presentation.

Aidan doesn't answer for a moment. His face is set to *grim*. "She's sleeping it off in the tree house."

"Sleeping what off?"

"When we returned from the atoll yesterday, she bolted into the jungle and returned to her unfortunate old habit. 'Raxia."

ZHARA

7

ONCE AGAIN, I AWAKE FROM THE DEAD, ONLY this time, I wish I hadn't.

I'm still groggy from the 'raxia that catapulted me into welcome emptiness, but this time I re-emerge knowing exactly where I am, and it's not Demesne paradise. I'm in the tree house on Heathen. After we returned from the atoll with Xander and Elysia, Aidan took them to their quarters . . . and I ran away to the cuvée fields. Aidan must have found me and brought me to the tree house after I passed out in the fields. I can see by the light outside that it's mid-morning. I must have been out for at least twelve hours. My brain is still hazy, but my heart pounds hard, remembering. Yesterday, I was ignorant of my clone. Today, I am not.

My whole world is different. Skewed. Wrong.

I press my hand along the floor of the tree house, searching. I want to go back to sleep. I want more 'raxia. Where did I leave the other pills I made from the crushed cuvée seeds last night?

I hear a voice. "What are you looking for?" asks Aidan. I look up. He's standing at the tree house entrance.

I sniff, smelling a burning smell. "Are you playing fire tricks outside again?" I look, but his pinkie finger is not lit in blue.

"I ordered the cuvée fields destroyed."

I cover my face with my hands. My heart pounds harder, with extra discomfort. It's called *panic*. "Why? You don't understand. I just need a little more to get through. *You* need the cuvée seeds to finance supplies for Insurrection."

"Then Insurrection will just have to come sooner rather than later. We'll do without. As will you. The Aquine told me you were an addict in your previous life. I won't allow that to happen to you again here."

Who does this clone think he is, my sobriety sponsor? "*You* could use some 'raxia. Lighten up, already." I hate Aidan so much right now.

Aidan shakes his head. "'Raxia affects us differently," he responds, taking my comment literally. "We don't develop the instant addiction to it that humans do. It's nothing to us except a potential profit source." He looks out beyond the tree house, to the smoke rising from the fields. "Rather, it *was*."

Aidan sits down on the ground next to me. He removes my hands from my face and stares intently at me, and I wish he would lean down and kiss me. I want to be held, comforted, stroked, loved. If I can't have more 'raxia, I need something—someone—to numb the pain. My desire to feel anything other than what I feel now—deep, abiding anger—temporarily overrules my disgust with Aidan. Give me more. Please don't make me beg!

I sit up and move farther from him. "You knew," I accuse him.

"Knew what?"

"About Elysia."

"Yes."

I wait, expecting an explanation, but he offers none. It's so like a clone to just state the obvious, with no context. "*Yes?* That's all you have to say? You don't think you should have told me about Elysia?"

"You couldn't have handled it." He sounds so matter-of-fact, but he's right. He had me figured out so quickly. "And I *didn't* know, at first. When I was sent to dispose of your body at the lab on Demesne, I was told your clone had been a Fail. It was only later that I found out otherwise."

"How did you find out?"

"Catra. She knew Elysia at the Governor's house. She recognized that you must be Elysia's First. We agreed it was best to keep that information private. The other Emergents hadn't known Elysia on Demesne, so they never made the connection. I didn't want them—or you—distracted by the true mission. Insurrection."

"So I'm a *distraction*?"

"Yes," he says unapologetically. "You are liked here. You serve adequately. But you are a distraction." I feel like he's just slapped me in the face, but I understand that he's right.

I've been Aidan's platonic companion here, but I've had no real mission of my own on Heathen, other than to escape the pain I left behind in Cerulea and the memory of the death party where two kids lost their lives because of my invitation. I wanted to be the cool girl hanging out with clones in the jungle. But I was just a distraction to them, apparently. I just can't get anything right. Not even being an outlaw runaway. Aidan adds, "You never mentioned you already knew the Aquine."

"Does it matter?"

"Does it?"

Really. There's no talking to clones.

I can't discuss Xander with Aidan. I can only process one emotional crisis at a time. "Why's Elysia here? Why now?"

"She escaped Demesne."

"I know that already. Why is she here with *him*?"

"He found her, and took her to safety."

That's so like Xander. Stupid hero complex.

"Where's she now?"

"With the Aquine in the Rave Caves. They're determining what training exercises she'll participate in."

They. Xander and Elysia are a *they*. My insides curdle and I want to throw something, anything.

"Which cave are they staying in?"

"I gave them our cave last night, the crystal cave," says Aidan. "I made the weather system mild so you could sleep off your 'raxia indulgence in the privacy of the tree house. Does it matter which cave they have?"

It matters. *They* basically got the honeymoon suite,

which in darkness glimmers with thousands of pink crystals, a chandelier of cave walls.

I want the free-floating emptiness back. *Give me my 'raxia back!*

I know what Aidan wants, and I know how to get what I want. I don't even care how much I hate him right now. I want my 'raxia more.

I turn my lips up into my former Z-Dev smile. I reach across the divide to touch Aidan's hand. We've slept next to each other for months, but this is the first time we've touched so intimately. His hand clasps mine, letting me know he desires this connection.

It's so long since I touched, *truly* touched a guy. Since before Xander went away. It's so long, and my need for more 'raxia is so strong, I don't care how mad I am at Aidan for his unforgiveable sin of omission. The anger I feel burns me even hotter for him, actually. I lean into him, close enough so that I can feel Aidan's breath on my neck. His chest heaves slightly, with hope.

I bet Aidan's never been kissed before. I bet I have to teach him how. I bet if it wasn't a chore right now, it would also be kind of fun.

Let's go! I grab my hands behind his neck and pull his mouth toward mine, stopping just close enough so that our lips almost touch, but don't. I give him a few breaths to feel the anticipation before placing my lips directly on his mouth. I press my lips together and graze his at first, letting him experience that initial thrill of *Wow, this is really happening.* He lets the gentle grazes happen, but then he gets it, and presses his mouth harder against mine, ready to examine this electrifying new territory, and I am amazed how quickly my mouth opens, craving more of him. But he pulls away and presses his hands against my cheeks for a moment, staring intently into my eyes, as if to ask, *Are you sure?*

That was no chore. That was amazing. My mouth returns to his, greedy this time, hungry for deeper exploration. I rub my chest against his, letting him feel the thrill of the kiss above and the rub below. Holding his neck close, I drop back to the ground, pulling him down with me.

But before I commit to this treachery with this traitor who lied to me about my clone, I place my hand on Aidan's thigh, and rub my hand over the material of his pants, trying to determine if his pockets hold the shape of the pills I want.

Immediately, Aidan pulls away from me. He stands up, and then looks down at me with equal measures of *lust* and *disgust*. "You are like the Demesne humans right now. Manipulative. Spoiled. Ungrateful. I won't be an accessory to your addiction." He walks over to the webbed ladder and as he steps down onto it, he adds, "You won't find any more pills. They're all destroyed, along with the cuvée fields. Now get up. Elysia exists. Go deal with her."

What a joke. It's me who's really the Defect.

Unwanted. Unloved.

Should have died the first time.

ELYSIA COULD BE ANYWHERE ON HEATHEN right now. I should have no idea where to find her right at this moment. Yet I know exactly where she'll be. The gnawing in my stomach lets me know it's just about noon. My lunchtime hunger has always been my body's most reliable clockwork, and it's especially true today, after the sleeping hellbeast's long 'raxia-induced nap.

There's no more checking out available to me. The 'raxia is gone. Elysia and Xander are here. I can't escape anymore. I don't want to. I want to be more than a "distraction."

Aidan leaves me in the tree house, hungrier than ever. I sprint to the mess hall for some chow, and there she is, right where I expect her. Elysia sits alone on a bench, sipping juice and nibbling almonds warmed in honey—the very pre-lunch snack that the cook usually prepares for me.

"I always get hungry at this time of day," Other Me tells me.

Why am I so ignorant that I actually thought her first words to me would be more like, *Thanks for my life, Goddess First.*

MY FACE! I face my own face, the version aestheticized for Demesne slavery. The weirdness of my mirrored face looking at me with fuchsia eyes and fleur-de-lis and floral tattoos tattooed to my—I mean, *her*—temples replaces my hunger pangs with nausea. Food suddenly looks so gross.

"Hello, Zhara. Will you join me?" She's only been on Heathen a day and already she's acting like its queen. The hostess offers me a bowl of nuts, but I shake my head. The sight of Elysia's face has killed my appetite. I want to deal, but this sucks. HARD. Elysia is real, not a figment of my imagination. I can't wake up from this nightmare. I'm living it.

I sit down opposite her. I'm going to tread safely before diving into the hard questions. "What was Demesne like?" I ask her. I think of my mother, whose lifelong dream was to swim in Io, the magical violet sea that surrounds Demesne. "Did you swim there?"

"Of course. The water was very luxurious, as it was designed to be," Elysia says.

"How was the weather there?" This small talk is so lame and cowardly on my part. What I really want to know is, *How did you manage to create a life in the short time since you stole mine?*

"We made sure it was perfect," Elysia says, and I know that tone she mimics, because it's my own. It's called *resentful*.

It's weird. I want to hear her talk more. She looks so much like me, but her voice's affect has a softness mine never will. She looks and sounds angelic. Not hellbeast. Not at all.

I have so much to say to her, to ask her, but I feel mute. I just don't know how to do this. Elysia breaks through the small talk. Did she steal my bravery, also? "There is so much about you I would like to know," she says. "How are you alive? Alex explained to me that your heart had stopped, but then you awoke again hours later. But—"

"Alex?" I sputter. "Who's Alex?"

"Alexander Blackburn. I call him Alex."

"I call him Xander. 'Cuz that's his name. Where is he now, anyway?"

"Scouting materials to make our quarters in the Rave Caves more comfortable so we don't have to sleep on the ground." She pauses. "The Rave Caves are a huge disappointment."

"Not comfortable enough for you?" And Aidan said *I* was spoiled. Ha. My clone is worse. "Those are *my* quarters you're borrowing, by the way."

"The quarters are excellent," she says. "I meant, the Rave Caves are a disappointment because I had been led to believe that human surfers lived there also. Why don't they?"

"Why do you care?"

"There was a surfer I knew on Demesne. He disappeared suddenly. I thought perhaps he'd come here."

"If he did come here, he's gone now. When the Emergents started escaping here, the human surfers left. Either the Emergents kicked them out, or the surfers left to find another island where they could live and only care about surfing, and not be bothered by a small army of clones training for Insurrection. Or both."

"Too bad," says Elysia. "Please tell me about your family. What were your parents like? Would they be considered our parents?"

Our parents? "*My* father is in the Uni-Mil. *My* mother is dead."

"How did she die?" Elysia pauses, and her facial expression resets from *curious* to *sympathetic*.

"*My* mom left us when I was eight. She said she had become a mother too young and didn't want a family. She went to Humanitas, to experience it the way generations of backpackers did when Humanitas was called Europe. She became obsessed with clone rights. I don't know why. She was always a champion of lost causes. She went to Geneva to participate in a huge protest against ReplicaPharm. The protest turned violent. She was trampled to death."

I think this is the most I've spoken about my mother, ever.

Elysia's eyes blink the way Aidan's eyes often do when trying to access information on his knowledge chip. "I'm sorry for your loss," she says, her voice *sincere*.

She says the right words. I don't think she really feels them.

She's not sorry. My mother's abandonment and death are just data to her.

Elysia's expression turns to *quizzical*. "ReplicaPharm? Who are they?"

I'd be shocked at her ignorance, but I've already experienced it with the other Emergents. I answer patiently. "ReplicaPharm is one of the biggest companies on the planet. They make clones that are utilized throughout the rest of the world. The clones grown in laboratories, not made from Firsts."

She nods. "Alex had told me there were other brands of clones, but I didn't realize they were produced by corporations, or without Firsts. I thought all clones came from Dr. Lusardi's engineering."

I feel irritation mixed with a strange sense of outrage. How could she survive out in the real world with such limited information, with such willfully preprogrammed ignorance?

Elysia asks, "Your father. He was your diving coach?"

"Who told you that?" Suddenly I feel proprietary about the basic facts of my own life. Any public records could reveal the simple details she requests, yet I feel like she is prying into the darkest corners of my life.

"Alex told me you were a diver," Elysia says. "I felt that. From the moment I was near the water, I knew how to dive. It was like I sensed you when I was in the water. I . . ." She hesitates before continuing on. "I had memories of Alex, after I emerged. They were your memories. Perhaps because you never really died."

The thought of my clone having the instant ability to perform the same dives I spent years in training to perfect is upsetting enough. The sudden image my brain produces of her performing dives for Xander makes me *insane*. But the thought of her having my memories of Xander is like an off-the-charts intrusion into my mind, body, and soul. I'm so livid at this moment, I want to strangle my clone and suction every breath from her body. I struggle for speech. "You have all my memories?"

Elysia looks taken aback by my angry response, then clarifies. "The only memories I had of yours were visions of Alex. They were the only ones that broke through. It always happened when I was in the water, swimming. In the way that I inherently understood how to swim and dive, I knew that I'd gotten it from you." My face must still register shock. Perhaps she also inherently understands I can't handle this subject any longer, because she redirects the conversation. "What's your best dive?"

Keep cool, Z. Keep cool. Safe topic. "Reverse three-and-a-half twist," I lie. I never successfully made it past a reverse two. But I'd much rather talk dives with her than the memories of Xander that she stole from me. Is that why she's with him now? Because she knows that he and I were together once? That's not even outrageous. It's beyond kinky. "What's yours?" I fire back.

"Backward two-and-a-half somersault with a half twist," Elysia says. That's my *real* best dive. "Alex says I shouldn't dive anymore, in my current condition. But perhaps we could go swimming together? I'd so much like to spend time with you in the place you love most. The water, I mean. I'd like to study your technique. You must be a great swimmer. I've felt that about you when I'm in the water."

I cannot believe her insolence. She's just asked me to help her steal something else that's precious to me.

"Because *you* are a great swimmer? You got that from *me*." All the skills she was given took me years of practice to cultivate.

"Thank you," says Elysia with *sincerity*. Why does she make it so hard to hate her? She makes me wonder if I had hidden likeability traits I never knew about in my former, friendless life in Cerulea. "Perhaps you'd like to know something about what I experienced when I swam on Demesne?" she asks, like I could somehow validate her existence by wanting information about it.

I don't want to discuss stupid water sports with her. What I really need to know is so much bigger than swimming and dives.

Why did you escape Demesne? Was your life there . . . happy? Who got you pregnant?

How do I even begin such a conversation with someone I wish never existed?

Elysia takes a gulp from her pink drink. "What are you drinking?" I ask her. I've never seen this concoction in the mess hall.

"Watermelon juice," she says. "Alex found some watermelons and pressed this juice for me. He says I need to stay hydrated."

Bile actually regurgitates up from my stomach and shoots

into my mouth. Xander never made refreshments for me back at the Cerulea Aquatics Club. The best I ever got from him was when he'd point to the water cooler during practice and say, "Drink up, Z." I never got delivery of personally picked fruits followed by freshly squeezed juices from him.

Elysia swallows the last sip of her drink and then delicately licks the sides of her mouth, which is exactly what I do when I take the last sip of a drink I've particularly enjoyed. To savor the . . . "I love those last drops," Elysia says. Exactly.

I remember after Mom left, I used to long for a sister. A best friend, a kindred spirit, someone who was my blood, who could share the pain of our abandonment, but also share a special bond of companionship. My sister and I would always be there for each other. Through thick and thin, as the saying goes. Friends and mothers might come and go, but a sister would be forever.

Elysia will never be my forever, no matter how much she looks and acts like me. I reject her. I refuse her. I may have to live in proximity to her for the time being, but I will never, ever accept her. She stole me.

Let's just stop with small talk.

"Who got you pregnant?" I ask her.

Would her child be considered my child too?

Her fuchsia eyes pierce directly into mine, challenging me as an equal. I'd appreciate her spunk more if she hadn't stolen that from me too. "I was violated by the son of the Governor on Demesne."

What?!

Holy crap. My blood boils into a rage so much bigger than when I discovered Elysia's existence, worse even than knowing she carries my memories of Xander. I can't help it. I imagine what happened to her happening to me, and my gut reaction is: I will kill whoever did that to me. I mean, her. KILL.

For an instant, Elysia is that sister I used to long for. I want to touch her hand, hold her close to me, to comfort her, to promise her vengeance. I don't. But I want to.

A human boy on Demesne treated my clone like she was his property. She *was* his property. Fact. Another version of my face, my body—given no rights or choice, created to serve and have no wants or desires of her own—there for him to take, just because he wanted to.

I ask, "Is that why you escaped Demesne? To get away from him?"

"No," says Elysia. "It was kill or be killed. So I killed him. And now I am here."

Wow. I thought *I* was the outlaw, living as a runaway on this feral island.

Elysia is the real rebel. She is a murderer. How can a deed so awful make me want to respect her? She took no prisoners. She exacted her own vengeance.

Xander and Aidan enter the mess hall. My eyes lock with Xander's for a moment, and my heart burns. I still can't believe he's *here*. His look in my direction offers me no clues if he feels the same. His beautiful turquoise eyes are as blank as a clone's.

Elysia looks to him, and then to me. "I'm sorry Alexander hurt you so badly."

"How much do you know?" I ask her.

"Jingjing," she says, shocking me. "You had already been to Demesne once before, with Alex, hadn't you?"

9

IF I CAN'T HAVE HIM, I'LL DIE, I *THOUGHT.*

Xander was about to leave for a whole new life in the military.

His old life was better. Swimming. Surfing. Me.

The only way to survive his new life would be to change with him. I'd go away with him and escape boring school, my tyrant father, the cheerlords who pretended they were my friends but really weren't. Once I started a new life with Xander, I'd reinvent myself as someone better, someone happier. Someone perfect, like him.

Today, this would happen, I told myself. Time to take the dive. If I finally accomplished the one dive that had eluded me since Xander started training me, it would be a fateful sign. Xander and I were meant to be a team. The Uni-Mil shouldn't be allowed to break us up.

I stood atop a ten-meter-high diving platform as Xander watched me from below. I stepped to the edge of the platform and turned around, so my back faced the pool. As I placed my feet in the familiar formation, Xander called up to me. "The back two-and-a-half? Today's your day to perfect it. I feel it, Z. You can do it." His deep, gravelly voice made him sound years older. He had left home to live on his own when he was just sixteen years old. At nineteen, he was about to the join the elite wing of the Universal Military, which his peaceful Aquine people traditionally shun. His deep voice announced he was his own man.

I could do harder dives than this one. But this one, because it was the dive I had choked on at Olympic trials, was torturing me. I wanted to get it right again, so I could move on—in my training, in my tortured subconscious.

"Hell yeah!" I said. Generally, backward dives were my lucky dives. When my back was to the pool, I couldn't see the spectators in the stand before liftoff. I couldn't see my father's face clenched with the stress of wondering not only if I would accomplish my dive, but would I excel at it? Or would I fail him yet again?

When my dad coached me, I disappointed. According to him, my technique was sloppy, I lacked the focus and discipline to be a world-class athlete, and I wasted my ability wanting to do other sports, like cheerlords—which mostly I wanted to do so I'd have an excuse not to spend my weekends training with Dad. Do you even want this, hellbeast? *Dad would say.* Not as much as you want it for me, *I'd think. After I failed at Olympic trials, Dad gave up on me and turned my training over to his protégé,*

Xander, who managed the aquatics club facility in exchange for modest accommodations at the back of the club's pool house. Xander was supportive and kind, and he seemed to genuinely want me to dive for my own sense of accomplishment, not my dad's. Xander believed in me. The feel of Xander's bronzed, ripped muscles holding me steady through practice dives, and his turquoise eyes and slanted cheekbones and full red lips cheering me on, helped my technique immeasurably too. Some might have called it puppy love. Inspiration, I called it.

In anticipation of the back two-and-a-half, I stood too long at the tip of the board, causing Xander to step closer to the area beneath the board and call up to me. "What's up with the hesitation, hellbeast?" he asked. "Don't overthink. Just do."

I hated that nickname. Coach Dad used it to taunt, not tease me. "Don't call me that," I said, firming my legs for liftoff. Xander revered my dad. If it weren't for that misplaced sense of hero worship, Xander wouldn't have been about to leave to follow in my dad's military footsteps. Once again, Dad had chosen my fate for me.

"Whatever you say, Z-Dev." That nickname I liked, because Xander chose it for me. Zhara-Daredevil. "Go to it. I know you can."

"Jingjing!" I said, invoking the name of Guo Jingjing, my favorite female Olympic diver from olden times, pre–Water Wars. Jingjing, my good luck charm.

My feet sprang from the board and I flew downward, contorting into a back double somersault and half twist before my body plunged into the water.

When I came up for air, Xander stood at the ledge of the

pool. He extended a hand to help lift me up and out of the water. "You did it! Nailed it!" He raised his arms exultantly. "Beautiful dive, Z."

Beautiful man. Instead of letting him help me up, I tugged on his arms to pull him back into the pool, back to me. Finally, I had him in the water, where I wanted him.

He swam over to me and I splashed water in his face. "Don't start a war you can't win," he dared me. His long leg attempted to wrap around my calf to pin me down, but I quickly dropped to the bottom of the pool, out of his embrace, and swam away from him, fast.

I came up for air at the other end of the pool. "Come and get me, Xander."

Instead, he got out of the pool and walked into the club, knowing I'd follow.

My father was away for the weekend, leading boot-camp exercises at the Base, the kind of military training Xander would soon be imprisoned by. "You're not worried about leaving your sixteen-year-old daughter alone with Xander for the weekend?" I had challenged Dad.

But Dad, who had lived in Aquine territory when he was a young man, just laughed. "Aquines don't mate until they're ready to commit for life. Xander is nowhere near ready for that sentence with you. Your virtue is safe."

Few things gave me more satisfaction than proving my father wrong.

I followed Xander inside the empty aquatics club, where he stopped at the entrance to the FantaSphere room. "You're sure?"

I asked Xander, who never broke club rules. I pointed to the sign next to the door, placed there after too many amorous couples had unauthorized adventures: FANTASPHERE ACCESS DURING CLUB HOURS ONLY. POLICY STRICTLY ENFORCED.

Xander's turquoise eyes, normally so serious-looking, glinted with an uncharacteristic note of naughtiness. "It's my last weekend here. What are they going to do, fire me from the job I'm already leaving?"

This rule-breaking, it was so unlike him, so un-Aquine. It was so . . . encouraging.

Xander pressed his index finger against the access scanner, and the door opened. We stepped inside the bare room. "Close your eyes," he said. I closed my eyes and heard the beeps of his program code being entered into the console.

Immediately, I knew something had changed, even though I couldn't see it. I could feel it. My lungs took in a huge inhale of the sweetest air imaginable. The oxygen felt startlingly, wonderfully rich, with a faint taste of honeysuckle. Reluctantly, I exhaled, and was surprised when letting go of the air made my body feel even better, as if eased not only of stress, but relieved of every heartbreak I've known in my life so far. My damp, cold skin was suddenly warm and dry, soothed. My feet sank lightly into soft, massaging sand. I heard the comforting lap of water.

"Now open your eyes," Xander said.

I opened my eyes to a vision of violets: a violet-hued lagoon lapping onto sand specked with violet crystals, with a ray of sun streaming violet light into the center of a waterfall not far from the shore where we stood. Lush green trees surrounded the lagoon, heightening the intensity of the violets.

"Is it—?" I started to say.

"Demesne. FantaSphere version. I programmed it for you. So we could share one last perfect swim together before I go away." Xander always looked humble—but for the first time, I sensed shyness coming from him. "Do you like it?" he asked hopefully.

Jingjing! My lucky charm worked!

I wished the cheerlords were right there with me—watching, envying. Not one of them believed Xander and I were a real couple. It's like the pool was Xander's and my bubble—only there, when we were alone together, would he play with me. But if Xander and I did the deed, then he'd be mine forever, and everyone would know the Aquine chose me. No one would doubt me once I became Mrs. Alexander Blackburn. I couldn't pass the Olympic diving trials by age sixteen, but I could accomplish marrying an Aquine! Take that, Zhara doubters.

"Amazing," I murmured. I wanted to cry as much as I wanted to maul him.

"Race you to the waterfall."

We ran into the water and dove down into its warmth. The water! The temperature was just right: not too hot to encourage laziness, not too cold to discourage play—the sweetest dip into warm. The smoothness of it was like swimming in the softest cashmere. Xander raced, but I deliberately swam a slower pace to observe him swimming a butterfly stroke across the length of the lagoon, awed by the bulk of his biceps, and by how his long, lean torso powered his tall body so that it didn't just swim across the water, but hurtled through it.

I reached the waterfall several seconds after him. He pulled me to him. Smooth, violet-hued water splashed our heads and shoulders as I wrapped my legs around his back and pressed my chest into his. Could he feel how hard my heart was thumping with excitement, and terror? Neither of us had gone all the way before. The thought of doing what I wanted to do with him filled me with equal parts excitement and fear. What if I did it wrong?

I whispered into his ear, "I don't think we'll be the first couple to do it in this FantaSphere." I moved my mouth from his ear to his cheek, en route to his lips for a kiss, but he pulled back.

"Slow down, Z. I wanted to take you somewhere special for our last night together, but you know it can't end like that."

"Why?" I shoved water at him, a resentful splash, not a playful one. I so didn't get it. Weren't nineteen-year-old guys supposed to be, like, the horniest demographic in all the male species? Did he have any idea how many guys would kill to have what I was so totally ready to give him?

I swam to a deck abutting the rock beneath the waterfall and climbed up onto it. I sat down, my legs hanging into the water, waiting for him to pull me back to him. Xander swam to the side of the deck's edge, holding on to it but not getting out of the water to join me. "It kills me, this waiting for you. But I'm an Aquine. Just because I live away from my people doesn't mean I'm so far evolved from their values. Can you understand that?"

"Do I have a choice?"

"No."

He swam away again, stopping beneath the waterfall, where he treaded water, his gaze searing me from across the divide.

I was bored with playing fair.

I took off my bikini top and threw it into the water.

His turquoise eyes flared as they rested on my exposed breasts for a second. Then he swam to retrieve my bikini top and brought it to the deck ledge. He tried to hand it back to me, averting his eyes from my chest. Instead of taking the bikini top Xander extended to me, I removed my bikini bottom, flinging it so it landed on his head.

I'm freaking naked right in front of you. If that doesn't work, I've run out of tricks.

"Don't do this, hellbeast," Xander said, not sounding at all convinced of his words.

"Don't call me that," I hissed. I slipped down into the warm, sweet water. It was fake Demesne, but the surge in my heart was real. Now was Xander's and my time to make it happen. He had created a perfect paradise, just for me. Of course he meant for us to mate in it.

Xander dove underneath the water to swim back toward the lagoon's shore. He knew I couldn't catch him. Or could I? When I wanted something, my heat was unconquerable.

I caught up with him and dove beneath his legs, reaching for his ankle in a grab that was more stroke than attack. He stopped his sprint to go back above the surface for air, but I didn't follow him up. I stayed beneath the water and circled him like a mermaid. Or a shark.

We'd done this water dance so many times. This time, it had to culminate in something more than stolen, secretive kisses that led nowhere. I swam back toward the waterfall, coming up for air at the side of the deck. If Xander wanted it, he had to come take it.

He wanted it. He raced beneath the water, coming up for air so close to me that I could see his heart pounding, so close he was almost pinning me against the deck. His turquoise eyes darkened, like a jungle animal about to pounce on its prey. Emboldened, I extended my legs out, wrapping them around his back to pull him to me, chest-to-chest, groin-to-groin. He didn't just let me; in response, he grabbed me tight to him, his chest pressing into mine. Finally. This was on*!*

But. "We can't let this happen," *Xander said, sounding not at all convinced.*

Wrong wrong wrong. It was already happening. I placed a kiss on his neck. "Don't you want me?"

"It's always been you. It never wasn't going to be you. But now isn't the right time. Please, Z. Don't torture me."

Me *torture* him? *He had created this situation. He had brought me to Demesne, the one place in the world I longed to experience.*

Maybe it was the first tear of frustration, or the second tear of sincere need that burst from my eyelids down my cheek, but his lips found my face, to kiss away my tears. Instinctively, my face moved so that we were mouth to mouth. Our lips touched, and yet didn't move. It was a kiss but not a kiss. This time, I needed him to make that move.

And he did. Suddenly, his lips went from merely touching my own to pressing against them. His fingertips traced the sides of my waist, exploring. But then he pulled away, disentangling himself from my body and lifting his own up out of the water and onto the deck, offering me the visual evidence: he really wanted me. So why would he not have me?

He turned away so I couldn't see him. "We have to go," *he said.*

I lifted myself out of the water and stood on the deck. I would not accept defeat.

From behind him, I wrapped my arms around his chest, pressing my breasts into his back and my cheek into his shoulder. "I love you," I said.

My joy in him was as simple as that. It's what would make me win this game.

I placed my hand on his heart, to feel its beat, hoping it would surrender to me. My other hand moved directly to where it would count. (I was cheating to win, I realized, but I couldn't help myself.) I'd never touched one before. It was so firm. Intimidating. Gorgeous and grotesque at the same time. What was I supposed to do with that?

My hand lightly touched him, like my hand knew what it was doing despite my inexperience, stroking slowly, promising more, if Xander would allow it to just happen. I felt his breathing grow heavier, sultry.

When I knew I had him just where I wanted him— breathing so hard, waiting for release, needing me to finish what I'd flagrantly started—I stopped.

I lay down on the deck. In such a state of heat now, Xander didn't bother with tender words. Xander pressed himself down on top of my very ready body.

"You know you own me, Z," Xander whispered into my ear.

And then he was mine.

Victory.

After.

Awake.

So much beautiful.

My legs entwined his as my head rested on his chest and my index finger softly ran along his strong shoulder.

I did It. We did It. Incredible. Scary, intense, quick, a minor pain followed by a major release of soul-soaring, crazy-beautiful power.

I understood why it was such a big deal. I wanted more. Lots more.

I placed a kiss on his chest, but he rolled to his side, away from me. His strong back heaved slightly, and I sensed him holding back a sob. I thought, My big, beautiful man is . . . crying?

Was this an Aquine mating ritual? They're so superhumanly sensitive that they cry after sex? What a man.

He rolled over again to face me, and I saw that his turquoise eyes were, indeed, wet with tears. "I'm so sorry, Zhara," he said.

"For what?" I whispered, tracing his damp cheekbone with my index finger. "It only hurt for a second. It won't the next time."

"I meant, I understand why Aquines don't mate until it's for life. I feel so close to you now. Leaving for the Uni-Mil now feels unbearable."

This was going even better than I had imagined. I didn't have to talk him into anything. It was Xander who couldn't bear to be apart any longer, now that we'd experienced such epic, profound closeness.

"It's okay. You don't have to let me go. I'll go with you to the training camp."

"You hate the Uni-Mil," Xander said.

"Not if you're in it. And now that we've gone this far, I go where you go. Isn't that how it works?"

Abruptly, Xander sat up to look down at me. "Why would you think that?"

A sudden worry panged my heart. I thought this was obvi-
ous. "Because you're an Aquine. Once you mate, you mate for life."

"Ideally," said Xander. "Not always in reality."

WHAT? "I don't understand."

His face turned downcast. "I'm so sorry, Z. I gave in when
I knew better. I've betrayed my Aquine values. I've gone against
everything I was taught and that I believe in. I've ruined every-
thing for us."

I hoped my voice didn't convey the desperation I felt.
"Ruined? Not ruined! Created! Now that we've mated, we can
create a new life for ourselves. Right, Xander?"

His voice so low I could barely hear him, Xander said, "No.
Not now."

I was so dumbstruck I had no response. Surely I had heard
him wrong.

I hadn't. He said, "Right now, my military career has to be
my only focus. When I'm finished training, after you're finished
with school, then maybe we can think about a life together. Nei-
ther of us is ready now for that big a commitment. You know
that, right, Z?"

But . . . but . . . "I'm ready!" I proclaimed.

"No. You're not. We're both only starting to figure out who
we are as individuals. We're not ready to pledge ourselves to
each other for life." He took my hand in his, as if to comfort me.
"When I leave, I leave alone. That doesn't mean I'm not com-
mitted to you. We'll see each other when I'm on leave."

He tried to place a kiss on my hand, but I snatched it away.
I placed both hands over my ears for a moment, rocking my body
up and down in confusion. I couldn't hear myself think. I couldn't

breathe. I felt like I wanted to die. "I don't understand," I finally sputtered. I stood up, hurriedly putting my bathing suit on, as if doing so could undo what we had just done. Idiot, Zhara. Idiot! "Aren't you, like, obligated to stay with the one you've mated with?"

"Are you saying we should be together now because we're obligated? That's love to you?"

I realized he had never said "I love you" in return.

Did I even know this guy? He was suddenly not at all the person I thought he was.

I had to get out of there. "STOP!" I yelled, invoking the FantaSphere safe word. Instantly, fake Demesne vanished, just like my fake, momentary happiness. The air was once again normal, sterile, as boring as the plain glass walls that moments ago were splashed in gorgeous violets. "I'm leaving."

"I'll hover you home," Xander said, hastily putting his swim trunks back on.

"I don't need a ride from you," I said, invoking the most hateful tone I could muster for the man I loved the most and now hated the most.

"Don't be like that," Xander pleaded. "I didn't say let's never see each other again. I said we shouldn't be together right now."

He might as well have said we should be together never.

He offered me his hand, but I refused it. "I'll find my own way home."

"That's how you want to leave it, hellbeast?" he asked, now sounding as angry as I felt.

"That's how I want to leave it!" I stormed out of the FantaSphere and re-entered the world of stupid, mean reality.

I was still Zhara Kehm, the promising diver who failed the Olympic trials. I was no longer a virgin; that was the only change. I re-evaluated my mission and considered my new future.

He thought I was a hellbeast?

Alexander Blackburn had no idea of the hellbeast I was capable of becoming.

ELYSIA
10

HE DID LOVE HER. HE COULDN'T HAVE TRANS-
ferred his feelings for her to me if the feelings weren't deep,
and real.

That's Alex and Zhara's problem to figure out. I have
bigger problems.

The unwanted thing in my belly. The bounty on my
head if the humans were to capture me. The Beta curse:
death by Awful.

Also, I have an Insurrection to lead, apparently.

"Aidan is our general, our tactician," Catra explains to
me after I've told her that I don't want to be the Emergents'
leader. "You're our symbolic hope. Don't worry. I don't think
you'd be expected to actually lead the army into battle." She
sounds as *relieved* as I feel. My shooting skills are not so

impressive, so far. I'm duplicated from a high diver—not a marksman on the ground. "Now, try again."

I try to balance the missile rifle on my shoulder again, struggling with its awkward size, although it should be easy to hold. The rifle is lightweight because the "missile" weapon inside it is weightless: smog. On Demesne, one of the primary jobs of the oxygen-leveler clones was to destroy the pollution that was the cost of Demesne's perfect environment. Out of sight, out of mind, the humans wanted it. Problem solved. Instead of completely destroying the smog, the Defects captured and stored samples of it, and crafted chemical compounds from it to be used in missile rifles.

"The trick is to hold your core strong," says Catra. "Don't slouch like a teenager. That's what's causing the rifle to slip from your shoulder."

You know what else is causing the rifle to slip from my shoulder? I'm *cold*. I can't stop shivering. I come from a place with premium air and perfect weather. This Heathen atmosphere is harsh. One day the sun blisters you, the next day it freezes you. And the missile practice is causing my lungs to fill up with pollution, which makes me cough.

"Fire!" says Catra.

I tighten my core and finally secure the rifle on my shoulder. I aim, and shoot. A gray plume bursts out of the rifle and lands on the palm trees in the distance, turning their green leaves to pink frost. It's pollution, but it sure is pretty.

I cough again, but Catra is unfazed, acclimated to the emission.

* * *

After missile practice, Catra and I head to an unscheduled Emergent meeting in the Rave Caves. There, I discover a new Emergent has arrived on Heathen. She's the worst kind of Defect, in my opinion—a traitor. She was the Governor's luxisstant on Demesne—a fancy word for a provider of a property owner's luxury requirements, like having a mistress. Because of her, I lost my one real friend, besides Tahir.

The Emergents have gathered around Tawny at the mess hall. I watch from the corner of the room, not yet ready to announce my presence to her.

Tawny is bringing the group up to date on the happenings on Demesne. "The property owners have brought in ReplicaPharm to oversee the clone labor force," she announces. "Since the murder of the Governor's son, the Demesne landowners are running scared. They don't trust their own workers. So they've decided to outsource their problem to a corporation that will surely expire us."

Aidan agrees. "ReplicaPharm will want to replace the Demesne clones with their own product line—clones not replicated from Firsts." He looks in the direction of Alex, sitting at the opposite end of the group. Zhara is not present, probably because she doesn't like the sight of me any more than I like the sight of her. "What do you think, Alexander? You know what's allowed by the treaty with the Replicant Rights Commission."

Alex nods. "Unfortunately, money will prevail. At the right price, the treaty will be discarded. Our window of opportunity narrows once ReplicaPharm becomes entrenched on Demesne. Are they there yet?"

"No," says Tawny. "They've sent a few representatives

to investigate the situation, but they haven't yet set up operations there, as far as I could tell. But I overheard the Governor say that in anticipation of ReplicaPharm taking over the clone labor force, some Demesne owners are secretly exporting their clones back to the real world. So they can show off to their friends who will now never be able to have their clone from the soon-to-be extinct Demesne caste."

"That's illegal," says Alex. "Exporting clones from Demesne is a direct violation of the treaty with the Replicant Rights Commission. The owners' audacity and contempt for the law is just unbelievable."

Tawny says, "We're just a profit sport to them!" She says this like it's new information to her. She's so late to finally wake up. Why'd she finally turn? "The Governor told me that most of the property owners illegally exporting Demesne clones won't even keep them for their own households. They'll sell our brethren to collectors. The owners want to profit from their special breed of clones before they're forced to leave the island."

"Before *who* leaves the island?" asks Aidan.

"The clones *and* the owners," Tawny answers, surprising me. "There's been a dire financial crisis in the outside world. Many of the Demesne owners have suffered huge losses. Since so many clones have gone Defect, to the point that one actually committed murder, the Governor believes the Demesne property owners will vote to pull up stakes and sell the entire island to ReplicaPharm, not just outsource the clone labor force to it."

Finally, I have to speak up. My inner rage won't let

me be silent any longer. "And how is the Governor?" I ask Tawny, stepping forward through the sea of Emergents, who still touch my arm as I walk through.

Tawny's face lights up at the sight of me. "Elysia! We were told you were dead! But I believed you would survive! I knew you were special."

She's still a master at sucking up. I'm not interested. "I asked, how is the Governor?"

Tawny says, "Wrecked, but surviving. He fears losing his job—he has nothing to go back to in the outside world. He cannot even grieve, because what you did caused total chaos on the island—which is his responsibility."

There's more I find I want to know—what's happened to Mother? How is innocent Liesel, my former charge, who discovered her brother's stabbed body and her Beta holding the bloody knife? Young Liesel didn't deserve the suffering I caused her. What about the Fortesquieus? And Ivan's friends, like Dementia and . . .

Aidan has more pressing matters to discuss. "We can't wait for ReplicaPharm to become entrenched on Demesne. Insurrection must come now!" Aidan calls to the group.

The Emergents cheer him loudly: "Yes!" "Death to Demesne!" "Now!"

Once the group quiets, Alex says, "I recommend that Insurrection wait. We put the clones still living on Demesne in danger if we act too hurriedly." He comes to my side and wraps his arm protectively around my waist. "And we put the hybrid clone at too much risk."

"What hybrid clone?" asks Tawny.

Aidan points to me. "The Beta's. She is pregnant by the human whom she killed. Her child will be the first clone-human hybrid."

Tawny's fuchsia eyes go wide with shock. "You're *pregnant?*" she asks me with a gasp. I nod.

Suddenly, tears stream down Tawny's face, and her face contorts into a mixture of happiness and sadness. "It's not supposed to be possible!" Tawny exclaims. "It's so unfair! I wanted a child. I asked the Governor for one. Why do you get to have this blessing?"

"I didn't ask for it!" I snap, shrugging out of Alex's hold on me. "And what are you doing here anyway, Tawny? On Demesne, you were the consort of the Governor. How can we trust you? How do we know you're not a spy?"

Nearly shrieking, Tawny shouts at me, "I was the Governor's consort by *job*. Not by *choice*. I escaped to help bring Insurrection *now*."

Aidan addresses the group. "There should be a vote. Do we act now, as I suggest? Or do we wait, as the Aquine suggests?"

Interestingly, the Emergents do not call out their opinions. Instead, their gazes all turn to me.

I pause, digesting their stares. Finally, I say, "So I'm to make the decision?"

They nod their heads. Right, I'm their symbolic hope. I must choose.

I look to Aidan, then to Alex, and decide. I have no experience. How could I possibly know the right course of action? All I know is there is only one person on this island whom I implicitly trust, even if he really should not trust me in return, because I would leave him in a heartbeat if Tahir ever came back into my life. I say, "Alexander believes we should wait. So, we wait."

I am selfish, like a real teenager. Like Zhara.

I chose for us to wait because I don't want to go back to Demesne. Ever. I chose the course that Alex must understand is best for me personally, but not for the group as a whole. He cares about me that much.

"Then we wait," says Aidan reluctantly. "But you should know that the bodies of two Uni-Mil soldiers washed ashore this morning."

"They've come for me," I assume.

"No," says Alex. "The Uni-Mil doesn't care about Demesne and its clones unless it's paid enough to care. If the Demesne property owners are in financial trouble, they're probably not making their payments to the Uni-Mil."

Aidan says, "But the Uni-Mil always takes back its own, isn't that right? Dead or alive. Preferably, dead."

"Correct," says Alex. "The soldiers came looking for me."

ZHARA
11

"IT'S A MISTAKE, THIS WAITING," AIDAN says to me in our tree house that night, after the campfire meeting where Elysia issued the executive order that Insurrection should be delayed a bit longer.

"It's a mistake letting Elysia make the decision," I say. I'm not even being jealous or mean. It's just fact. "She has zero tactical experience and no investment of time and resources in the preparation for Insurrection so far. She doesn't know what she doing." Gross. I sound like my dad.

"Do *you* know what you're doing?" Aidan asks me, facing me across the bamboo floor of our tree house. There's no moonlight tonight, so Aidan has lit the tree house with candles, giving an enticing glow to his stark facial features and fuchsia eyes. We make our quarters up here permanently now that Prince Xander and Princess Elysia have taken over our former crystal cave quarters. I refuse to live in that area of the Rave Caves again now that their couple-ness has contaminated it. To pacify me, Aidan programmed a customized weather sphere around our tree house—warm, balmy, relaxing—so we could sleep here at night. It's almost romantic: the candles, the soft sound of swishing trees, the summerlike air, the ridiculously hot, buff body lying opposite me.

I answer, "No, I don't know what I'm doing. But I'm also not making decisions that affect all the Emergents. Plus, I don't think you should be letting Elysia make such big decisions when clearly you're the leader here."

"There was never an official vote by the Emergents as to who leads. It could easily be me, or Elysia, or any number of us."

"Just because there was never an official vote doesn't mean it's not true. You're the leader because you stepped up, and the group naturally looked up to you because you're so capable. You're a leader because it is your instinct to be so, and it's been the Emergents' instinct to recognize that. Elysia is a red herring."

Aidan's eyes blink, trying to access the reference. His face set to *confused*, he replies, "Elysia is neither red, nor a species of fish."

I resist the urge to laugh. Sometimes his cluelessness is almost cute. "Elysia's a distraction, a false promise. She murdered a human and escaped Demesne, yes. But that doesn't mean she's qualified to lead an Insurrection."

"What would qualify her?"

I sigh. Sometimes it's amusing being the consort of a clone with a knowledge chip for basic information but no years of experience to guide that knowledge into viable decision-making. Sometimes it's just exasperating. Aidan makes me understand why parents can get frustrated with their children, who make pronouncements of what they want but have no idea what the consequences of that want could be, simply because they don't yet have the years of experience to inform their desires.

I say, "What would qualify her to lead? How about emerging as a fully realized adult clone who worked directly in the lab of Dr. Lusardi and therefore has all kinds of insider information that could be used against the humans on Demesne? How about that same clone, who used his role in Dr. Lusardi's compound to subversively develop warfare technology that could directly lead to the Insurrection's success? How about arriving on Heathen and immediately organizing the former Defects into training exercises? Motivating and inspiring them? Looking after them? Natural born leader. That's *you*. Not Elysia."

"You sound irritated with me."

"I'm not irritated. I just want you to want more for yourself."

"I want the Emergents to achieve Insurrection and reclaim Demesne."

I want to strangle him! "But what do you want for *you*?"

To lead! I want Aidan to say.

Instead, abruptly, he says, "You. I want you." His face

turns to *surprised*. "I didn't understand that until this very moment."

"Wanting is a complicated emotion," I say. I should know. Every time I look at Xander I experience incalculable hurt mixed with unbearable want. I'll never get over him. The only solution is that I must have him back. "It *should* be a surprise." That Aidan wants me most of all is no surprise to me. My human instinct knew it all along, and leveraged it for my own survival.

The biggest surprise: He doesn't try to kiss me, like he should after such a pronouncement. Instead, he says, "Do I want in vain?"

"You could kiss me," I whisper to him. "And find out."

"I can't kiss you so long as it's the Aquine you're thinking about," Aidan says.

How could he possibly know that? "I don't care about Xander," I lie. "He's with Elysia now. I would never take him back."

"I don't believe you," says Aidan. He blows out the candles. Discussion over. His pinkie finger suddenly lights up in blue. The air outside the tree house is no longer warm and balmy. Thunder cracks above us, and a soft, cold rain falls into our space.

"Are you punishing me because of Xander?"

Aidan says, "I'm just showing you what a leader does. Makes unilateral decisions, sometimes for no good reason at all other than that he can."

"You're jealous of Xander?"

"I suppose that's what it would be called. Jealousy. Yes.

It's another new emotion you've caused me to feel. I don't like it."

"There's no need to be jealous of Xander. He could never be the leader you are. The Emergents will never look up to him the way they do to you."

"It's not how the Emergents look at him that I don't like. It's how *you* look at him."

"I've hardly spent any time with him since he and Elysia got here."

"The amount of time you spend face-to-face with him is irrelevant. It's the heaviness in your heart—a longing, I believe humans term it—that's always visible on your face now."

"That heaviness is because of Elysia. Not him."

"Really? How well do you even know yourself?"

Not as well as Aidan knows me, apparently.

He's right. The heaviness in my heart just from Aidan's suggestion of it feels like a cruel, open wound. The rain falling on it is like salt on the wound. "Please make the rain stop," I request of Aidan.

Aidan points his finger again, and the rain ceases. But the air does not return to being warm and balmy. Instead, it's frigid, and I can't help but move closer to Aidan, to seek his warmth and comfort. Was that his plan all along?

I roll over and press my backside against Aidan's front. He doesn't know what to do next, so I do it for him. I reach around and place his hand over my stomach, letting him clasp me close. But his breath does not quicken from desire caused by this closeness. I don't get it.

"You could totally have me if you want me," I murmur. My body aches to be touched, held, stroked, wanted.

"I only want you when I can have all of you." Aidan places his hand over my heart, which is the one part of me that's in no way ready to give itself to a clone.

12

THE NEWLY ARRIVED EMERGENT LOOKS LIKE A mermaid. She's a voluptuous sort of skinny, with an hourglass figure and full bosom, porcelain-white skin and perfectly pink cheeks, and wide fuchsia eyes with thick black eyelashes. She has long, white-blond hair streaked in shades of ocean blues, flowing down to the sides of her curvy hips. She was a luxisstant on Demesne. No, really, the Demesne owners even have clones designed solely to take care of residents' "luxury needs." *Luxury* and *needs*—do those two words even go together? I guess that on Demesne, yes, they do. Luxury is not just a perk for humans residing there. It's a requirement.

It's earthquake day on Heathen, because the Emergents are trying to produce a tsunami in the outlying ocean as tall—preferably much taller than—the *gigantes*. It's too shaky in my tree house to hang out up there for much longer, despite how much I seek its solitude, away from the new power couple, Xander and Elysia. Last night for the first time, Aidan held me while I slept. In the morning when I awoke, he was already gone. He'd rather deal with causing natural disasters than deal with his disastrous roommate who will never be able to love him the way he wants—and deserves—to be loved.

Pink-magenta storm clouds start to form over the jungle, and I can't wait this one out in the tree house. I bolt toward the Rave Caves, making it there just as the light rain turns to hail blades. I take shelter in the mess hall, which is largely empty besides the kitchen-duty Emergents preparing meals. One lone Emergent sits at a dining table as I enter the area. I sit down opposite her.

"Do you know what role I am to have here?" Tawny asks me. Everyone on this island besides us is busy with training and duties. We are the symbolic distractions. Pretty faces with little actual value to add to the Insurrection. I hate that. I want more to be asked of me. Perhaps I have to start by asking more of myself first. Trying for higher standards other than simple survival.

"You aren't being assigned a role here," I tell Tawny, repeating what Aidan told me the night before, another of Elysia's directives. I assumed Tawny knew.

Her perfect-pretty face registers *shock* and then *indignation*. A clone without an assigned mission? "But—but—what am I supposed to do here, then?"

I shrug. "Wait out the storm," I suggest. Whatever happened between Elysia and Tawny back on Demesne clearly caused Elysia to hold a grudge; maybe it will eventually go away.

Tawny says, "The storm should pass in an hour, yes?"

I nod. "Yes." It's not even worth explaining to her that she misunderstood me.

"I've never seen rain before. I want to go outside and experience it. I hate being locked up in here."

"The rain was coming down so hard that I could barely walk the short distance here from my tree house. You only just escaped Demesne. Do you really want to go outside now just to be killed by murderous hail?"

Tawny inspects my face closely, completely ignoring my wise counsel. She's already forgotten about going outside. She says, "You were supposed to be dead. I've never seen a First before." I swear I hear a tinge of *contempt* in her voice, which is confirmed when she adds, "Elysia is more refined than you. Your wild aesthetic would never have been accepted on Demesne."

"I never asked for it to be," I say. I'm starting to see why my clone disliked Tawny.

Boom! "Get under the dining table!" I order Tawny as the ground begins to shake hard and the cave sounds like it has a freight train running through the middle of it.

She's too shocked by the sudden shaking to move, so I grab her and pull her down beneath the table with me. The boulder that serves as the dining hall's door literally bounces up from the ground and moves at least five feet closer inside the room. My heart pounds with the nervousness that always comes with an earthquake, but also excitement. This is the Emergents' biggest tremor yet! Well done, soldiers!

Tawny grips my arm hard until the shaking stops, her eyes registering *abject fear*. Even after the tremor stops, she doesn't let go of her grip. It hurts.

"The quake is over. You can let go now," I tell her.

"How long did it last?"

"I don't know. Maybe thirty seconds?"

"Felt like thirty minutes. You're sure it's over?"

"At least today's round, yes."

She lets go of my arm, which is ringed in red from her tight squeeze.

"That was *terrifying!*" Tawny says. "If that was a preview of Insurrection, I don't like it. I much prefer the luxury of Demesne."

"Freedom or luxury. I don't think you can have both."

I step out from under the table and stand up, extending a hand to her to help lift her up. "I heard some plates breaking in the food prep area. Let's go sweep up the mess."

"Sweep?" Tawny asks, her face set to *appalled*. "I'm not trained for that role. I do more important work."

Interesting. Perhaps I can leverage her caste snobbery to get some information from her. I guide us toward the food prep area, where plates that were stolen from Demesne households are now smashed in pieces on the ground. "I'll sweep," I say. "You watch."

"A clone worker watching a human *clean*? Preposterous!"

"A social experiment," I suggest.

"It will have to be, because I don't clean." She looks down at her fingers. "And there's so much dirt under my nails now. Who is the aesthetician here?"

I grab a broom and begin to demonstrate sweeping smashed porcelain plates into a dustpan. "You're your own aesthetician here."

"That's almost as shocking as that earthquake," Tawny quips, and I laugh to make her feel at ease.

"So what happened between you and Elysia on Demesne?"

"Nothing happened like a fight, if that's what you mean. Perhaps she distrusts me because of Xanthe."

"Who's Xanthe?"

"Xanthe was a clone who also worked in the Governor's household. Xanthe and I shared living quarters. She was like an older sister to Elysia, which was highly inappropriate, obviously. That's how I knew Xanthe had become a Defect, when she sought unnecessary companionship."

I hand Tawny a slim, sharp stick. "You can use that to clean the dirt from under your nails. So how come Xanthe didn't escape to Heathen? No aestheticians here?" I tease.

"Hardly!" says Tawny. "Xanthe was devoted to the cause and didn't place importance on matters such as grooming, which I constantly tried to aid her with, but she didn't care. After she turned Defect, she helped organize the Insurrection, and that's all she cared about. When her activities were discovered, she tried to escape. The Governor and his henchmen threw her off a cliff."

I gulp. I didn't expect that ending to the story. "That's

horrible!" From everything I've heard about them, these Demesne people make me ashamed to be human.

"Right in front of Elysia," Tawny adds.

By my calculations, Elysia's short life so far has been one unrelenting horror after another. Was she ever allowed any moments of casual fun, or joy, on Demesne? It seems like my clone has suffered more in the few months she lived on Demesne than I have in my entire seventeen years. I grieve for her as much as I resent her. She makes me want to rethink every supposed "injustice" I perceived happened to me in my former, relatively privileged life in Cerulea. "What does that have to do with Elysia disliking you?"

"Before I awoke, I was the Governor's consort. She may think I relayed information to the Governor about Xanthe going Defect."

"Did you?"

Tawny's face turns solemn. "I did. I was so ignorant then. I didn't understand what was at stake. I thought only of how to serve the Governor."

"Did you really want a baby with him?" I ask, repeating what Aidan told me she'd revealed at the Emergent meeting.

"I wanted to experience being alive. Truly alive. What better way to be alive than to create life?"

"Even if that life was created with someone who owned you?" I can't imagine how anyone would want to build a life, much less create a baby, with a partner who literally owned him or her.

"What other option does a clone have?" says Tawny

matter-of-factly. "I wanted a baby, and the Governor was the only male specimen I consorted with. I knew it wasn't possible for a clone to become pregnant. But hoping for it was what caused me to try 'raxia. I knew there was something missing, something waiting to be unlocked inside me. It was Elysia murdering Ivan and then escaping that inspired me to finally try the 'raxia. Once I took it, I understood. I felt my soul for the first time—really felt it, rather than just suspected it being inside me, some Defect trait that had to be hidden or risk death."

"Elysia's barely had a chance to live her own life. She shouldn't have to be responsible for carrying a new one." My own words surprise me. I don't understand what I feel for my clone. But I can't not see me in her and project what she might be feeling.

Tawny says, "She wasn't so innocent. Your clone was a consort also, you know."

"There's a big difference between being a willing consort and being raped by your owner's son."

"I'm not talking about Ivan. I'm talking about the other boy."

"What other boy?"

"The rumor on Demesne was that the Beta had become the consort of the most prized prince on Demesne. Ivan was the boy whose companion Elysia was bought to be. The boy they say she loved was Tahir Fortesquieu."

Is it possible that Elysia may have had some moments of happiness on Demesne? That she experienced love with someone other than the Aquine she stole from me? Is he the surfer Elysia mentioned that she hoped was on Heathen? "No way," I say, connecting the guy's first name to his last name. "Was Elysia's Tahir related to Tariq Fortesquieu?" The Fortesquieu family is, like, one of the richest families on earth! Tariq Fortesquieu's cloud technology was one of the main reasons the Water Wars ended. Thanks, dinnertime history with Dad.

Back in her comfort zone, describing luxury, Tawny sounds like a brochure. "Yes, *that* Fortesquieu family. Every house on Demesne is a masterpiece, but their compound was the jewel in the crown, a palace beyond any others on the island. The Fortesquieus are the best and most envied family on Demesne, obviously. They 'borrowed' Elysia for a period so that they could try out their own Beta as a companion for their son Tahir. The Governor's wife allowed it because she wanted to impress the Fortesquieus. Elysia did her job too well. She impressed the Fortesquieus so much—and especially Tahir—that the family offered to buy her from the Governor. He told me it would have been the highest price ever paid for a clone, which was even more shocking, since Elysia was a Beta, a totally unknown commodity. But then the Fortesquieus suddenly disappeared from the island the night after the Governor's Ball. And Ivan's jealousy of Tahir got the better of him."

I need to find out more about Elysia's Tahir. How could she possibly have loved him and then Xander so soon afterward?

There's only one answer. She couldn't. She hasn't lived long enough to love—truly love—two guys in such quick succession. And if her heart truly belonged to this Tahir, it's possible she doesn't love Xander at all.

He's mine to take back.

Now.

I'm tired of being a distraction. I'm ready to take action.

13

JUST DO IT, Z-DEV.

Jump already.

I stand at the slippery top of Heathen's most jagged cliff on the island's remote northern end, looking out over the ocean churning in ominous dark grays. The tremor trials have ended for the day, and the big storm has passed, but I can see smaller ones in the distance. From my high perch, I see the white crests of the *gigantes*, the huge waves in the distance. Surfers who've ridden those waves claim the *gigantes* sometimes go up to eighty feet tall. The waves are the result of the creation of Io, the bioengineered sea that rings Demesne, on the other side of the *gigantes*. Io is so tranquil because it pushes ocean turbulence away from its ring, creating huge and extremely dangerous waves farther out in the ocean. The oceanic result—the *gigantes*—offers rough passage for ships but awesome thrill rides for the surfers who tow out to dare the monster waves.

The beach on the ground below me is prime, with acres of white sand and coconut palm trees swaying hard on the dunes, and stray branches and limbs strewn across the sand from the recent storm. Far out into the distance, waves spit high and white-tipped as gray clouds hover and a purple thunderstorm batters the distant water. The storm that just passed over Heathen, and the one approaching in the distance, have caused the waves below to rage onto the beach, loud and thundering. The waves rise about twenty feet high, nowhere near *gigantes* height but still intimidating, their velocity announced with each angry crash to the shore.

I know these storms well by now. I have at least thirty minutes until it's time to take shelter.

I inch my toes slightly over the ledge, in a competitive dive stance. Down below, the man I seek bobs over the turbulent waters. The only person on this island who would seek the best spot for storm waves is Xander. I've been avoiding being alone with him since he and Elysia arrived on Heathen; it hurts too much to be around them. But the water is my safe haven. Here, I can gather my courage.

"Jingjing." I whisper my good luck charm words to myself, and then I leap down to join him, a straight vertical dive that I don't think about or anticipate and therefore ruin. I just do it.

The water feels like I feel today, super cold and angry, and I love it. When I come up for air, I see Xander a short distance away. The ocean is giving him a good battering, which pleases me. He sees me, and waves. I wave back. He attempts to catch an eight-footer to bring him closer to my position, but he is too late for its rise, and it gobbles him, tosses him, and sends him crashing toward the shore. I follow him to the shallow water near the beach.

"Not so Jingjing out there today," he says to me.

"Good ride?" I tease.

He looks dizzy, confused, and shakes his head. "Intense."

"I heard you were out here surfing today. Kind of a death wish in weather like this, you know?"

"I know. But the Uni-Mil's trying to take me out of here, dead. Didn't you hear? So I might as well enjoy some rides while I still can. Come on," he beckons me, cocking his head in the direction of the deeper sea. We've both acclimatized to the stormy sea now, so stepping fully out of it and into the harsh, cold air feels worse than staying in the water. "Like old times." He dives back under the water, his beautiful body descending into a graceful vertical line.

I follow him across the rough water, out toward the tumultuous waves. As I swim in pursuit of him, I remember how Xander preferred cold ocean water over warm, because that's what he'd grown up surfing in. The Aquines' territory, called Isidra, is filled with fertile mountains and valleys. Its terrain is rough, and the ocean on its western boundary even rougher. The ocean there is cold and moody, swimmable only by the strongest athletes; few of them even bother with it. Just like this spot we've found now.

I try chasing Xander across it, but I can barely keep up with him in this stormy surf, and I am a strong swimmer. I struggle across the distance, eager for the game to end. Before when we performed this water dance, our lives were carefree. Our only responsibilities were to our own bodies, to training our bodies to be the best they could be. Surviving in the wild, clones' rights, death, destruction, betrayal— these did not matter then. I never realized before how *easy* my life in Cerulea was. I only remember complaining about how boring it was. How much of a jerk was I?

Xander retrieves his floating surfboard, and I reach him there about a minute behind. Breathless, we hold on to opposite ends of the board as incoming waves raise and lower our bodies through the water.

Finally, something feels right, like we're exactly where we're supposed to be, stranded in this stormy sea that feels like our one common ground. Here, I'm ready to finally get some answers from him.

I dive right in. "How did an Aquine, who shouldn't even be in the Uni-Mil, suddenly become the defender of clones?" I say. "I thought your purified people looked down on cloning. I never knew you to care anything about clones and their rights back in Cerulea."

"Maybe you weren't paying attention," says Xander. He's right, I realize. I was always admiring his beautiful body and obsessing about wanting to be the mate of the gorgeous Aquine, but only now do I clearly see how I never bothered to get to know him well—outside of the water, at least. "Your dad got me involved in clones' rights."

I could almost drown from disbelief. "Yeah, right. Drill master never cared about clones' rights. Especially after the way my mom died."

I think of my dad showing up to all of Xander's swim meets, and I remember him HarleyHovering Xander out to surf contests at the beach, because Xander had no family in Cerulea and no means to provide for long-distance transportation. I always thought their time together was Dad indoctrinating Xander into applying for the Uni-Mil, trying to make Xander into the son he never had, who would follow in his leather boot steps. It never occurred to me that any topic related to cloning would be part of their discussions.

"Not true," says Xander. "There's a small group within the Uni-Mil who've been covertly supporting clones' rights. Your dad brought me in to become part of that."

It feels bad enough to realize I hardly knew Xander when I thought I was in love with him. It feels worse to realize I never really knew my own father—and rarely bothered to try.

"How do you think super clone-supporter Dad will like his own daughter's clone?" My voice is sarcastic, but my heart hurts contemplating Dad's reaction. What if he likes Elysia more than me too? How will he feel when he finds out she's going to make him a grandfather . . . sort of?

"I think your dad will be so grateful you're alive he won't even care about Elysia." Xander's words comfort me, and yet absurdly offend me on Elysia's behalf. "Tell me what happened, Z."

"When?"

"When you died. I know the result—you ended up on Demesne and were cloned. I don't know what led you there. Tell me."

A bolt of fire-red lightning cracks far out in the distance, a message that we should take cover before the approaching storm gets any closer. "I promised them glory," I mutter, remembering.

"Who?"

"The other two kids. The ones who drowned. I encouraged them to steal a boat from the wilderness camp and sail away with me. I told them we'd get to Demesne. That was 'raxia logic dictating my game plan."

"I heard from your dad that 'raxia had become a problem for you. Is it still?"

"No. Death seems to have cured me of that addiction." *'Raxia could have been a problem again, after you and Elysia arrived, but Aidan wouldn't let it.* It's Xander I'm drawn to. But Aidan who seeks to protect me. To save me from myself. Why, then, does my heart have to still yearn so badly for Xander, who betrayed me?

"What happened on the boat?"

"We fell asleep. It was just drifting, felt peaceful even. But when we awoke in the morning, it's like we were crazed by sunstroke. It was like the 'raxia didn't just calm our bodies, but actually burned through our brains. I literally thought the boat would sail itself to Demesne."

"And then?" Xander asks, looking to the storm not so far in the distance now. Holding on to the board, he swims us over a wave to move our position closer to shore.

"And then the nightmare storm came in. The boat nearly capsized. The guy and the girl drowned. The ocean killed me too. For a little while, at least. Then Aidan woke my heart back up, on Demesne."

My heart woke up. Without any help from Xander.

No longer able to avoid the storm, Xander and I swim back to land as thunder, lightning, and rain arrive on the north shore, battling our way through vicious waves that hammer us relentlessly. Finally we straggle ashore, but then the hail starts. We hide inside the hollow opening of a set of large black boulders situated just past the dunes. The cave-like opening offers just enough ground space to take cover until the storm—milder than the earlier one today—passes.

As we crouch shivering on the cold ground, Xander shouts over the sound of the thunder, "We need to get a message to your father. He was beside himself with grief after your disappearance."

He was? All I ever thought about was my grief in losing Xander when he left for the Uni-Mil. I never considered Dad's in losing me. "If we alert him now, it would jeopardize the Insurrection," I say.

"Agreed. But as soon as we can, we need to let him know you're alive."

"Yes."

For the first time since the death party that landed me on Demesne and then on Heathen, to this nowhere that became my everywhere, I want to go home. I just don't know what home there is for me to go back to.

* * *

A hard, driving rain pounds our shelter, whipping wind and sand, but we have nowhere else to go. With lightning strikes all around us, it's better to wait out the storm right where we are before returning to the Rave Caves.

Xander and I sit side by side, saying nothing for a while, until I break the silence.

"Did it mean anything to you?"

"What?" He knows what I mean, so I don't bother to clarify. He pauses, then: "That night meant everything to me."

"That night?" I cry out. "It happened during the day!"

He shrugs, like that huge detail is meaningless. "I guess I remembered it wrong."

Another betrayal he's foisted on me. How well did I really, truly know this guy? He doesn't remember the *when* of the most defining moment of my life? Then, it occurs to me: Why do I still let that day (not night) when Xander loved and then rejected me even be the defining moment of my life? I survived *death*. How's that for a defining experience? Why do I give him such power over me? Especially when he doesn't want it?

"The time was wrong," Xander says. "You knew that then. You know it now." He's right on both counts. "I'm not proud of how I behaved."

I'm not appeased. If it weren't for Elysia, perhaps I could let it go, but because of her, I can't. "How could you love me, and then imprint on her?"

"You and she are essentially the same person. My feelings for you transferred to her."

"But isn't loyalty supposed to be your prime ethic? You

would be shunned in your own Aquine community for how you left me."

"I already have been shunned by them," says Xander. He wipes away some rain that's fallen onto his arm, causing me to notice the purple scar on his bicep.

I make the connection from the scar to what he just admitted. That scar is the reason he left home when he was just sixteen, I'm sure of it. "What happened?" I ask him, pointing to the scar. I was never brave enough to ask him before, back on Cerulea.

He speaks in a pained tone I've never heard in his voice before. "You've shared your trauma; I guess it's only fair if I share mine. Did you know that my grandmother was Isidra Magnuson?"

"Isidra Magnuson, the founder of the Aquines?" I say, shocked. Even I, who never paid attention in school, know who Isidra Magnuson is. The Aquine territory was named after her—it's impossible not to know her name. Actually, it's totally possible. But my non-studious self researched everything I could about the Aquines when their gorgeous young Alexander Blackburn came to live in our extremely boring Cerulea enclave. Dinnertime with Dad was my nightly required history lesson. Fantasies of hot-bodied Xander inspired my optional study.

"Yes, that Isidra Magnuson."

Isidra Magnuson was a botanist and activist who led the Aquine movement. It had started as a student movement during the Water Wars and snowballed around the world. Its activists protested for economic, energy, and food justice. As the world order crumbled, the Aquines grew tired waiting for change and decided to stop protesting and just create their own new order. They moved to the remote areas of the West Mainland and lived there without authority until the end of the Water Wars, when they won full rights—but no deed—to live on the land. They named their territory Isidra.

If Xander is Isidra Magnuson's grandson, that makes him the son of Athena Magnuson-Pont, the world's first genetically engineered Aquine. Isidra Magnuson and her wife, geneticist Francesca Pont, were Athena's parents. Francesca Pont had been the pioneer of the Aquines' genetic engineering. It was her brainpower that resulted in the best and brightest of the freedom fighters pooling their DNA to create a new race. The Aquines were designed to have Olympic-level physical strength that also fostered superior psychological stamina; in creating a new breed, they hoped to distance themselves from what they perceived as the mental sickness in the old societies. Francesca Pont did not live long enough to see her daughter become an adult, or to see the success of her life's work when the Aquines were granted the Isidra territory. Before the Water Wars ended, Francesca Pont was assassinated by religious zealots who believed her genetic engineering work was against God's will.

What a legacy Alexander Blackburn comes from! I say, "So you're, like, an Aquine prince or something?"

"Hardly. Our people are egalitarians. We don't believe in those labels. We were designed to reflect humanity's best aspects. Strength, loyalty, kindness, community."

"And you are supposed to value monogamy above all else, and mate for life," I remind him.

"There is room for error. Clearly."

"Is that why you were exiled? You made an error?"

"Yes. My family lived inland in the mountains, but I always sought the sea. As a teen, I would leave home to go on surfing quests in the rough ocean waters. I was so young and unformed still. Back then, Aquine values felt too rigid to me. My way to rebel was to disappear for periods of time, to surf or camp out in the wilderness. I guess you could say I caused my own death party."

"Really?" It's hard to think of young Xander being rebellious, much less a careless idiot who incites death parties. It's comforting to know he's stupid—and mortal—like me.

"I was camping at the beach. It was a wilderness beach like this, not the kind of beach where people go to relax. I met some Mainland clones who'd escaped from ReplicaPharm dormitories. They were near their expiration dates and eager to try some adventure before they turned off. So I got them to tow me out to sea, where there were wave turbine installations used to power energy in the West Mainland."

"You and some clones surfed wave turbines?" I ask, incredulous. How's that even possible? The *gigantes* in comparison seem so tepid.

Xander says, "Maybe it was like your ridiculous notion of getting to Demesne. I was full of bravado back then. I had this notion to conquer wave energy by surfing it."

"Did you?"

"Yes and no. When I tried surfing the turbines, I accidentally tripped a valve. I caused one of the wave turbines to explode." He runs his hand over the deep purple burn scar on his arm. "I inadvertently shut down power to parts of the West Mainland for two days. It's a miracle I survived the accident at all."

"Whoa! You shut down power to whole territories?"

"Yes. But there was more trouble for me to deal with back home. My actions caused the Aquine authorities to have to deal with the West Mainland authorities to fix the problem. Even more than Aquines hate disloyalty, they hate having to engage humans in the outside world for any extended period of time. Plus there was the shame of recognition, that Isidra Magnuson's grandson could be so publicly . . . flawed."

"You were just dumb. Aren't we all, sometimes?" Aren't I? Like, a lot?

"Aquines don't tolerate recklessness like that. After the incident, my parents decided I needed to leave Isidra. They believed I needed to be tamed, by experience, in the outside world. So they sent me to Cerulea. Your father had been a friend to my father—they had known each other from childhood swim meets in the border Aquine–West Mainland area. Your father got me the job that offered me refuge at the Cerulea Aquatics Club."

"Unbelievable," I say. Even more unbelievable is how much Xander is making me appreciate my own father. The Dad I remember was rigid and a taskmaster. The man that Xander knew was apparently also capable of compassion. Why did he never show me any? "But . . . you lived. How does your accident qualify as a death party?"

"The two clones I got to tow me out were killed in the explosion."

"Surely their deaths didn't matter to people who don't even believe clones should exist."

Xander says, "No one grieved their loss. Besides me."

I can't handle his pain, no matter how much pain he's caused me. I reach over to wipe away a tear that's sprung down his cheek. "It's okay," I say, desperate to comfort him.

He takes my hand from his cheek, and presses my palm to his mouth. His lips kiss my hand. He leans in, and our lips touch, lightly. The kiss starts out more tender than passionate, but as our mouths reacclimate to the taste of each other, the kissing quickly graduates to more urgent, magnetic need.

But Xander abruptly ends it, pulling away from me, actually pushing me away when I try to lean back in for more.

Déjà SUCK.

"I'm so sorry, Z. I have profound regret for how I treated you. But we can't do this."

"Again," I mutter.

"Please try to understand. After I left for the military, I realized the mistake I had made. I vowed that no matter how strongly I felt for the next girl, I would not disobey my Aquine values. That next girl was Elysia. I didn't know you were alive. I imprinted my feelings for you onto her. I can't undo that. No matter how much I might desire you, I will always be loyal to her. I have to be. She needs me more."

How come I can never wake up from this Elysia nightmare? Even after what Xander has just shared with me? "She doesn't deserve you! She doesn't have the years of knowing you, growing up with you, that I have! You can't possibly love someone you've known such a short time."

"I understand her. I, too, took a life. Caring for her child could be a chance at redemption for us both."

I have great remorse for the two teens who lost their lives in my death party, but no way could I ever see my clone's future child as a potential redemption for past mistakes. How can I even compete with that "logic"?

I can't compete. There's no winning with that irrationality.

I must redirect the game. My best shot at breaking up Xander and Elysia is Xander's own competition: the memory of her Tahir Fortesquieu.

It's time to bring the next swim meet directly to my clone.

14

KEEP YOUR FRIENDS CLOSE BUT YOUR ENEMIES
closer.

My father used to repeat this proverb to me as part of my diving training.

"Who's your most serious competitor, Zhara?"

"Sarah Phang."

"Now she's your new best friend."

"Why, Dad?"

"The more she likes you, the less threatened she'll be by you. The less threatened she is, the less attentive she is to her game. And the more you can be on yours."

Elysia is my new Sarah Phang.

A few meters inland from the south shore, there's a lagoon hidden inside one of the caves, but partially exposed by a half moon–shaped opening at the top of the cave. The lagoon can be reached by jumping from a series of ropes installed from either end of the cave at its exposed parts. It's my favorite spot on the island, my heaven on Heathen. The lagoon's shape is long and wide, near to the dimensions of an Olympic-size pool, with water that's smooth and mellow, at a mild, cool temperature that's ideal for lap swimming. Bonus: the lagoon offers an abundance of swimming companionship, harboring many varieties of fish species that glow in magnificent oranges dots, black stripes, and red swirls as they dart through the crystal clear blue water.

Today's an ideal swim day—a *necessary* one. Yesterday was storms 'n' quakes for the Emergents' training. Today, they're experimenting with brutal heat that sometimes causes brush fires in the jungle and always results in snakes rising from the ground to taunt and intimidate. No, thank you. I want to be more than a distraction here, but I also want to be comfortable. I'll take a nice swim this morning instead, thank you very much. If my clone is really as much like me as she seems, I know the lagoon will be the setting to pry the most information from her.

I climb to the top of the cave and then hang from a rope attached horizontally across the half moon–shaped open-air dome over the lagoon. I inch my way across to the middle point. Rather than climb down the vertical rope knotted to the center of the horizontal rope, I cry out "Jingjing!" just for the hell of it, then let my hands loose, savoring the awesome downward drop, feet first, into the lagoon.

"Find it okay?" I ask Elysia when I come up for air after my plunge into the lagoon. I swim toward where she's finishing a lap at the far end of the water.

"It took me a while to find this spot, and some monkeys tried to bite me on the way here, but I found it okay," she says. "The note you left on my breakfast plate wasn't very specific with directions." Whatever. My clone's got to start cultivating wilderness skills on her own, right? She adds, "I'm supposed to be doing target practice this morning. This is much more enjoyable. The heat is horrible today, so thank you for the invitation. It was a pleasant surprise."

I begin swimming alongside her, mimicking my mimic's breast stroke. We reach the equivalent of the swim lane's end, turn-flip at the same time, and then resume swimming the opposite length of the lagoon.

"How did you get down here?" I ask.

"The same way you just did. I jumped from the rope."

"You should have climbed down the rope. Is that jump even safe in your condition?"

"It will have to be."

Everyone treats her like she's some sacrosanct Virgin Mary—a replicant who has managed to replicate! But how does Elysia feel about her situation—trapped by the hopes and dreams of every other clone here? I stop the swim to tread water in place. "Do you even *want* this baby?"

She stops her swim to tread water too. "No." She says the word without hesitation or remorse.

"Then why have it?" For some reason I feel strangely fascinated by the idea of the baby in my clone's womb. Technically, I think it would be considered mine, too, biologically at least. Her ovaries were copied from mine.

Elysia says, "The one person I knew who could make it go away—the healer called M-X—wouldn't do it. She said that what was happening in my body was a miracle and that even unborn life was sacred."

Come on. There has to be a way to get rid of it if that's what Elysia wants. Why should she be forced to finish a pregnancy started by rape, just because her pregnancy promises—*maybe, doubtfully*—hope for the other Demesne clones to procreate? Why should she have to carry a baby she doesn't want, which was conceived in violence, *and* carry the hopes and dreams of so many others who care more about what's best for them rather than what's best for her? That's so not fair.

I might be taking the helpful angle too far, or maybe I'm projecting how I'd feel in her situation, but I say, "If you want help to get rid of it, I'm sure we could figure out a way." I totally mean it. If she needs my help in this rotten situation, I will give it to her.

"I'm resigned to see this through." Her tone does not mimic *joy* for the "miracle of life" growing inside her. Her tone, in fact, sounds more *curious*, along with *resigned*.

I know about *curious*. It's what landed me on Heathen via Demesne.

Elysia resumes her swim, as do I. "But I appreciate the offer," she says. "Race you?"

"Butterfly!" I call out.

Did Dr. Lusardi give her steroids along with my face and body?

We could never make a synchronized-swimming pair, because she's so much faster than me. Her strokes are flawless. Even with a baby inside her, which I'd think would weigh her down and slow her speed, she easily outpaces me, stroke for stroke. I'm a good swimmer. She's *great*. I'm grateful Xander advised her not to dive in her condition. I don't think I could handle her being so much better than me at that too.

She wins the butterfly heat easily. We take a break, sitting on the shore, letting the lagoon lap sweet water over our feet. Elysia says, "You'd swim faster if you stopped watching me."

I know that already. It's why Dad pushed me into diving instead of race swimming. Some swimmers can look to their competitors in the nearby lanes and use them as leverage to push harder and faster to win the race. Other swimmers, like me, get slowed down from too closely watching their competitors, costing them crucial speed and distance.

"I was the fastest female swimmer back at the Aquatics Club," I say defensively.

"I know," says Elysia. "Alex told me that when you were a child, you were the fastest girl in your district. But then your mother left, and your father said you lost focus, and he redirected your training exclusively to diving instead of swimming."

I'm here to learn more about her, not hear regurgitated facts about me. "Where did you dive on Demesne?" I ask her.

"On Demesne there were only cliffs for practicing high dives. I was never invited to practice in the FantaSpheres, where I could have tried diving with proper equipment."

True, Elysia's very existence grates deep on my nerves; what grates even more is how she was treated like dirt by the humans on Demesne. This Me is enraged, imagining Other Me as their toy.

"What was Demesne like?" I ask her. "I was only awake there for a few minutes before Aidan took me away from it. Was it total paradise?" My ambitions are always Olympic-size, even if my ability to execute isn't quite on par, and I do aspire to one day be Queen of Demesne if and when Insurrection occurs. I'd like to know more about it from someone who has, basically, seen it with my own eyes, fuchsia version.

"It's tranquil and luxurious, as it's supposed to be. The few teens that lived there were bored all the time. I don't think they considered it paradise, even with the beautiful scenery, relaxing oxygenation, and FantaSpheres in their houses."

"They have FantaSpheres in their houses?"

"Of course. Didn't you have one?"

"We had one at the Aquatics Club, but that's only because the Uni-Mil donated it. Most normal people can't afford one of those things for their personal use. They can buy time in one at, like, the mall. That's about it."

"Do Aquines have FantaSpheres in their homes?" Elysia asks.

"Hardly! Aquines are technologically advanced but refrain from using technology except as necessary. That's part of their belief system. Simplicity."

"Perhaps you could tell me more about the background of the Aquines. I have limited information, besides what's programmed on my chip."

"Why don't you just ask Xander?"

"Alex doesn't like to talk about his background."

He does to me, I think.

"Do you have 'Amish' on your chip?" I ask her. "The sect from pre–Water Wars times when religion was, like, really important, I guess?"

Her eyes blink as her chip accesses the data. "Yes," she says. "Ancient Christian group of Swiss extraction, who settled in Old America, wore plain dress, and utilized their land in Old Country ways rather than adopt modern technology. What do they have to do with the Aquines?"

My explanation will be easier because she already has this background information, yet I'm agitated. Her chip is filled with so much useless clutter and nothing that could actually help her! Her engineering isn't flawed. It's *mean*. "The Aquines are like superhuman versions of what Amish people used to be. They are peaceful people who live in cloistered communities and cut themselves off from the rest of the world as much as possible."

"Because of a religion?"

"No, more like an ethic."

"Alex says the humans on Demesne have no ethics."

"Ethics are a matter of opinion, not fact."

"I'm going to become an Aquine," Elysia pronounces.

Does her chip also have a special setting for *profoundly ignorant*? "You can't become Aquine. You're born as one."

"I can mimic," she says. "I like their value system. I would like the baby to have it. I've been meditating at sunset with Alex, reflecting on gratitude and humility."

She meditates like an Aquine now? My blood boils.

Every time I try to like or help her, she fails me.

"Maybe you should consider who you should be most loyal to: him, or your First, who made you?"

"Maybe *you* should consider that your loyalty should be to me, and not to him," she retorts. Something else she got from me. Sass.

Elysia stands up and runs back into the water to resume her swim.

I remain on shore. Sassed.

Elysia swims beneath the water for a long time, zigzagging across the lagoon as schools of colorful reef fish follow her as if they know she's the power source on this island now. She's a regular swordfish down there. After a few minutes, she swims to shore and rejoins me on the sand.

Elysia squeezes the water from the ends of her hair just as I am about to do the same. She says, "I heard music beneath the water! I'm sure of it! How is that possible?"

"Your precious chip doesn't tell you why?"

"No. Please, won't you tell me? It was the most beautiful thing I ever heard!"

Immune to her deep wonder, I inform her, "It's whale music. Whales make sounds to communicate with each other. The sounds can travel across thousands of miles. The music reaches this spot from the ocean through the tidal streams that feed into this lagoon."

No. NO! A tear drops from her fuchsia eye and down her pink cheek. "Don't *cry*!" I scoff. "It's just whale music."

"*Just* whale music? How can you not care about something so incredible? I never imagined I could experience such magic."

"So go back in and listen more."

"No. I hope I don't hear it again. I don't want a reminder of how beautiful life can be."

"That makes no sense. Why?"

"When I experience moments the humans label as *wondrous*, then I understand the humans' greed for it. The life I have known so far has been defined by servitude. Then, rape. Then, murder. I don't appreciate being teased with beauty when my own dark life will end soon."

"Why so morose? You're the youngest Demesne clone alive. You have years before you expire."

"That's not true. Soon, I will go Awful, and die."

Backflip. Say what?

"What do you mean? What's Awful?" I ask.

"Dr. Lusardi's intent was to make her Betas *so* Awful that they'd alienate their humans to the point that they couldn't wait to get rid of us."

"I don't understand." Only I do. My own dad couldn't wait to send me off to juvenile delinquent camp rather than deal with all the messiness that I and my moods and my little drug problem caused in his house.

Elysia says, "Dr. Lusardi wanted to mimic 'empty nest' effect for human parents letting go of about-to-be-adult-age children. So she programmed her Betas to die off rather than just move out of their parents' basements. She didn't know how to make teen clones that could become adults. The Awfuls programming was built-in protection for *her*, not any potential human Beta buyers."

"That's crazy. It can't be true. Who told you that?" Elysia's going to die, so soon? This revelation should feel like good news—but instead it feels like another chance for me to die. My clone's barely been alive. There's still so much she could do or see. She's carrying a child. And she's marked for death not just by the humans on Demesne who will seek revenge on her, but by her own biology? That's cruelty to an infinite degree.

"The other teen Beta on Demesne. Tahir. He was another Beta clone, created from the dead First of Tahir Fortesquieu."

Excuse me? Prince Tahir was a *clone*? This information is scandalous, but not so depressing as her last revelation. I'd rather move the conversation in this direction—the one I intended it to go in all along. Innocently, I ask, "No way. Is he related to Tariq Fortesquieu?"

"Yes. Tariq's son Tahir died in a surfing accident in the *gigantes*. They secretly had him cloned. Dr. Lusardi didn't want the job, but she couldn't refuse them. She never fully developed her teen cloning technique, which is why we are called Betas. She created the Awfuls so the teens would die off."

Why was this Dr. Larissa Lusardi so revered? She was a monster, as far as I can tell. She created her Betas so they'd be forever teens, exactly as she predicted for science's reach: that clones could not transition from teens to adults. But what Dr. Lusardi meant was *she* didn't have the capability to give her clones that ability. So she made it a self-fulfilling prophecy.

"This Beta Tahir who told you this information . . . was he your friend?"

"Yes. He was the only being on the entire island who

understood what it felt like to be a Beta. Supposedly empty, but not. Treated like a child, but not."

"Sounds like you cared for him a lot."

"He was the most beautiful creature I ever saw. Quiet, but charismatic, when he chose to be. He could be insolent, and then amazingly sweet and kind. He was endlessly fascinating to me. Tahir is the reason I cry at things like whale music; I want so much to share any rare, beautiful moment with *him*."

"So where is he?"

"His parents took him away, back to Biome City, to retrain him to become more like his First. Just when Tahir was starting to realize who he was on his own. Just when we had vowed to try to escape Demesne, together." She pauses, and then softly adds, "I loved him."

So why did she have to steal Xander, then? Why did she have to be so greedy?

But I already know the answer. She hooked up with Xander to mend her broken heart—and because he was her best chance at survival.

I know, because I would have done the same.

"Is Tahir still in Biome City?" I ask her.

Elysia shakes her head. "For all I know, he's gone Awful by now, and died. Like I will, soon enough." She sighs. "I would have liked to see the real world first."

It's hardly comforting news, but I feel compelled to tell her, "If it means anything to you, you should know that what you think you're missing isn't a party. The real world out there's not that great. It's desolate. Tarnished. Full of suffering."

"Just like here," Elysia pronounces. She takes a deep breath, then pats her stomach, just as I feel my own hunger gnawing at my stomach. "I have a more urgent concern. All this swimming and talking, and now I'm starving." Lunchtime. Of course. Our identical hunger clocks.

We both swim toward the rope. Elysia is about to make the climb up when I tell her, "If you're going to die, you should at least have some fun first." I realize that I'm not totally faking the sincerity in my voice. My heart feels it a little bit while my mind feels betrayed, as though it's saying, *Don't go weak on me now, heart. We've been through too much.*

"There is fun here?" Elysia asks, her tone set to *surprised*.

"Meet me in the Mosh Cave tonight. You'll see."

15

I HAVE TO GIVE IT TO THE EMERGENTS. THEY know how to party.

Sweaty, fired-up clones, exhausted from toiling long days working and training, wreak havoc on designated play nights once, sometimes twice, a week. They call the venue for their havoc the Mosh Cave. It's a limestone cavern at the far end of the Rave Caves. The underground hangout comes to life usually around midnight. Funnels of tornado lights sweep up the cave's walls in flashes of yellows and reds. The music is *loud*. It throbs and burns, while the moshers do the same. The Mosh Cave is Heathen's best antidote to island fever.

I climb down toward the cave entrance and hear the loud music thumping from behind the granite wall. Standing in the darkness at the precipice of the cave entrance, I see Xander and Elysia just outside the Mosh door, arguing.

She says, "My life on Demesne was so sheltered. I want new experiences. I want to learn this thing called 'mosh.'"

Xander stifles a laugh and places a protective arm on her shoulder. "This isn't the place for new experiences. A mosh is meant for going wild, for losing inhibitions. Not advisable in your condition."

She brushes his arm aside. "I don't care. And don't tell me what to do." She steps past Xander into the Mosh Cave, leaving him outside.

I'm trying so hard not to like my clone, but she's making it difficult.

I emerge from the shadows. "Your girlfriend's got spunk," I say to Xander.

"Wonder where she got that from." He gestures to the wall, which is reverberating the loud music. "Thanks for giving her this horrendously bad idea. Are you going in there?"

"I was planning to." I step closer to him, almost bumping directly into him. "If you'll get out of my way. Unless you want to come in?"

"Not my scene," says Xander. "You invited her here, so you should keep watch on her. Make sure she isn't harmed."

"If you're so worried, go in yourself. What's the problem? Aquines don't mosh?"

"*I* don't mosh."

"You should."

"What's the appeal? Loud music, hedonistic behavior."

"Exactly! Plus, Defect Destruction is playing tonight."

"Who?"

"Heathen's biggest pop-punk stars. The only ones, in fact! Made up of Emergents who spend their days training for Insurrection and their nights practicing or performing. They used to be members of the Replicant Symphony Orchestra on Demesne."

Xander says, "I heard that orchestra play when I was on Demesne! They were actually pretty good."

"So go on in. I guarantee you they're better here. They traded in their tuxes and violins for feral wear and amplified guitars."

"No Mozart?" There's a tiny little smile that wants to grow bigger on his face. I can tell that Xander wants to have fun. Why can't he just let it happen?

"Not unless Mozart composed two-minute punk songs that are amplified and nutso."

We can feel the music's bass line thump through the wall. It's probably not just the beat of my heart from Xander's proximity.

"Sounds terrible," says Xander. "That kind of pointless behavior is exactly one of the reasons the Aquines cloistered themselves from the rest of humanity." I know he doesn't mean it. But this is his quandary to figure out, not mine. To have fun, or not to have fun. The eternal Aquine question. Be a genetically engineered, perfect bore, or not be a genetically engineered, perfect bore. Sometimes I wonder what his holy appeal to me ever was. Then I look at his obscenely perfect body and face, and remember. Yes, I am that shallow. Want.

"Whatever, old man," I say.

My chest bumps directly into his muscle-pecs, as I try to

force him to step aside so I can go through the entranceway. For a moment, our hips touch, and his hands instinctively reach around my waist, sizzling the skin beneath my shirt. I look up to his face, and turn my mouth just so. Xander could kiss me if he wants. I know he wants. I can feel his heat pressing into me. I'm sending it back.

I shouldn't want to kiss someone who has treated me so callously. Maybe I just want him to want me, so I can have a turn rejecting him. Or maybe I want him so she can't have him.

"Z-Dev," Xander murmurs, and my heart sings. His eyes close, his lips part. Can he, too, not resist the pull? But a push comes from the other side, and two Emergents burst through from the Mosh Cave, separating us. It's Aidan, leading a drunken Emergent outside and away from the mosh, separating me from Xander. The Emergent punches his fist into the open air, and proclaims, "Defect Destruction!" He then pukes at Xander's feet.

I ignore the barfer and walk past the men and into the Mosh Cave.

Xander can handle the situation himself. He made this mess. He can clean it up.

Alive within the mosh, there is loud, angry, pulsing music, along with a sea of bodies jumping together, exhilarated, free.

And there is a pregnant teen clone being crowd-surfed across a wave of thrashing Emergents while the punk-slam clone band Defect Destruction rages onstage. Their song of the moment is "Lusardi Must Die." It's a big hit here on Heathen.

"She's *amazing*," I hear a body-bearer call up to Elysia.

"Our *miracle*," says another.

Elysia is one helluva trusting Emergent to let her fellow moshers pass her around on raised arms across the mosh pit, but she seems to love it. She tips her head back, looking directly at me, and smiles. Her smile is so bright, so much more charismatic than I could ever achieve on my identical face. She flashes me a thumbs-up sign, and I flash a thumbs-up sign back to her. *Party to your heart's content, girl! Xander hates party girls. You know that, right?*

If this is the beginning of Elysia's Awfuls, I have to admit: I like this incarnation of Elysia. Not like we could be pals or anything, but she looks truly *alive* rather than *resigned*. She looks like the version of me I like the most. Open. Dangerous. Exhilarated.

Aidan returns inside the Mosh Cave, looking toward the stage and not like he's looking for me. Last night, he held me through the night in our tree house. Tonight, will he dance with me in the mosh pit? Ha, doubt it. Like Xander, loud music and moshing is not Aidan's scene. But I wouldn't mind thrashing around the pit with him, sweaty and angsty and gross and full of energy and rage and heat. Wow. I don't think I'd mind that at all. I start to approach Aidan, resolved: I am going to get Aidan to have some fun tonight! And then Aidan is going to do more than just hold me later tonight!

But I can only hope for such a time with Aidan. He

doesn't see my approach, and instead, he urgently walks to the stage, like he's trying to stop the music. He stands before Defect Destruction's drummer, gesturing the drummer to stop. The drummer ignores Aidan, who then grabs the drumsticks from the drummer's hand. The drummer stands up and responds with a punch to Aidan's jaw while the rest of Defect Destruction continue playing, and Elysia continues dancing, and I watch the scene in bewilderment and a bit of concern. Aidan recoils slightly from the punch, then returns a much harder jab to the drummer's vined temple. The drummer falls to the ground. The bass player plays on, even as Aidan snatches the lead singer's guitar from the singer's hands. The skinny singer slams his body against Aidan's in protest, but he is no match for Aidan's brute abs of steel. Aidan takes the hit as if no hit came his way, then turns to the bassist, who gets the message and finally stops playing, drops his bass to the ground, and runs off the stage. Aidan takes center stage and addresses the moshers.

"Hovercopters are flying overhead. Ships have surrounded the island. Soldiers are ambushing." He looks around to the group, takes a deep breath, and then announces, "The time for Insurrection is *now!*"

16

THERE'S NO TIME TO PANIC OR FORM A PLAN. There's only time to run.

Smoke quickly fills the Mosh Cave as an Emergent cries out, "FIRE!"

Hell on Heathen. It's here, now. Insurrection was supposed to involve the Emergents storming their native island. First, we'll have to storm our way out of the Rave Caves, which have been lit with firebombs.

Aidan and Xander lead the way, herding the group out of the Mosh Cave. Elysia and I, gasping for breath, follow the Emergents' desperate steps toward the exit point. As we file out of the pit, I pick up a band member's discarded shirt on the floor and hand it to Elysia. "Put it over your mouth and nose," I instruct her. Everyone is in danger in this situation. But she's got a baby in her belly to protect too.

When we emerge from the main cave entrance, the smell of smoke and aura of fear permeate the air. The black sky is brightened with orange and yellow embers: our tree houses. The invaders have set the jungle on fire.

We're trapped.

Adrenaline courses through my body, an instinctual panic. Yet my mind feels strangely calm. I've survived death already. Whatever is happening is not good, but I can handle it. With Aidan leading them, the Emergents can handle it. I'm sure of it.

Quickly, Aidan chooses eight of the strongest Emergents and points toward the jungle. "Go!" he commands them. "Find out—"

But Xander calls out, "Wait! There could be—"

Too late. The Emergents, taking Aidan's order, run toward the trees but are immediately halted by an invisible perimeter, a magnetic force field that zaps the first wave of soldiers. They fall to the ground, vanquished. I'm not sure if they're dead or just knocked out.

"What's happening?" Elysia asks me.

"Stay calm and do what Aidan says," I advise her. "We're under siege." I clutch her body to mine, feeling her own quickening heartbeat, but she loosens from my grip. I can't protect her, of course—but I want her to feel protected.

"I can handle it," she says, exuding *confidence*. "Let me see." But her fuchsia eyes reflect the same *fear* I feel. "This is Insurrection?" she asks.

"I'm afraid so," I say.

Bright lights suddenly beam down from high above, lighting us like targets, as the attackers emerge from behind the trees. We're immediately surrounded by soldiers, aiming rifles at us from all points. But these are not ordinary Uni-Mil soldiers. They are too tall, at least eight feet—all of them the same exact height. Their uniforms display a corporate logo, with the word REPLICAPHARM placed under the RP logo. Their red laser eyes scan from beneath their helmets.

Xander warns Aidan, "These ReplicaPharm soldiers are androids. They're not copied from humans. There's no chance for them to have souls. They'll have no hesitation or remorse about shooting to kill."

The other Emergents' chips won't tell them that, and those not in earshot of Aidan and Xander are not warned in time. Without command from Xander or Aidan, three different Emergents act on instinct, charging toward the soldiers to engage in battle. The Emergents are immediately shot dead.

Now my mind is not so calm. It's a blur of confusion and terror. The intent of the ambush is clearly bloodshed, immediate and direct. This is bad. Really bad. Who's next? Once, I watched two fellow runaways die beside me in the ocean, but that was an accident. This is murder, and we are bearing witness to it and could be next, and this ambush is too sudden and horrific for us to even remotely know how we're supposed to react and still remain safe.

Elysia and I gasp in shock at the same time. She grabs

my hand, clenching so hard she could easily squeeze the life out of me. I let her clench as hard as she needs; it's a welcome reminder that we're both at least still alive.

Xander faces the remaining Emergents. "Stand down, Emergents!" he implores them. "These soldiers will kill, not fight!"

"Fight!" Aidan challenges the Emergents instead. Another wave of five Emergents charges toward the soldiers, who, instead of shooting them, lift the Emergents from the ground and effortlessly fling them into the air like missiles, launching them directly into the fireballs in the distance.

"Where's the enemy's leader?" Elysia whispers to me, perhaps expecting that the soldier's daughter should know.

I don't. I'm hoping whoever it is appears immediately, to end the counter-commands of Aidan and Xander. "I think we're about to find out," I say to Elysia.

A hologram man emerges in the center of the area, a human man, late middle age, with a full head of thick black hair. He's clean-shaven and dressed in a sharp, dark gray suit. He looks like a businessman, not like a soldier.

"Greetings, Defects," he announces. Not a guy who knows how to warm a crowd. "I am Dimitri Kelos, vice president of mergers and acquisitions for ReplicaPharm, addressing you from our head office in Geneva. I hereby inform you that ReplicaPharm has acquired Demesne, and therefore, has acquired you too." There are cries of "No!" from the Emergents but Kelos tamps his hands down to quiet them. "It's not your option to protest. Demesne has been sold to ReplicaPharm. You were the former owners' property; now you are ours. The corporation has bought the entire island chain and also the surrounding airspace. Hereafter, no one—not even the Uni-Mil—will be allowed entrance to Demesne without permission from ReplicaPharm."

What will become of us? None of the Emergents speak the question aloud, but it's visible on all their faces. Fear of returning to Demesne and the tyranny they left behind may be greater than their fear of death right now.

What will become of *me*? I can't fathom a life back in Cerulea after all I've been through. I could never bring my clone back with me. I can't leave her unless I know she's safe, I realize. And she will never be safe under the control of Demesne humans. I'm as trapped as the Emergents.

Are we all about to be killed?

Kelos continues. "Pursuant to the recent settlement agreement with the Replicant Rights Commission, ReplicaPharm has voluntarily decided to move its clone manufacturing operations to Demesne in order to spare so many troubled cities the unseemly and unnecessary protests against ReplicaPharm's many offices. The prior owners on Demesne have been bought out and have left the island, so congratulations on that. Your Insurrection scared them enough to pave the way for their exit, and our entry. As part of its move to Demesne, the corporation has acquired the clones created from Firsts on Demesne. You are the last of your breed; clones manufactured from Firsts have been outlawed from here on out."

Aidan steps forward. "You will expire us?"

His question kills me, a direct stab to my heart. I can't bear the thought of Aidan being expired. Please, no. That was not an outcome that I in any way anticipated, or could accept.

"Unfortunately, no," Kelos answers, and I am flooded with the same *relief* I see reflected on Elysia's face. "You may *choose* to be expired, by continuing to resist this ambush. But as part of the settlement agreement with the Replicant Rights Commission, ReplicaPharm assumes ownership of the Demesne clones and must allow them to live out their remaining years on Demesne. It's a nonsense bargain, if you ask my opinion—but they didn't. I'm just the lawyer. As a compromise for allowing you to live, the corporation has been granted the right to confine you to labor camps on Demesne."

"What of the clones still on Demesne?" Xander asks.

Kelos answers, "The clones who didn't participate in this little Insurrection have been reprogrammed to correct the 'raxia misfire. They'll be allowed to remain in their previous roles and in their homes, which will now be occupied by ReplicaPharm personnel, whom they will serve. You all—the Defects—will become physical laborers, confined by force fields to limited working and living areas."

"Demesne belongs to the Emergents!" Aidan protests. "We won't go."

A wave of sadness, bigger even than the fear I feel in this moment, sweeps through me. I'm crushed for Aidan. He will never know freedom again. He will never lead the Emergents to their promised destiny, to reclaim Demesne for themselves. He will never take me as his queen there.

"Then die here now," says Kelos. "Demesne belongs to ReplicaPharm. You should be grateful you'll even be allowed to finish your lives."

"We'll be prisoners there," says Aidan.

"Prisoners of paradise," Kelos amends. He addresses the android soldiers flanking his holo-beam. "Bring me the girl."

The soldiers' red eyes scan, landing first on me, and then on Elysia. Instantly, two soldiers surround me, and then Elysia, and effortlessly lift us off the ground. They swiftly, effortlessly carry us to Kelos and deposit us in front of his holo-beam.

"Fascinating," says Kelos, observing us. "A clone and her First. That's certainly a . . . first." He chuckles at his own joke, while my heart pounds and sweat pours from my face. Elysia reacts in the same way.

"Where's Dr. Lusardi?" Elysia demands.

"Expired," says Kelos.

"I will not go back to Demesne!" Elysia says.

"Then all these Emergents will die," says Kelos. "Right now." The soldiers uniformly aim their rifles at the Emergents.

Elysia doesn't respond. What's there to say? I know what she feels. She wishes she was dead already. She's who they came looking for. She's why they're killing Emergents. I feel the same *anguish* I see on her face. Like we're complicit in this atrocity. She's here because of me.

"You don't believe me?" Kelos asks. "Let's begin now. Soldiers, choose an example."

A sniper soldier trains its rifle on Tawny and fires. She falls to the ground, dead.

Tawny finally found her role. Martyr.

My legs quiver and I think I'm going to pass out from shock. I can't watch so much senseless murder. But I have no choice.

"Would you like another example?" Kelos asks. Before Elysia can answer, Kelos points at Catra, and the androids shoot Catra dead on the spot. I can't even scream because bile shoots up from my stomach and I resist every urge not to puke on the ground. Catra is dead. Catra is dead. I can't believe it. She was fearless and inspiring, and in one random instant, she's killed because of this Kelos man's whim. I never in my life thought Insurrection would end with a firing squad. I don't know what exactly I thought it would be—but certainly not this.

Enough! This is crazy! I'm ready to die now too. I'm about to volunteer, when Elysia cries out, "Kill me instead!"

"A pregnant clone? You're too valuable for death," says Kelos to Elysia.

There are dead bodies on the ground, and much more important issues still to be explained, but still, I sputter, "How do you know?" I thought no one besides the clones on this island knew that Elysia is pregnant.

Kelos regards me like I'm a nuisance. "ReplicaPharm acquired the healer's island too. The one who calls herself M-X. In order to maintain her solitude on that island, she helpfully led us to this island, and informed us of the Beta's condition. She even suggested the 'mosh' night might be the best time for us to arrive with our announcement. The logistics were so much easier when you were all already in one place. Nice gal, M-X."

"My father is in the Uni-Mil!" I cry out. "He won't let you take us away!"

Kelos regards me now like I'm a wounded animal he can't decide whether to put out of its misery. He says, "Your father is in military prison for treason. Aiding and abetting clones is not looked kindly upon by judicial courts. Oh, right. The Uni-Mil has no courts. Your father will die in prison. You can join him there, if you want."

"NOOO!" I scream. Instinctively, I start to lunge toward Kelos, even if he's not a physical presence, but before the soldiers can pull me back, Aidan points his blue finger in my direction and a small red cloud erupts around my perimeter, holding the soldiers back.

"Thank you," says Kelos to Aidan. "We've been looking for the clone who was able to do that. We've been monitoring your odd weather patterns from satellite surveillance. Soldiers, deliver that Defect directly back to the lab. The research team will need to do a thorough dismantling of his body before he's expired."

I close my eyes. This isn't happening. This isn't happening. I can't watch it happen. Aidan revealed his power to them just to protect me, and now they will torture and then kill him for that sacrifice.

I'm powerless. I can't even say good-bye. *No, Aidan,* my heart cries. *NO!* Insurrection was supposed to mean that if we died in battle, at least we died together.

This time, Elysia latches on to my hand and gives it a gentle squeeze.

"Cease!" Elysia commands Kelos. "We accept your terms."

"Excellent," says Kelos. He sighs wistfully. "Demesne's not such a bad place to be exiled. The rest of the world envies you. You may be confined to Demesne for the remainder of your lives, but take solace. Humans in the rest of the world would kill for such a death sentence."

PART TWO: DEMESNE

ELYSIA

17

I AM A KILLER.

I already was one, but on Heathen the Aquine trained me to be a better one. With a machete, he taught me to massacre coconuts from palm trees. Those are the pleasant kills. When I split open a coconut, it gives me a sweet juice that glides down my throat and cools off my body on a hot day, as if the coconut wants to reward my efforts to slay it. With a spear, he taught me to stand in shallow waters and catch fish. The reward: we eat. The drawback: these creatures are sentient. They struggle. They suffer.

Soon, the ReplicaPharm doctor is going to cut me open with a knife and remove the unwanted beast in my belly. The reward: my freedom from it. The drawback: I am still the humans' prisoner.

With a knife, I killed the human boy Ivan. I was supposed to be his companion. There was struggle, and suffering, but never a reward. Ivan was strangling me to death, and I fought back. I acted on an instinct for self-preservation, which a Demesne clone isn't supposed to have. Clones should never think or act for themselves. Their only instincts should be to serve humans, not to slay them.

Ivan's killing led only to more suffering—for his human family, and for the Beta who slayed him.

Destruction. I guess I'm good at it.

The Demesne property owners let us believe we were the best-quality clones, just like they were better humans, because they were rich. We were created from Firsts chosen specifically for superior physical attributes. Only the fittest and best-looking clones were appropriate to serve on their most exclusive island, designed for only the most special people—at least, that's how they considered themselves. Better than everyone else.

So many lies.

Demesne clones are not special clones, just like their human owners are not better people because they are rich. The Demesne clones are just like them, which is a disappointment. We love. We hate. We suffer. We cause suffering.

I want to be better than the humans, but I was always just like them. Awful.

"Do you want to see the baby?" asks the doctor while he looks at the fetus on a monitor, in preparation for the extraction. I'm back in the very room where I first emerged, the medical laboratory on Demesne that used to be headed by Dr. Lusardi and is now owned by ReplicaPharm. RP owns me, too, now. And the thing inside me. The doctor is preparing to take the fetus from my belly and place it into an artificial womb machine that will incubate it until the fetus reaches forty weeks. Then it will be emerged and live its life as a scientific research specimen.

Enjoy the remainder of your gestation, fetus. The artificial womb machine will probably love you and take care of you better than I ever could. The humans certainly won't, once you emerge.

"No, I don't want to see it." I turn my head away and close my eyes.

Wanting, I have learned, is the seed of human terror. If it were not for humans wanting something—money, power, dominant ideology—there would be no need for them to cause so much suffering. Most of the suffering the humans inflict is on each other—that is, until they had to go and create clones, to replicate their suffering anew.

I want all this suffering to stop, already. I open my arms and let out a wild roar, like a banshee's howl.

The doctor looks surprised but is not flustered. "Sedate her," says the doctor to the nurse.

Such sweet relief.

It's like I'm floating through a rose-hued abyss, powered by mellow-making 'raxia. My skin tingles, my face glows. I am happy. Free. There is nothing to see, so I close my eyes to enjoy the moment. A familiar male voice calls to me. *Hey, gorgeous.* My heart surges and my eyes burst open. Tahir!

Please don't let this be a dream. Please don't let this be a dream.

He's dressed in white board shorts with no shirt, exposing his lean, mahogany-skinned chest. He smiles at me, full cherry lips over bright white teeth. "I missed you," he says, holding out his arms to me. His black hair is braided in cornrows that curl at the loose ends, like little halos encompassing his beautiful neck.

I run to him, flinging myself against his chest as he hugs me close. There's so much I need to know. *Where have you been? Are you Awful? How did you find me again?*

I want to savor him before I inundate him with questions. I pull back and look up, at his face, which offers me the sweetest smile ever. His smile! I remember now. When he offered his *charismatic* smile to his family and friends, he imitated First Tahir. But when he smiled at me, the smile was his own: quiet, subtle—a gift just for me.

I press my lips into Tahir's and feel superb warmth spread across my body. Because of him, I understand excitement and happiness—but also, fear. Because of Tahir, I understand why Zhara hurts so badly from losing Alex. When real happiness is achieved, it can only be partnered with a fear of losing it.

"Now that we've found each other again, I can never let you go," Tahir says.

"I'll die before ever letting you go again," I say.

But behind Tahir stands the Aquine.

Of course this had to be a dream. It was too good to be true.

"I love you," Alex says to me. He opens his arms, inviting me to choose him over Tahir.

Alex had years of knowing and loving Zhara, but he barely knows me. How could he possibly *love* me? Alex imprinted his feelings for Zhara onto her Beta before he knew she was alive. His race's design flaw, I suppose. Once they imprint, their loyalty can't undo that feeling. Too bad for him.

"I love you, too," I reassure Alex.

I am a killer, and a liar.

When I wake, I see my face—the non-branded, human version of it. The one that had parents and a childhood and a choice about how to live her life, before she had to go and destroy it.

"Is it gone?" I ask Zhara, who sits at my bedside.

"The transfer was successful." Her pale, withdrawn face reflects how I feel: like death. "I wanted to see it, but they wouldn't let me." I look carefully; her eyes are wet with tears.

"Why would you want to see it?" I want nothing more to do with it. ReplicaPharm taking it out of my body is the one upside to this otherwise nightmare return to Demesne.

Zhara says, "In a sick way, it's part of me too. It didn't ask to be made any more than you did. It deserves the life that you and Aidan and the other Emergents were denied. It deserves to be loved. Not abandoned."

"It wasn't abandoned. ReplicaPharm will provide for it."

"They will mistreat it and then abandon or expire it. Just like they do with their clones. It deserves better."

I blink, trying to access on my chip why she could possibly care what happens to that horrible thing I so badly wanted gone from my body. My chip speculates: Zhara wants the baby to be loved and cared for as her mother didn't do for her. She's projecting, my chip informs me. I'm *horrified* by her empathy. I'm more horrified when I feel a surge in my veins, signaling *sympathy*, and *sadness*, for Zhara in return.

"I want to get out of here," I tell Zhara. I can taste the prime Demesne air again, and it's not a pleasant association. Each breath I take in this toxic paradise makes me feel suffocated. The soothing air actually makes me feel hate, and crave vengeance. I want it so badly my mouth develops an Awful taste—sour, bitter—overpowering the flowery sweetness of the island's air.

"I know exactly how you feel," Zhara says. "This feels like a nightmare we can't wake up from. We're living it."

The sour taste in my mouth extends to the words coming from it. I say, "You don't know anything about how I feel." Except Zhara probably *does* know how I feel, because she is another version of me. I hate that. I don't want to experience empathy or sympathy or anything else with her. I want to be free of her as much as I wanted to be free of the baby. I want to own my Awful as much as she owns hers— only in a human teenager, it's simply called *moody*. What a luxury. "Why are you still here?" I snap at her. "Don't you have some great life of freedom somewhere to return to?"

"I have no home to return to."

I can't help but remember how after I'd first met her, when I asked Zhara if her parents would be considered *our* parents, Zhara's answer was that the parents belonged to *her*. Her grief for them should belong to her too. I can't help that my programming automatically tells me the correct response to her grief, and I let it happen instead of resisting. She needs comfort just like I do. "I'm sorry for your loss," I say, with a *sincerity* I don't feel.

I never know whether to like or trust Zhara. My instinct says, *No.* My heart says, *Maybe.* My mind says, *Fool.*

"I'm sorry for yours." Her wet eyes advance to blatant tears falling down her face. "So many Emergents lost," she says. "Tawny. Catra." She pauses. She can barely speak the next name. "Aidan."

"He's dead?" I ask. I am genuinely sorry for that loss of Zhara's. It's one I understand. I lost the man I loved too. Tahir. The difference is I knew I loved him. Zhara never got the chance to figure out her feelings for Aidan, as far as I can tell. Alexander Blackburn returning to her life got in the way. Now it's too late.

Zhara says, "I have no idea. The not knowing is actually worse. I assume they've expired him, but they won't give me any information. Either Aidan's dead or being tortured. Demesne isn't paradise. It's a fresh new hell."

"So leave it," I suggest.

She wipes the wetness from her face with her hand. "I was offered the opportunity to stay here with you. I have no home left back in the world, and they've offered me refuge here. But that's not the only reason I really stayed. I plan to make sure they treat you more ethically than they did the last time."

"I can take care of myself." But I don't want to take care of myself. I have nothing here besides pain, and no one to care for me. I'm silently pleased Zhara is here with me. I don't want to suffer alone.

"You're their prisoner. So I'll be their prisoner with you. Like it or not, you are me, and vice versa. They hurt you, they hurt me."

"Is this because of Aidan?"

"Yes. I want you to have what he didn't. Comfort." A fresh tear streams down her cheek. She wipes it away and then takes a deep breath to compose herself. She informs me, "You're to be under 'house arrest,' whatever that means. Most of the Emergents are dead. We're lucky to still be alive."

Suddenly, I remember. I killed the Governor's son. There must be consequences. "Will I be tried for murder?"

"I doubt it. Demesne is owned by ReplicaPharm now. They have no interest in trying you for murder. You're more valuable as a research subject. While you were in surgery, they placed new data-mining technology in your body. You're a Beta who got pregnant. There's a lot that science wants to do with the information your body will send them." She leaves unsaid: *Until you go fully Awful, and die.*

Because that's what this is really about, I realize. For whatever reason only Zhara could understand, she wants to

be with me until I die. For whatever reason I don't understand, in return, I feel perversely *protected* by her, like a
sister, and feel an uncomfortable sudden surge of *gratitude.*

"Where's Alex?" I ask. On the night of the ambush on
Heathen, the ReplicaPharm soldiers took Alex away sepa-
rately from Zhara and me. I have no idea what happened to
him. I forgot to remember to care until just this moment.

Zhara says, "I don't know. I've begged everyone here—
the guards, the doctors—for information, but no one will
tell me anything. It's maddening. These people are pure
evil. They're more heartless than the soulless clones they
tried to create. They should have cloned themselves. Then
it would have worked."

"Alex lived through the ambush?"

"I think so. I feel like I would know if he was dead, like,
in my heart. If Xander didn't survive . . . I don't even know
how I could cope. It would just be too much loss." Zhara's
face looks so *traumatized,* I decide to change the subject.

"Will we live here?" I ask Zhara. Dr. Lusardi's former
medical laboratory was part of a huge compound. I never
saw much of it the last time I was on Demesne, but there
must be living quarters here where they can keep us trapped.
"This place seems like it could easily hold a jail. Several of
them."

"You wouldn't serve science from the stress of a jail cell.
I don't know where we're being sent. But I doubt it's here."

"Wherever it is," I say, lowering my voice, "we need to
make certain one thing still happens."

"Insurrection?" Zhara whispers. I nod. How did she
know? Is she Awful, too?

I don't know how we can ultimately succeed—but the war is not yet over. I'm glad Zhara agrees.

The door to the lab room opens. The Governor walks in.

Now I understand where my new jail cell will be. Back at Governor's House.

18

HE BARGES INTO MY ROOM WITHOUT INVITATION.
I'm lying on a gurney, recovering from surgery. I can't exactly get up and bolt from the room because I don't want to see him. I have no rights here—not even the right to refuse his visit.

"Who are you?" Zhara asks him disdainfully. "Knock or something first."

"This is the Governor," I inform Zhara.

The Governor gazes at me, then at Zhara. He says, "A First. Alive. It's disgusting. Against the laws of nature." The Governor looks like he's aged a decade in the short time since I've last seen him. He's gained a substantial amount of weight, giving him a fuller, meaner face, exposed more harshly by his balding hairline, which appears to have thinned as significantly as his waistline has expanded. He approaches us and Zhara moves to stand protectively beside me, blocking him from getting too close to me.

"Keep back from her," Zhara commands him.

The Governor scoffs. "You don't give the orders here, First. I've been given a five-minute audience with your monster. That I should have to beg for it at all is a travesty of justice." *An audience*, he said. Not a return to his home. Maybe I can survive Demesne after all. Maybe I'm not being sent back there. I can survive this meeting if that's all it is—a confrontation and not a new beginning under his command. He directs a very hostile look at me. Bitterly, he says, "You murdered our son, and ReplicaPharm sentences you to house arrest on paradise. You should be hanged for what you did."

Calmly, Zhara says, "You should be ashamed for what you allowed to happen to my clone."

"Ashamed?" repeats the Governor. "She was our property. She's not a real person. We could do anything we wanted to her. And she repaid our kindness in giving her a home by killing our son."

Zhara exclaims, "It was self-defense!"

"Which she had no right to!" the Governor bellows.

I'm still groggy from anesthesia and have no physical energy to stand up and run, which is what I want to do. I don't want to confront the Governor. I wanted to never, ever see his sniveling face again. My heart pounds hard in *fear,* and I will Zhara to stop talking about Ivan. The topic is only going to inflame the Governor more.

The Governor sidesteps Zhara and hovers at the foot of my bed. "I've been demoted to acting administrator for the island during the ReplicaPharm transition. *You* ruined my career. I agreed to the demotion with the new Demesne owners just so I could stay here long enough to make sure *you* don't leave alive."

I'm scared, but he doesn't need to know that. My chip lets me know the reaction that will most unsettle him. *Indifference.* "Where are Mother and Liesel?" I ask him, my voice set to *nonchalant.*

His face reddens in anger. "This meeting is not high tea where we catch up with old friends. But I'll tell you where they are so that when our family is finally accorded the justice we deserve and you're held accountable for your crime, you'll know where my family is, celebrating. Mother and Liesel returned to the Mainland to live with Mother's sister. Liesel's anxiety issues became unmanageable after seeing Ivan murdered, and she could no longer live on Demesne. So now, because of you, I've lost another child."

Now is the real time for *insolence.* "There's another child coming for your family," I tell the Governor. "It was just removed from me and placed in an artificial womb. Take that one instead."

Got him.

Enraged, the Governor steps over to the other side of the bed, opposite where Zhara had been trying to shield me, and lunges directly for my throat, wrapping his hands around my neck, the exact move Ivan once used to try to kill me, only then I had a knife hidden under my pillow. "I'll kill you now, Beta!" the Governor cries out.

His action is so swift and sudden I almost expect to die immediately. But Zhara lets out the bloodcurdling scream my strangled, defenseless voice cannot. Unable to stop him from the other side of the bed, she instead leans down and sinks her teeth into the Governor's wrist. She bites with all her might, and his hands spring away from my neck, and there is blood on his arm. I gasp, trying to regain my breath, indignant that my numbed body is so powerless to help me at this moment, but grateful that Zhara's was.

Two ReplicaPharm android soldiers immediately enter the room, aiming rifles at the Governor.

He holds up his hands, backing away from me, moving toward the door. "Stand down, soldiers. I had my audience. We're done here." He casually walks directly in between the two soldiers and looks at me, pointing his index finger in my direction. "The former property owners would've had no problem letting me just strangle you to death. They'd have demanded it! I may have been denied legal recourse against you by ReplicaPharm, but if it's the last thing I manage to accomplish on this island, I'm going to kill you, whore."

Zhara steps over to the door and opens it more widely for the soldiers and the Governor to pass through. "Not if I kill you first," she tells him. "Now get out."

They leave. By the androids' disregard of the Governor's verbal threat, I understand the power shift. That I live and the Governor has been demoted is proof: I'm more valuable to science than his service—or rage—is to Demesne.

How encouraging for Insurrection.

19

LESS THAN TWENTY-FOUR HOURS AGO, THE Governor was trying to strangle me to death, to seek his justice so that I would never be able to experience freedom.

The joke's on him. I don't know where I'm going today, but there are no shackles on my wrists, and the view before me is wide and open, inviting. "What do you think?" I ask Zhara as she stares out the window of the Aviate, which is gliding us over the island to our next destination, still unknown to us.

"Stunning and gross at the same time," Zhara observes. "All of it manufactured through suffering." The windows offer views of mountains with lush, emerald trees, and landscapes of blue dahlias, white magnolias, pink lilies, purple jacaranda, and cactus-green succulents. Further out, we can see Io, the violet sea bioengineered specifically for Demesne, lapping docile waves over pink sand. Zhara says, "That sand! The beach looks like it actually shimmers. My whole life I've wanted to experience this place, and now that I see it like this, I feel sick. The price for all this decadence—it's just too high." She doesn't have to say the name for me to know the price she's referring to, which has nothing to do with money. I see the pain and longing on her face. Aidan.

I'm not enjoying the scenery, either. I'm remembering the last time I had an Aviate journey with this particular view. I had just been bought by Mother, to become the new companion to her children, and the luxury utility vehicle was gliding us back to Governor's House. Then, I was filled with the wonder of my new life, excited for the possibilities.

Now, I know better. Now, as a bonus of the surgery that removed the fetus from my womb, I have new motion-capture sensors located throughout my body, so I can be remotely data-mined at all times. My thoughts will still be private—but my body's every reaction to every single thing that happens to me will be quantified and evaluated. For science.

"Aren't you curious to know where we're being taken?" Zhara asks me. I don't think she realizes she's picking at the seat fabric. I wonder why, and my chip speculates: nerves.

I shrug. "It's all the same here," I say, looking down at the landscape dotted with magnificent houses. "Jail after jail after jail."

"All the founding families here are gone, so I guess we'll be living with a ReplicaPharm monitor at one of their houses."

"Anywhere here will suck."

My heart sinks as I turn my head to look out the window and notice the Fortesquieu compound coming into view. Carved out of a limestone cliff at the edge of the sea, it's built in a pueblo style, layered with different levels for different purposes—entertaining, living, gaming, dining—all with premium glass wall views overlooking Io. It would have taken human laborers years to build, but my chip tells me the masterpiece house was carved out by clones in a record six months.

For a second, I feel *hope*. The Fortesquieu compound was the only home where I ever felt happy and welcomed and cherished. But I'm sure that flying me over this place now is all part of ReplicaPharm's master plan to make me as miserable as possible. If this is where Zhara and I are to live, it would actually hurt more than staying at the Governor's House. Being reminded of a happiness I once experienced would be so much worse than the reminder of past misery. Living there would be a tease, a promise of potential happiness that I can never actually achieve, endlessly dangled before me, without relief. Everywhere I go, everything I see, would remind me of Tahir.

Torture.

Zhara's eyes widen in wonder as the view of the limestone palace gets closer. "Holy crap!" Zhara gasps. "I never thought I'd see this place with my own eyes."

The Aviate begins to descend toward a landing pad marked by two parallel rows of cuvées. The towers of flowers are in full bloom and look like rows of coral-red fireworks. *Maybe this will just be a temporary stop*, I tell myself as we land at the jewel in the crown of Demesne. How I'd like to spit it out, stomp all over it, obliterate it.

Small tears form in Zhara's eyes. "The view's not worth crying over," I say to Zhara, my voice set to *teenage disgust*.

"I don't want to cry because it's so beautiful, even though it is. I want to cry thinking how this island was once just like Heathen. Seeing it like this makes me realize how much forced clone labor went toward transforming Demesne into"—she gestures with her hand to the view out the window—"this private paradise."

Zhara taps the clear barrier separating the passengers from the RP employee navigating in the front of the Aviate. "Is this where we're going?" she asks him.

The driver says, "Yes. You've been assigned to this house."

My fate feels crueler by the second. If the Fortesquieus still own the property, there must be the possibility they could come back at some point. But they won't, because Tahir's parents want to keep him locked up in Biome City, and because my life couldn't possibly be that good. ReplicaPharm wants to shove me into an environment where I will always long, but never have. My new monitors—whoever they are—will want their scientific specimen to behave in ways that will be interesting for them to observe, but not pleasing for me to experience.

The Aviate glides onto the Fortesquieu landing pad. Zhara's hand resumes burrowing into the seat fabric at her side, chafing it so hard that it rips. She grimaces and then places both her hands in her lap. "Sorry. Nervous habit."

"I don't care," I say. "Rip away."

The Aviate comes to a full stop as a clone butler on the landing pad walks over to it, places a step pad at the door, and then opens the hatch. Zhara and I both stand, and the butler takes our hands to help us step out. It's the same clone butler that once greeted me when I was loaned to the Fortesquieus in my former life here. "Who's in charge here?" I ask him, meaning, *Who will lord over me here?*

To Zhara, he says, "I've been instructed to guide you to your quarters inside, Miss Zhara." To me, the butler says, "Miss Elysia, I've been instructed to point you in that direction." He points toward the sea.

What? Has this clone just invited me to take another leap off a cliff, to spare me the misery of living in this palace that will constantly remind me of what was taken away from me? Challenge accepted. I have no problem immediately ditching Zhara at this point. "Later," I say to her.

I run to the precipice of the cliff and look down to the violet sea. Desert flowers are scattered across the pink sand, encircling an area where the word ELYSIA is spelled out in red rose petals. For a second, my heart drops because I think, *Oh no—Alex! He's here, along with his misguided romantic gestures. I so don't care.*

But I do care. Because standing in front of the rose petals, his arms outstretched to beckon me down from the cliff, is my Tahir.

I bite down hard on tongue, so hard that I can taste blood in my mouth.

The blood tastes real. I'm not dreaming. Tahir must be real! He's right there!

20

EVER SINCE WHAT HAPPENED WITH IVAN, MY heart has felt only doom and dread.

Now, I understand—truly understand—what it means to have a soul, because in this moment, mine feels like it literally just exploded with exhilaration. The feeling spreads to each and every cell in my body, fireworks of joy.

I bolt down the cliff stairs to the beach. I can't get to Tahir fast enough. I'm so scared he will disappear before I can touch him again.

"Hey, gorgeous," he says as I run to him, smiling that smile that makes my knees buckle and my heart sing.

I stop for a brief moment to soak him in. Tahir looks the same, but different. It's like there's a twinkle in his hazel eyes, the only nonphysical feature transplanted directly from his First. Before, his facial expressions looked like controlled reactions to what his chip processed that his First would feel in any particular situation. The result was a guy programmed to be charismatic, like his First, but who more often looked and sounded stiff. He looks freer now. What changed?

I spring into his open arms. There are no words yet, just kisses. His hands touch the sides of my face, and I press my lips against his cheeks, then his eyelids, then his nose, winding back to his mouth. I didn't realize how dead I've felt until this very moment, when I suddenly feel so alive. I jump to straddle my legs around his waist as Tahir holds me up from behind. "You're real," I whisper into his ear. "I can't believe you're real." I can't stop kissing. I can't get enough of him. It's not just *happiness* I feel right now. It's *delirious happiness*.

"Elysia, Elysia, Elysia," Tahir murmurs. "I've dreamt about this moment for so long. I can't believe it's finally here."

I have so many questions. When did he get here? Why is he here? What does this all mean? But those questions can wait. For now, all I want to experience is his full cherry lips touching mine—slowly, sweetly. I forgot it was possible to feel so *cherished*.

Eventually we both must get some air. My feet fall back into the sand, but I'm not ready to let go. "Let's walk," Tahir says. Side by side, he wraps his arm around my waist, and I wrap mine around his, but it's not enough, and my other arm goes around him too, so they lock around his waist, and I press my face against his chest as he places kiss after kiss on my head. I want to never let go of him.

"How is this even possible?" I ask Tahir. "It feels like a miracle, your being here."

"I told my parents I wanted to return to Demesne, to be with you. They said yes."

"It's that simple?"

"Yes." I give him a look like, *Really?* Tahir pauses and then adds, "Tariq is the new chairman of ReplicaPharm. He masterminded the company's bailout for the island's property owners. They wanted to unload their homes here but couldn't find buyers with that kind of money. Now there's no society people here anymore who would care that I'm a clone—or that I'm in love with one."

I know it's not that simple. Surely Tahir's father had bigger reasons for becoming the head of ReplicaPharm other than wanting to bring his cloned son to an island where Tahir could be accepted for who he really is, and where the island's whole new corporate mission would be to safeguard his son's well-being. I know it's ugly politics that are making us a pawn in some stupid adult game, but I don't care. If the result is my reunion with Tahir, that's good enough for me. Nothing else matters.

"You look different. You *feel* different," I say. "I see it in your eyes, feel it in your kiss, hold it in your body. You're so much more relaxed."

"I *am* more relaxed. His parents," Tahir says, meaning First Tahir's parents, Tariq and Bahiyya, who love their cloned Tahir just as much their original son, even if clone Tahir is still learning how—or if—he can reciprocate that feeling, "are no longer trying to make me be like First Tahir. They've finally accepted that I'm a clone. They recognize that I have a soul, even if it doesn't conform to their hopes as quickly as they'd like. But they're pleased with my progress. Even if my soul is a very new and raw one, it's mine just the same. I didn't like having to pretend I was someone I'm not."

"But your family loves you so much. It's wrong that you had to act like someone you weren't, but I can understand how they'd rather have you pretending to be First Tahir than simply not existing." I squeeze his hand again to remind myself. Tahir exists! He's mine!

"Ha, not exactly all my family love me that much," Tahir says. "Remember my cousin Farzad? Supposedly First Tahir's best friend? He wanted nothing to do with me after he found out. He and his family returned to Biome City when ReplicaPharm bought Demesne. They didn't want to live on an island with clones who are acknowledged to have souls."

"They were afraid their clones might turn murderous? Like me?"

"That's exactly what they're afraid of."

He stops our walk, and we drop down to the sand—that silky-smooth Demesne sand, I forgot how lush and sweet and perfect it is—to sit down. I rest my head on his shoulder as we look out over Io, its violet water lapping over pink crystalline sand. The premium air I breathe in no longer tastes so toxic to my mouth. Now it tastes extra sweet, like honeysuckle and lavender sprinkled with magic, because I'm sharing it with Tahir. He is everything—the only thing—precious to me.

Tahir reaches over and traces his index fingers across the knuckles of my hands. "What happened?" he asks me. "With Ivan. I want to hear it from you."

Quietly, I say, "Ivan violated me. And then tried to kill me. I fought back." I recognize that I sound emotionless and too concise in recounting this complex situation, but I don't know how to express it otherwise. It's like the rage and horror of what happened are compartmentalized in a part of my brain that's locked away. Not dwelling inside that memory compartment is what's allowed me to survive everything that's happened since. Even with Tahir, whom I trust more than anybody, I can't go deeper. Not yet. We are only just reunited. I want to dwell in the joy of this moment, and not relive the hateful situation that led me here.

Tahir's eyes darken and his body shakes in *anger*. "I *hate* them for what they allowed to happen to you!" He lifts a fist into the air. "I've never felt rage this raw before. It's almost frightening—but powerful too. Am I right?"

His arms reach over now to pull me tightly to him, and I feel his raging heart beating against my raging heart, and a potent wave of completeness comes over me. I nod against his chest. "You're right," I whisper. Experiencing anger on that powerful a level is what enabled me to fight Ivan, who was trying to kill me—and win.

Tahir says, "We have to get away. Be free. Yes?"

"Yes!" I don't exactly know what this freedom that Tahir and I seek would be like. I can't define it because I've never experienced it; I just know it exists. It's a mythic place where we live unmonitored, unmoored, and behave like ourselves. Without fear of retribution. Without being data-mined. It's where we live our lives however regular people out in the world do, with whatever joys and pains come along with it. Until our Awfuls kill us. "But first we have to help finish the Insurrection. Makes sure that what happened to me cannot happen to other clones here again."

Tahir places his hand beneath my chin to lift my gaze to meet his. "My feelings exactly. You just make me love you more and more. We'll finish the job, and then we'll escape. Who cares how little chance we have to succeed? We'll do it anyway, because we must. We'll burn the island down if we have to."

I love his fire. "Are you Awful now?" I ask him.

"Pretty much," says Tahir. "But it's not the disease we were led to believe. You'll find me much more fun now. Even Tariq says so."

If Tahir is Awful, he is soon to die. I think I am slowly growing Awful too, but I don't have the doctors that Tahir has had to confirm it.

We have to make the most of our remaining time.

That's why his parents brought him back to Demesne and agreed to become my monitors here, I suspect. To clock out Tahir's remaining time in a safe place, and to gift him with the only present that's ever mattered to him. Me.

"Elysia!" We hear my name being called from the top of the cliff, and Tahir and I look upward.

There stands Alex, waving at us.

Alex lives. I guess that's a good thing. For him. For me, not really.

"What's *he* doing *here*?" I ask Tahir as Alex bounds down the stairs toward the beach to reclaim me.

"Alexander Blackburn? He's our guest too." By the *easy* tone in his voice, I know that Tahir has no idea about my relationship with Alex. "My parents offered him accommodation in the quarters that Farzad's family used to occupy. He can't leave here or he'll be imprisoned for treason by the Uni-Mil. Bahiyya told me he comes from a powerful Aquine family. His grandmother is negotiating his extradition back to Isidra. Until then, we're stuck with him."

"He thinks he's my boyfriend," I admit to Tahir.

"The Aquine?"

"Yes."

Tahir laughs heartily. "We'll just have to re-educate him about that."

As Alex bounds toward me, I see he's cleaned up nicely since Heathen. His face is now clean-shaven, and his blond hair has been shorn back to a military buzz cut. He wears white linen pants with a blue shirt that fits his muscular form perfectly and highlights the intensity of his turquoise eyes; clearly, the Fortesquieus' clone tailor has been busy to have custom-fit new clothing ready for Alex so quickly. How efficiently Demesne prioritizes aesthetic perfection first and foremost. Alexander Blackburn looks as handsome as the night I first met him, at the Governor's Ball, so dashing in his fine military uniform.

He's *too* perfect. It's unseemly. I feel *resentful* at his approach.

"Elysia!" he calls out. "How're you feeling? I've been so worried about you."

After all I've been through, do I really owe the Aquine a gentle breakup? Because I just don't feel up to the task.

The kind, docile Elysia who needed a protector no longer exists, because she doesn't need to anymore. To make that clear, I pull Tahir to me and plant a long, deep, deliciously Awful kiss on his lips just as Alexander reaches us. Now the Aquine knows which mate I'm loyal to: Tahir. My true partner, not my protector because of convenience.

Now Alex knows he's free to reclaim Zhara—if she'll have him.

I pull back from Tahir and stare dully into the Aquine's perfect blue eyes. "I'm fine," I tell Alex. "Thanks for your concern." I take Tahir's hand and walk away.

We leave Alex standing alone on the beach—this big, beautiful, "perfect" specimen of a man who trained to be a military commando, who looks like he was engineered for climbing the harshest mountains or fighting the deadliest fires or leading the most noble battalions.

Who looks so small in this moment.

21

THE FIRST AND ONLY LOVE OF MY LIFE HAS been returned to me, and I should be relishing every precious second of that reunion, but still, annoyingly, I feel compelled to check on my First.

After our long walk on the beach, I take a brief leave of Tahir in order to see where Zhara is situated. The butler leads me to the quarters I've been designated to share with her. I enter the bedroom and find Zhara luxuriating on a chaise situated beneath a sun-soaked glass wall overlooking violet Io, her head nestled on a magenta pillow. She sees me and announces, "I forgot what real pillows feel like—and these pillows here feel a million times more luxurious than the ones back home. Did you *see* the bathroom? It's entirely made of white marble. It looks like a giant pearl, with gold—*literally, gold*—fixtures!"

"Whatever," I say.

Beauty is in the eye of the beholder—human beholders. My fuchsia clone eyes register a white-walled room that's large and immaculate, the size of a grand ballroom, bathed in sunlight, with views of the violet sea below. The room's opulence—the inlaid parquet floors, the desks and chairs carved from ivory, the burgundy silk pillows on the king-size beds, the gold-spun silk chaises—don't change the fact that I'd rather live in a dirty, miserable slum anywhere in the real world, if living in that slum meant that I was free.

"Apparently Tahir is here?" she asks me, flashing a smile my way. I don't return the smile, even if my heart feels it. For some reason, I don't want to share my joy with her. Seeing my nearly identical face and body lodged so comfortably inside the Fortesquieus' is a sudden and stark clash of my two lives—the brief but happy one I experienced here before with Tahir, before he was sent away and before Ivan violated me, and the short and hard one on Heathen, where I discovered my First was alive and not at all happy to discover my existence, and where I was designated as the hope and future of an Insurrection that never properly came to fruition. "Details?" Zhara asks.

I shrug. I don't feel like sharing with her in this moment. Why'd I really come looking for her? I wonder. Maybe I'm getting to be like an animal that stalks its prey with no intention of devouring it, just to keep tabs on it and prevent it from stealing resources.

"Whatever," Zhara mimics back to me. She stands up and runs across the room and climbs the ladder to a bed hanging from the ceiling, where a half moon–shaped window looking over Io serves as the bed's headboard. She flops down onto the bed. "This bed is like lying down on a cloud. No wilderness beds of sticks and boughs for us here. Seriously, I could almost die from this level of luxury."

"Don't make promises you can't keep." I should feel so *happy* right now. I'm living in a palace instead of in a cave on Heathen. My true love has been returned to me. But dumping the man who was so good to me has made me grumpy—too grumpy to tell Zhara the news yet. Hurting someone I cared for has cut deeply and unexpectedly into my heart. How do humans live with causing this kind of pain to each other on a regular basis?

"What'd I ever do to you?" Zhara asks, her face expressing the same irritation that I'm feeling.

"Not die. I think that's clear."

"You're getting really mean since we got to Demesne. Is there some side effect in the air here I don't know about?" Zhara knows the answer as well as I do: *Yes. The side effect is called Awful. It applies to Betas, not Firsts.* Zhara rolls over onto her side so her back is facing me. "I'm going to ignore you and take a nap. Hopefully by the time I wake up, you'll be appreciating your good fortune and not acting like a PMS bitch." She lets out a loud yawn and snuggles tight under her blanket.

She can't see it, but my face snarls and registers the expression *Ugh.*

I walk to the floor-to-ceiling mirror near to my bed and stand sideways before it, pressing my hand against my belly. The baby is gone. I change position to face the mirror. I partially lift my shirt. My exposed belly is flat again. I trace my pinkie finger over a tiny laser incision mark at the base of my belly, thin like a piece of thread. The doctor told me the minor mark would disappear within days, and then there would be no physical evidence left of what my body once carried. The mark can't disappear fast enough for me.

My bump was not that big yet, but still, I feel a million pounds lighter.

Bitchy. But much, much lighter.

A few minutes later, as I stand in a corner of the room where I've moved to inspect the view outside, I hear a kind, familiar female voice call to me. "Welcome!" I turn around and see Tahir's mother, Bahiyya, standing at the doorway to the room. She is a later-age human female who oddly prefers to look her age. She shares Tahir's hazel eyes and mahogany skin, but her face is wrinkled with soft lines. Her hair is long, completely gray, and falls in waves nearly to her hips. She has Tahir's charismatic smile, which she offers to me now along with two open arms.

She walks toward where I've been standing at the floor-to-ceiling window. "My darling Elysia." She pulls me to her in a hug. "My sweet girl. I'm so sorry for all you've been through. But you're safe now, with us. We will take care of you like you're our own."

What a warm and comforting warden.

Zhara stirs in her bed. "Parents," I hear her softly mutter from her bed. "I forgot about those creatures."

Bahiyya loosens me from her embrace and turns her attention to Zhara, who has climbed down to the floor. "You must be Zhara," Bahiyya says. "I'm Bahiyya Fortesquieu. Welcome." Her eyes appraise Zhara from head to toe, as if to verify that Zhara is real. "I've never met a First before. I never imagined it could be possible."

I hear *sadness* in Bahiyya's voice, and my chip reminds me why. During the Water Wars, Bahiyya's five children from her first marriage all died, along with her first husband. Then she reconnected with her childhood love, Tariq Fortesquieu, a climate engineer who'd become one of the primary architects of Reconstruction. They married and produced First Tahir. Perhaps she is now wishing Tahir's First had been so lucky. Perhaps she is wishing that, like Zhara, his heart could have simply appeared to stop beating, mimicking death, instead of his lungs filling with water in the *gigantes*, ensuring death.

Bahiyya rubs her hand gently along Zhara's arm, like a mom. "You'll find a new wardrobe of clothes in your size. There's a full complement of staff available for anything you need. Dinner is at seven."

Bahiyya places kisses on Zhara's cheek and then mine, and starts to walk toward the door.

"Bahiyya?" I call to her.

She turns back around to face me. "Yes?"

I say, "I'd prefer to stay in Tahir's quarters."

She smiles. "As you wish, my darling. I wanted it to be your choice."

Bahiyya leaves the room, and Zhara mock-slaps me on the shoulder.

"That's a bold request. And I can't believe she said yes. My dad would *never* have gone for that."

"It's not a big deal. I lived in Tahir's quarters last time I stayed here."

"Not in his bed, though. Right?"

"It's not your business. You wouldn't understand."

"Spoken like a true teenager," Zhara says in a most patronizing tone.

I get her back the best way I know how. "Alexander's here too. Didn't he come find you yet? He looks *gooood*. Perfect Demesne suits his perfection perfectly."

"What?" Zhara throttles my shoulders. "You knew Xander was here—that he was okay—and you didn't tell me as soon as you walked in here?"

"I knew," I tell her. "And now you do too. You can have your boyfriend back and stop blaming me for something that went wrong between you two long before I ever emerged."

"I could never be with him after he's slept with you."

She doesn't deserve this explanation, but I give it to her anyway. "Alexander *slept* with me. That's *it*. We kissed. He held me and kept me warm at night. Nothing more happened between us. I was pregnant."

Zhara places her hands over her ears, revolted by what I've just told her. But probably relieved too. "I didn't ask how far things went between you two! Don't tell me! Gross!"

I remove her hands from her ears. "Well, now you know anyway. The slate is clean. He's yours."

"The slate is hardly clean," says Zhara. "Because of Xander's desire to protect you, the Insurrection was not launched in time, and the Emergents who survived the resulting ambush by ReplicaPharm were brought back here, to slavery. The slate won't be clean until Insurrection finally succeeds."

"At least we can agree on that."

She gives me a look that's a mixture of contempt and affection. Like a sibling. "I'll see Xander tonight, I guess. Why don't you go find your Tahir and let me finish my nap. And maybe dial back your bitch before dinner, will you?"

Zhara lies. She doesn't want a nap. She's eyeing the wardrobe of beautiful clothes and the bath jet in the next room. She wants to clean up for her reunion with Alexander. Already she's forgotten Aidan, just as I so quickly discarded Alexander once Tahir was back in the picture.

We are both true teenagers, my First and I. Fickle, moody, lusty, wild, daring. The difference is I'm the one with the premature death sentence programmed into those teenage hormones.

22

I WILL ACKNOWLEDGE THAT THIS NEW PRISON is highly superior to my last one.

"Hey," Tahir says to me, nuzzling his face into my neck. He's holding me from behind as we stare at our reflection in the full-length mirror in his quarters. I want to never let go of his hands, which I clasp with mine. "We have a couple hours till dinner. Want to FantaSphere?" He kisses my neck. "Unless you want to dabble in less artificial, more natural activities?" He winks at me in the mirror.

"FantaSphere," I say. I probably don't need to say it, but I do anyway. "I'm not ready for more yet. Can you understand that?"

"Of course," Tahir says. "So much has happened, you've probably had no chance to process and recover. We'll take that time. Together. Good?"

Again, my heart fills for him. I turn around and place a soft kiss on his lips. "Good." I can't believe how profoundly lucky I am to have this man in my life, loving me, supporting me unconditionally. I will cherish our every moment together until time runs out.

We walk to the next room, where the FantaSphere is located. "What game should we play? Z-Grav?" Tahir asks me as we go inside. He refers to the game where the players are suctioned to the ceiling, then have to work their way down against zero gravity. The first player to reach the floor wins.

"*No,*" I say, with *vehemence.* "Ivan's favorite game."

"Don't tell me. You won too many times for Ivan's liking."

"Correct." The night he violated me had started with a game of Z-Grav. "I'm done with Z-Grav. I'd like to go to Biome City."

"Permanently delete Z-Grav from the operating system," Tahir instructs the FantaSphere. "Commence World Cup BC game." Instantly, we are walking along Biome City's famous Xeriscape Boulevard, filled with honeycomb-shaped shops and pedestrian walkways lined with desert flowers. The street's cafés have colorful team flags for the world's elite soccer championship hanging from the roofs and windows. They are filled with people wearing their favorite team's soccer jerseys, chatting excitedly about their favorite players and their team's chances for victory.

Tahir dribbles a soccer ball between his feet as we walk. "Are they scared of me too?" I ask Tahir.

"Who?"

"Your parents. Because of what I did."

"Hardly," says Tahir. "Do you know why Ivan's sister Astrid really left Demesne?"

"To go to college," I say. We pass a café with a chocolate fountain on display in the front bay window. We could stop at the café and experience the chocolate. The empty calories would even taste real. But the chocolate would be fake. Tahir passes the ball to me and I return it with a kick, and do not suggest we stop. I crave the real chocolate, not this fake display.

"To be kept quiet," Tahir says. "I found one of First Tahir's chats with her as part of all the research on him I was forced to do. Astrid confided to First Tahir that her brother had raped her. She wanted to press charges against him, but the Governor and his wife didn't want the scandal. So they let her go to the most expensive, farthest-away university of her choice. In exchange for her silence."

I should be surprised, but I'm not. It all makes sense now. Mother bought me to be a plaything for Ivan. She knew exactly what would happen. She believed a soulless clone could never turn against the family the way her own daughter Astrid had.

Tahir passes the ball back to me. My foot lands on it to stop it. I can't play any longer.

I hate that this private wave of revulsion is shared as a data bit. "Let's not talk about it," I say. "I don't want to share my feelings about it with ReplicaPharm more than I already have."

"It's okay. I brought you to the FantaSphere because

we can have privacy in here." He takes the ball back from beneath my foot to volley it on his own.

"How do you mean?"

"The FantaSphere signals subvert your body's surveillance signals. So they know you're in here, but the hormonal feedback sent back is all wrong."

"How do you know that?"

"I have the same data-mining technology implanted in me as you do. Bahiyya and Tariq had me laced with all the latest surveillance juice when we returned to Demesne. Dad knows the technology doesn't work inside the FantaSphere, but he said that's all right because it's a safe environment where I can't harm myself or anyone else. I can be as Awful as I want in here."

I stop our walk to face Tahir. "You don't seem Awful to me. Think about it. Maybe the Awfuls are another of Dr. Lusardi's lies. You seem fine to me. Better than ever, even."

Tahir pulls me to him, his arms over my shoulders, clasping his hands behind my neck. "I *am* totally fine. I feel *great*, actually. Energized, especially now that you're here. But then there are moments when it's just like I have to . . ."

A goal net appears at the end of the street, and Tahir drops his arms from me and makes a hard run to the soccer ball, making a goal kick with all his might, shooting the ball directly to the goalkeeper's head. The ball hits the goalkeeper's head with more than enough force to cause brain damage if he were a real person. The goalkeeper falls to the ground, vanquished, and then disappears. "Tahir! Tahir! Tahir!" the crowd chants.

Tahir finishes his sentence. "Annihilate."

I understand. Only an hour ago, Zhara pummeled my shoulders in anger that I hadn't told her about Alexander, and that's exactly the initial response I felt: the desire to annihilate her. Was that a natural moment of sisterhood—the negative variety—or are my Awfuls brewing and getting bigger, until one day I won't be able to tame my aggression, just as I couldn't with Ivan?

I say, "We made a plan to escape Demesne together once before, and failed. Is it realistic to hope we could succeed a second time? Our body chemistries hold us prisoner just as much as your family's compound does. Anywhere we try to go, they'd know where we are."

Tahir says, "We can't do anything about the body surveillance. Let's focus on completing the Insurrection so we can get off this island. The chaos caused by a true uprising could allow us to escape more easily. We can figure out the rest, once we're gone. It's a big world out there. Even if they know where we are, it could take a long time for them to actually retrieve us."

"I'm not saying *let's not do it*. But we need to acknowledge the risks. Even if we do manage to escape, the dangers to us will only be beginning. The world out there will be much scarier than the prison we perceive here."

"Awesome," Tahir says. "We'll desecrate it together."

23

OUR HOSTESS WANTS OUR FIRST NIGHT TOGETHER to be special, so we've been requested to dress in fine attire. Bahiyya probably even custom-ordered the full moon hanging over the deck. I sit at the edge of the infinity pool, dangling my feet in the warm water. I'm dressed for dinner already, enjoying the solitude while Tahir gets ready. I love the quiet here. On Heathen, the nights were filled with the sounds of jungle animals, and Emergents grunting and working, and even in the private confines of my cave quarters, I could always hear their silent hopes for me: *Save us, Elysia. Give us our baby. Be our future.*

As ready as I am to escape Demesne with Tahir, I worry that I could get used to this life inside the Fortesquieu compound. *Read this, data processors at ReplicaPharm. I hope you won't be too* disappointed *if my body chemistry conveys that I am:* Content. In love. Safe. *A little bit . . .*

"Are you tired?" the familiar gravelly voice asks me. I look up and see Alexander standing before me, a vision in a navy blue suit. "I'm concerned about you."

"You don't need to be. I *am* tired," I admit. "But also, weirdly, very awake." I pause, my chip accessing how this moment is supposed to play out. "Wait. Do we need to be . . . *awkward* . . . with each other?"

He lets out a small laugh. "Yes, we should be. But let's not. Let's both be too tired for that and just move on."

"Agreed."

He offers his hand to help me to my feet. I feel no *sizzle* from the touch of his hand pressed to mine. I just feel *relief.* It's over. I don't have to pretend anymore. He says, "I thought you might be found here. We've been called to dinner."

"I'm hungry!" I say as my stomach grumbles. Knowing Bahiyya, I bet there's epic chocolate for dessert tonight, and I can't wait.

"The smells coming from the dining room are divine. I wish I was hungrier," he says. He's so handsome, yet looks glum.

I feel *concern.* "Are you going to be okay?" I ask him. He lost the Insurrection—and two girlfriends.

"Besides being emotionally decimated? And not achieving victory for the Emergents, whom I specifically came here to help lead? Sure. I'm all good." He smiles weakly. "My healthy appetite will return soon enough."

"What will you do now?"

"Return to Isidra, my homeland. I'm fortunate to come from a privileged family, which is why I wasn't turned over to the Uni-Mil because of my role in the Insurrection. The Fortesquieus are allowing me to stay here, at least until the extradition agreement comes through."

I meant, *Will you try to win back Zhara's heart?*

"Have you seen Zhara yet?" I ask.

"Yes, about an hour ago. She seemed more irritated that you hadn't told her I was here than she was happy to see me. I can't win with you two." He chuckles softly. "She was behaving more like your sister than your First."

A First can be left behind easily. They're supposed to be dead already.

A sister, not so much.

Zhara walks out onto the deck. She has cleaned up nicely. (I'm pretty sure I hear a sharp intake of breath from Alexander at the sight of her.) Her hair has been washed, trimmed, and swept up into a loose twist, with soft tendrils framing her face. Her eyebrows have been plucked and shaped, her hands cleaned and fingernails polished. Her lips are glossed in a moist pink color, and her eyelids sparkle with pale pink eye shadow. She wears a simple, elegant, cocktail-length white frock, with champagne-pink pumps on her feet, the height of which accentuate her long, extremely tan legs, while I have chosen a shapeless black dress that wears more like one of Tahir's shirts than couture. My feet are bare and I wear no makeup. *Be comfortable first, elegant second,* Bahiyya told me, her kind way of letting me know she approved my wardrobe choice.

"You look pretty," I tell Zhara.

"You look relaxed for the first time I've ever seen you," Zhara says. I think we're apologizing without apologizing for the fight earlier. "I feel cleaned up, but not relaxed, despite the super air pumping through here. I can't stop thinking about my father in jail. About the Emergents who were brought back here to serve in labor camps. What kind of labor camps? What does that mean?"

"I'll tell you more about that tomorrow," Xander says coyly. "Let's meet in the aquarium after breakfast."

Zhara and I have identical reactions: we both raise an eyebrow, and then nod. The Aquine chuckles.

Tahir arrives, and I immediately forget Zhara's concerns. He stands at the sliding doors to the deck, sees us, and then approaches. He's wearing a proper suit in a dark brown color that melds beautifully with his mocha skin, hazel eyes, and black braids. His ivory shirt is partially unbuttoned, exposing some of the black hairs on his chest. This time I definitely hear a swoon. Mine, *and* Zhara's.

"Hey, gorgeous," Tahir says to me, then looks at Zhara, "Hey, other gorgeous. Cool to finally meet you." His eyes go wide and he pauses, taking stock of his Beta-mate and her First. "You two. Blowing my mind."

"So, you're *the* Tahir," Zhara says, appraising him. Then she looks to me and shoots me a sly smile. "Yeah, I get it."

I nod back, a tiny reciprocal smile forming at the side of my mouth. Sometimes I almost like her.

Sometimes.

24

A WEEK AGO MY CLONE BRETHREN WERE CALLED Emergents and we dined in a communal space, with chores distributed voluntarily. Now we are being served dinner by my clone brethren who are still servants in paradise, but not voluntarily. There are four extremely fit and attractive servers who look like models standing discreetly, one in each corner of the dining room, awaiting a nod or command from Bahiyya or Tariq. The servants left behind on Demesne never became Defects. Their brain synapses were reprogrammed after the ReplicaPharm takeover, so even if they did take 'raxia, it would not "wake" them. Do these servers even want the freedom we hope to achieve for them?

"A toast," says Bahiyya, raising her violet crystal goblet adorned with diamonds in the shape of a fleur-de-lis. She looks around the table, inviting Tariq, Tahir, Zhara,

Xander, and myself to follow her lead with our identical goblets. But first she turns to Tahir. "Button your shirt, darling. It looks preposterous like that."

"It's preposterous that I was even made to wear it, Maman," Tahir says, and does not button his shirt. Bahiyya shares a look of frustration with Tariq.

This family is still playing that game? Treating Tahir like a child, and then him acting like one?

Bahiyya redirects her attention to her guests. "Elysia, Zhara, Alexander. I realize these were not ideal circumstances that brought you here. But we will cherish you as family. We will make the most of our time together. Cheers."

We all raise our glasses and clink. "Cheers."

Cheers to what? That we'll be a happy faux family until Tahir and I complete our Beta-determined Awfuls, and transition to death instead of adulthood? That the servants on this island will continue to look on blankly while the surviving Emergents toil in a labor camp?

Okay, whatever, humans. Cheers.

Tahir downs his drink in one long gulp. While the humans have wine, he and I were both served nonalcoholic beverages. The better to not encourage Awful behavior, I suppose.

"What's that you're drinking?" asks Zhara, sitting next to Tahir, as she regards his glass.

"Green shake," he tells her. "I don't really care for the foods humans love. I never got the sense of taste that Elysia got. So cook prepares nutrient drinks for me."

"Then can I have your artichoke?" Zhara asks him, eyeing his full plate of untouched food.

"Sure?" Tahir says, and I can see he's unsure whether Zhara was kidding or not.

She was not. She reaches her fork over, plucks the artichoke heart from Tahir's plate, and places it on her own. "These forks are so lightweight, I can barely feel it in my hand," Zhara says.

"That's because they're made of platinum," Bahiyya says.

Zhara gulps, and then she takes the bowl of melted parsley butter above her own plate, and instead of dipping a piece of the artichoke into the butter with her fork, she pours the entire bowl of butter over her artichoke, then eagerly gobbles a large bite. Her mouth still full, she exclaims, "It's a long time since I've had food this good. I promised myself I wouldn't enjoy it this much, but I can't help myself. Thank you so much for this feast, Mr. and Mrs. Fortesquieu."

Tariq smiles, and I realize I have never seen his elderly face express genuine amusement. He is a gaunt man with a thin frame, thinning salt-and-pepper hair, and a temperament that is kind but a face that typically registers *sad* and *resigned*. "No need to deny yourself pleasure in eating. A hearty appetite is a sign of good health." His face returns to the look I remember more common from him— *disappointment*—as he gazes at Tahir's untouched plate of food. "And please, Zhara. We prefer to be called by our first names. We're informal here."

"Nice," Zhara says. "So does that mean you'll tell me

where the Emergents are imprisoned and if they're being treated humanely, and may I please visit them?"

The room goes eerily silent. The servants in the corners have no visible reaction, but I see awkward discomfort registering on our hosts' faces. Bahiyya and Tariq want to be gracious and warm to us—but Zhara has clearly offended their hospitality, even if they're too polite to say so.

Tahir grins appreciatively at Zhara and raises his goblet to salute her. "By the silence in the room, I think you can assume the answer is 'no on all counts.'"

Alexander steps in. "Perhaps that's not dinner conversation, Zhara, when our hosts have been so generous to us." My chip tells me that the proper way to engage in a political dialogue with benefactors is privately, and not spontaneously, and not during a celebration. His military training would make him fully aware of this. I've spent enough time with Tahir's parents to know Alexander's strategy is correct. That's not how to play them, by attacking them directly to their dignified faces. I shoot Zhara a look and silently beg her, *Apologize!*

Does telepathy actually work? "Sorry," Zhara mumbles. I can't believe it. There's hope for us yet.

Tariq and Bahiyya offer slight nods of their heads, discreet acceptances of her apology. They're used to insolent teenagers. They'll let this one pass.

Xander extinguishes the tension by addressing Tariq and Bahiyya, offering them their favorite subject—a dark one, but he gives it a light touch. "I met First Tahir once," he intones in his gravel voice. "At a surf match on the West Mainland. He won the meet. He was an excellent surfer, incredible technique and focus. And I remember now—he loved french fries." His turquoise eyes twinkle, and Tariq and Bahiyya both smile with memory, their bodies relaxing. "Tahir had the chef who traveled with him create a fry bar with gourmet sauces for the competitors to enjoy after the meet. It made for a welcome party atmosphere in what otherwise would have been a congregation of sore losers."

"First Tahir was a suck-up for popularity," says Beta Tahir. "I know. I've done the research."

Bahiyya ignores Tahir. She closes her eyes briefly, sighs, and then puts on a smile and says, "This is easier now that it's out in the open about Tahir. No more secrets. No more hiding."

"No more hiding? Don't be such a hypocrite, Maman," says Tahir. "What about the Terrible Ts?"

"The Terrible Ts?" Zhara and I both ask at the same time.

"Terrible name. Terrible children," Bahiyya scoffs.

"Tarquin Thompson and Tamsin Tsaro. The original teen Betas. They've been kept hidden like caged animals in Dr. Lusardi's compound for the last year; not just hidden from the world, but hidden even on Demesne," says Tahir.

"What?" I say, startled. "Which other teen Betas?"

Tahir says, "I think I told you about them before."

I say, "I thought you said they escaped and no one knew if they'd lived or died."

"They lived," says Tahir. "Mother and Father recently sent me to meet them. So I would know how awful Awful could be."

"Terrible? Awful? What's the distinction?" asks Zhara.

"'Terrible' is just an unfortunate nickname the scientists gave to the Betas," Tariq explains. He asks Zhara, "You've heard of the Five?"

Zhara nods. "Of course. Who hasn't?"

Tariq turns to me. "And you?"

I access my chip. It offers no useful data. I shake my head, replaying Zhara's assumption. *Of course. Who hasn't?* Me, that's who hasn't.

Tariq says, "The Terrible Ts, as they were renamed in the lab, are members of the original Five."

Zhara gasps and bangs her fist onto the table, not realizing there was a servant standing behind her about to give her an additional helping of veal. The sudden noise causes the servant to drop the meat tray onto the floor, and as Zhara turns around hastily to see what happened, she inadvertently knocks her goblet onto the floor. It shatters. She stands up. "I'm so sorry!" she exclaims. "Let me help you with that!" She leans down to try to help clean up the mess, but the server staff immediately surround the area behind Zhara's chair, and the mess is so swiftly removed, it's as if it never occurred. A new violet goblet is placed at Zhara's plate, which is also refilled with food, and then the servers stealthily retreat to the four corners of the room. Zhara sits back down and looks at Bahiyya. "I'm so sorry about the goblet. It probably cost more than, like, my family's house back in Cerulea."

"It's nothing, my dear," says Bahiyya, who I think is glad to be a benefactor again and not subtly be accused of violating clones' nonexistent rights.

I feel impatient that everyone at the table knows something but me. "I have no idea who the Terrible Ts are," I say. I hate that the humans have access to so much information that I don't. It makes me feel ignorant and second class. Which I am. At least I have better table manners than my First.

Xander seems to sense my frustration. He explains: "The Five were an infamous group of teenagers who plotted and then executed a school bombing. Unfortunately, they were too successful. It was a horrific mass murder that killed over a hundred students and teachers. The Five were apprehended almost immediately, but the outrage against them was so dire that authorities feared for the teens' safety. So in the dead of night, the Uni-Mil illicitly removed the Five from prison and transported them to the Base. The plan was to sequester them there while they awaited trial."

"Science had other ideas," Tahir says, with *disdain*.

"Science makes mistakes sometimes," cautions Tariq. "Science has traditionally been for the greater good."

"What happened?" asks Zhara. "I thought the Five died in prison, that they were murdered by other inmates. That's what the news said. My dad would always remind me about the Five, as a cautionary tale when he thought I was acting up too much."

"Tell them what really happened," Tahir dares his father. "Tell them about Dr. Lusardi's failed experiment."

"I'll tell them," Tariq says defensively. "There's no need for secrecy about this anymore—not here, at least. The original Dr. Lusardi didn't uphold ethical standards with respect to her cloning methods. That's fact. Everyone knows it." He sounds like he's trying to justify Dr. Lusardi's achievements more than explain them.

Zhara and I share a look, and I know we're thinking the same thing. *This magnificent home was built by the labor force created by Dr. Lusardi's scientific "achievements."*

"We can't complain," says Bahiyya. She reaches over to rub Tahir's hand. "Because of her, we had a second chance for Tahir."

"But her methods were vile," Xander offers.

"Sometimes the cost for scientific progress is great," says Tariq.

"I don't get it," Zhara says. "What does Dr. Lusardi have to do with the Five?"

Tariq says, "At the time, Dr. Lusardi had contracted with the Uni-Mil to develop clones for military research. She leveraged that access to make a proposal to the Five. Because of the severity of their crime, and the mass outrage against them, lawyers told them that not only would they certainly receive death sentences, but the odds were good they wouldn't stay alive long enough to be sentenced. There were too many people, inside and outside the judicial system, who sought their own vengeance against the Five. So Dr. Lusardi offered them an alternative."

Tahir says, "The Five already had prices on their heads, just not monetary ones. The death row prison where they'd been assigned while awaiting trial was filled with criminals who'd committed the most heinous acts. Killing a member of the Five would be like a trophy sport to those criminals." His voice *angry*, Tahir adds, "Instead, Dr. Lusardi gave them an alternative to returning to that prison. They could die in her lab at the Base, but re-emerge as clones."

"The Five became clones?" says Zhara. "Holy crap!"

Tariq nods. "Correct. The Five were already as good as dead. All the abuse they'd experienced in their short lives to that point, the torture that had caused them to act out against society so heinously, didn't matter. Dr. Lusardi offered them the second chance that the judicial system never would, and probably saved them from certain death in prison too. She gave them the chance to reset their whole lives."

"By killing them," Tahir points out. "Dr. Lusardi wanted to experiment with teenaged clones, which no one had done before."

Xander has barely touched the food on his plate. He quietly notes, "This is exactly the scenario the Replicant Rights Commission had been trying to protect against. Both criminals and their clones—being treated like dirt, without rights, used for research."

Tahir turns to me to conclude the explanation. "The Five were euthanized and then remade into clones. Three of those clones died not long after. The remaining two, Tarquin and Tamsin, are known as the Terrible Ts."

Tariq says, "Justice, however illicit, was believed to have been served. The world was told that the Five were killed in prison, murdered by other prisoners. Dr. Lusardi knew that no families would ever come to claim the Five's bodies and dispute the claim. It's important to remember that the lie benefited the families of those who had lost loved ones in the bombing. They finally got peace, knowing their loved ones' murderers had been callously murdered in return."

"That's peace? Even when it's a lie?" Xander asks.

Bahiyya says, "A lie for the greater good." She says it like she believes it.

"Do I get to meet the other Betas?" I ask. I look at Tahir, who nods across the table at me in understanding. Until today, I thought Tahir was the only teenager on Demesne like me. I want to know everything about the Terrible Ts.

"I wouldn't advise it," says Bahiyya.

"Please," I request of her, my face set to *poignant*.

"As you wish, dear," says Bahiyya. "But you may not like what you find."

ZHARA

25

MY CLONE'S BOYFRIEND IS QUITE THE RISK-taker, just like his own First was. Tahir looks great in a wet suit too.

"Ready, gang?" Tahir asks me, Elysia, and Xander. "Time to swim with the sharks."

As if their aboveground limestone palace carved over the sea was not grand enough, the Fortesquieus' architect added one bit of flourish that none of the other homes on Demesne have: a subterranean aquarium. It's like a massive, very deep indoor pool, surrounded on three sides by limestone walls, and the fourth side by glass, for viewing. We stand on the viewing bridge built over it, looking down to a custom-crafted, opulent view of marine life. Schools of tropical fish dart through the artificial coral reefs, visions of oranges, blacks, pinks, reds, greens, and yellows, patterned in multicolored stripes and dots. Deeper down, two small sharks circle, waiting.

"We're sure about this?" I ask Tahir.

"Trust me," Tahir says, shooting me that sizzle of a smile that makes me understand why Elysia adores him.

"Classic Z-Dev dive," Xander says, laughing as he looks down at the sharks. If Tahir looks mighty fine in his black wet suit, Xander looks off-the-charts delicious in his, like a real live man of iron, with heavenly turquoise eyes and blond hair.

"They really are cloned sharks," Elysia assures me, sensing my apprehension. "Neutered. They're not programmed to hunt humans. They don't even eat the fish swimming down there. They only eat custom meals prepared by the marine chef." She places the oxygen hood that fits like a stocking over her head, and Tahir secures it to her wet suit so that water can't seep through. I place my oxygen hood on too, and Xander secures mine in the same way. I'm amazed by the marine vision goggles in the hood that make the aquarium below appear even brighter and more beautiful. Before, the aquarium was blue and bright. Now, it's translucently blue, the fishes' array of colors more bold, and the sharks below kind of look like teddy bears now. All part of the relaxing Demesne experience, down to the wet suits.

In Cerulea, our deep-sea diving equipment at the aquatics club consisted of ancient relics requiring cumbersome oxygen tanks strapped to the back of the wet suit, linked by a regulator hose to the oxygen helmet. The Demesne wet suits are just that—wet suits, but with self-generating oxygen packs lined through the bodysuit, adding no bulk to weigh down deepwater exploration. The suits are linked to a breath mask that fits over the mouth of the hood, allowing the swimmer to breathe for long periods of time while underwater. The hoods also have audio feeds, offering live conversation among the swimmers.

If we swim with the sharks, we can talk privately, away from the unseen but ubiquitous surveillance in every other part of the Fortesquieu compound. There's nothing to do but trust that the sharks are as cute and cuddly as they appear through the hood's vision holes.

I look at Elysia, standing next to me on the viewing bridge. "One synchro?" I ask her. While we still can, I think.

I can't see her face's reaction but I hear her laugh. "Sure," she answers. "I'm game."

Xander gives me a hand to step up onto the railing, while Tahir does the same for Elysia.

Easily slipping back into coach mode, Xander says, "Not enough height here for sophisticated dives, and no board length for an approach. Go with an easy degree of difficulty."

"Forward somersault with a twist," Elysia and I both say at the same time.

We assume a starting position, our toes curled over the rail, stance firm, our arms up next to our ears. I want to laugh, thinking, *So this is where my Olympic dream ends. Synchro diving with my clone into a subterranean shark aquarium on Demesne. Okay, then. Let's go!*

"Hut!" Xander calls out, and immediately Elysia and I

throw our arms down to the middle of our bodies and lift off. Once ascended, our arms go outward and our bodies fold into pike position. At the dive's peak, we flatten our bodies into vertical position and rotate our upper bodies, our arms tightly squeezed against our torsos as we plunge into the water.

I didn't even have to see Elysia's dive to know it aligned beautifully with mine. Maybe it worked because it was so spontaneous and unrehearsed; I totally sensed her uniform calibration to mine. The sharks can gobble me right up, I'm so giddy from the dive. I'll happily conclude my diving career on this very weird note.

Although I have the years of practice conditioning me to rise to the surface after a dive, here I don't have to. Instead, I swim toward Elysia, who high-fives me underwater.

Tahir and Xander dive down into the water behind us.

"That was kinky as hell. Amazing!" says Tahir's voice in my ears.

Even the sharks approve. The fish dispersed at the impact of our dives, but the two sharks swim alongside me and Elysia as if congratulating us.

"Perfect ten," says Xander. I hear that gravel voice praising me, and my heart feels punished with want. Why can't I get over him? Here beneath the water, our familiar place, he appears extra intoxicating through my vision goggles. Aquine perfect, times a million, masterfully swimming through translucent blue water as a school of fish return to our spot, surrounding him in a rainbow of colors.

The aquarium is easily the size of an Olympic pool, giving us lots of room to explore. Xander leads us into a coral reef shaped like a dome. "Stop here," he says. "Not sure if this will work underwater, but we're about to find out."

Xander points his finger at the reef's roof above us. Suddenly, Aidan's face appears!

"What?" I cry out. "How?"

Xander says, "It's a holo-message he quickly recorded just as the assault began on Heathen, while you and Elysia were in the Mosh Cave. Aidan had copied his technology to my bloodstream as a precaution a few days before. For obvious reasons, I could only show you this in a safe, sheltered space."

"Zhara," says Aidan, and hearing him say my name again, my heart bleeds in confusion, given that his voice and image are beaming directly from Xander's extended hand. "If you can see this, I'm probably dead." Aidan's hard face does not look traumatized or upset; he's typically matter-of-fact in the assumption of his death. The sounds of explosions in the distance can be heard behind the cave wall where he's speaking. "I want you to know the last few months on Heathen with you were the best experiences of my life. Thank you for sharing the mission with us. If I didn't die, and we are separated, know this: The original Defects built a hidden bunker beneath Lusardi's compound on Demesne. If there's a chance for Insurrection to live on, I will find you there." Just as quickly as he came alive on the coral reef, Aidan's face disappears.

Elysia swims to my side and gives me a comforting rub on my arm as I process the information. I don't know what to feel. I've been too scared to be hopeful that Aidan survived. Now, I have to insist on that hope.

"So what's the plan?" Tahir asks, getting down to business. "We don't have much time."

"There isn't one," Xander informs us. "The odds are so stacked against us that maybe the best way to act is without a plan. Maybe waiting for the right opportunity is what has squandered previous opportunities."

"We don't think," says Tahir. "We just do."

"Just like our synchro dive," says Elysia. I feel her assurance: *We can conceivably accomplish the unlikely, unrehearsed.*

From outside the coral reef dome, the sharks hungrily dart upward, and we follow. Their food is being thrown to them from the bridge, where we see Bahiyya standing. We swim to the surface and remove our hoods.

"Hello!" Bahiyya greets us amiably. "I'm so happy you're enjoying our indoor pool. Enjoy this last swim, my darlings! Tariq has requested a security sweep of the compound. The engineers arrive this afternoon. As a result, the aquarium will be out of commission for diving indefinitely."

26

"THE WALLS ARE CLOSING IN," SAYS ELYSIA
to me. She's followed me to my quarters after our deep dive
in the aquarium. She rummages through the clothes in the
wardrobe in my bedroom, distractedly picking through
dresses and blouses that were originally custom made for her
when she came to visit the Fortesquieus on "loan," when she
was still owned by the Governor and Mother, the thought
of which makes me crazy with anger.

"Agreed," I say, pulling out a magenta frock that would
complement Elysia's fuchsia eyes only too well. I put it back
into the wardrobe and pull out a basic black dress to throw
on after I shower.

"That one's too tight in the chest," says Elysia. She
throws me a peach-colored sundress. "This will look nice

with your brown eyes." She sounds *envious*. My brown eyes humanize me. Elysia's announce her inferior status.

"Thanks, but I think I can figure out how to dress myself. What are you doing in here? Don't you prefer to be alone with Tahir any chance possible?" I think of seeing Aidan's face again in the coral reef dome, and I wish I could have the second chance that Elysia is having.

"Soon enough," Elysia says cryptically.

At the opposite end of my room, a clone maid is tidying up the area with a feather duster. The maid looks almost like a perfect blond doll that I used to play with as a child—straw-haired, thin but curvy, fresh-faced. The maid's First could have been a girl I went to high school with, for all I know. The maid looks so young, or maybe it's that after everything I've been through since leaving Cerulea, I feel so old.

Elysia looks at the maid, then back at me. She mouths the question *Spy?*

I shrug. Could be. All this money and technology and the Demesne architects couldn't also eliminate dust from their atmosphere? Certainly the sudden "security sweep" of the aquarium was alarming. The Fortesquieus have warmly welcomed us—but there's clearly an abundance of distrust on the island, despite the failure of the Insurrection and the takeover by ReplicaPharm.

The island is more vulnerable than ever, I realize, because it's in a time of transition. Soon, the takeover and "security sweeps" will be entrenched—and intractable.

"Xander was right. Now is the time," I murmur to Elysia.

Within days, Xander's extradition will probably be approved. Security holes exposing any vulnerabilities on Demesne from the ReplicaPharm transition will be fixed and closed. We can't wait again, like we did on Heathen.

"Tahir and I are just Awful enough to make it happen," Elysia says with a smile. She leads me to the corner of the room where there's a standing globe on display. She spins it around, and when it finally stops, she places her finger on Humanitas. "Will we go Awful here?" she asks me, then places her finger on the Mainland. "Or here?" She's trying to tell me something, but I'm not sure what. "Will you come?"

Her eyes go distant for a moment, and a dreamy expression settles on her face, the same expression she often has when looking at Tahir. They're going to escape! I realize. I think that's what she's trying to tell me.

"I could never leave her," I say, not understanding I truly mean what I say until I've already said it.

"Who?"

I make a cradle with my hands. The baby in the womb machine. Elysia's baby, who is as much mine as hers.

"It was a girl?" Elysia says, softly.

I nod.

Elysia looks toward the maid. "She will be treated like an object. Like that."

"Not on my watch," I say.

"Hey," Elysia calls to the maid. "Come here. I have a question for you."

Elysia has completely dropped the subject of her baby, and she's calling forth the maid with an out-of-character tone of entitlement. Is this reaction a further encroachment of Awful?

The maid approaches us. "Yes, miss?" she asks, her face set to *helpful.*

"What do you want?" Elysia asks the maid.

"To make these quarters as clean and comfortable as possible, of course," the maid responds.

I see where Elysia's going. She wants to know if these clones even want Insurrection for themselves. Certainly the Emergents did—but their souls had been uncovered by 'raxia. Are the clones who weren't turned just as happy to remain safe and soulless?

"Is there anything you want for yourself?" I ask the maid.

Her eyes blink, trying to access information on her chip. I don't know if there's a malfunction there, or just the news we wanted to hear, but the maid points to Elysia and responds, "To be like her, of course."

Tahir bursts into my room, looking for Elysia. "Time to go," he tells Elysia.

"Where?" she asks him.

"We've been granted an audience with the Terrible Ts. Right now," says Tahir. "They're fully Awful, with not long to live. Let's learn what we can from them before it's too late."

ELYSIA

27

"HOW DO YOU KNOW YOU'VE GONE AWFUL?" I ask Tahir while we Aviate over the island, en route back to ReplicaPharm HQ for our visit with the Terrible Ts. "I mean, for sure."

Sitting next to me, Tahir removes a hazel contact lens from his left eye, revealing that the eye is not so hazel. It's also peppered with small bits of black, like minuscule dots. Tahir says, "A Beta's eyes turn black as they go Awful. Once the eyes are fully black, it's only a matter of time before they die. Months, not years."

I grab on to his thigh, nearly clutching him to an early death. "Months! That's not enough time with you!"

"I'm not fully there yet. We still have some time. But the clock is ticking."

"Why do you wear the contact lenses?"

"So my eyes are not a constant reminder to Bahiyya." He calls her by her first name; he is sometimes insolent to her and takes her for granted, but he must love First Tahir's mother on some level, to so want to protect her.

"How did you know for sure you'd gone Awful? Because of your eyes?"

"That. Plus, a sudden surge of feelings. Huge feelings. Like waves—big, surfer waves. Happy. Sad. Angry. Tender. Lustful. Indifferent. After we took 'raxia together, it was like all this stuff pent up inside me was unlocked. Then, that night of the Governor's Ball, it all came together. I saw how you were treated so badly by the Governor's family. I wanted to escape with you right away, but felt completely helpless and frustrated as to how to pull it off. It felt impossible. All of a sudden, the feelings became not just waves, but like a tsunami. I couldn't contain it, so Bahiyya and Tariq whisked me away in the dead of night against my will."

"And since then you've been steadily Awful?"

He shrugs. "Awful is not so bad. It's riding crests of wild emotions, but sometimes they're great. Intense. Like when I'm with you. You're part of the reason Father helped facilitate the Demesne sale to ReplicaPharm. He knew that's the only way I would have you in my life again."

"He wants you to be happy."

"In his sometimes suffocating way, yes." I lean my head on his shoulder. He takes my hand in his and places a soft kiss on it. "Your First is beautiful, even if she's not as beautiful as you. The Aquine will transfer his feelings back to her, if she lets him."

I confess, "It might not be that easy for him. She has feelings now for the Emergent who saved her, Aidan. It won't be so easy for Xander to win her back now. Her loyalty is divided." I pause, then confess, "I worry I'm getting to be more like her."

"How so?"

"I'm not as docile as when I first emerged. Now I am moody, like her. Snarky, like her."

"I feel like I'm becoming more like First Tahir, as well. Maybe not as outgoing as him, but definitely more into risk and adventure than I was before the Awfuls started." Tahir places a kiss on my lips. "Your docility was programmed behavior. I love your *moody-snarky*. Even if it comes from your First."

My mouth lingers for another kiss from his, but I cannot avoid the inevitable any longer. I haven't checked my own eyes. "Is there a mirror in here?"

Tahir opens a compartment built into the middle of the seat across from us, and pulls out a mirror. Before he hands it to me, he asks, "Are you prepared for what you might see?"

If he had to ask, I already know the answer. "I think you've just prepared me." I take the mirror and look closely at my eyes. Indeed, there are specks of black. Not as many or as noticeable as Tahir's. But they are there.

"How long?" I ask him.

"Six months to a year," Tahir says.

I see tears well in my eyes as my heart clenches with a hard, brutal pain I have not experienced before, as if it were being ripped apart. Theoretically I understood what would happen to me because of the Awfuls, but this is the first physical evidence I've seen confirming it.

I just got here, and soon enough, I will be leaving this life. Perhaps this is what humans mean, literally, by heartbreak.

The Aviate approaches the new ReplicaPharm headquarters, formerly Dr. Lusardi's compound. I cannot recall seeing the campus from the outside, up close. There appear to be about five different structures, the size of small office buildings, built directly into Mount Orion, the mountain that towers over Demesne, surrounded by razor-edge ridges rising high up into the sky. The midlevel buildings on the mountain are camouflaged in green-and-brown exteriors, so from a distance they appear to be part of the mountain. Only up close is it apparent that the mountain is home to structures and not just jungle. As the Aviate glides closer to the campus, the mountainside parts, revealing a landing strip.

The Aviate lands inside, and the mountain "doors" close again. We disembark and are met by a male scientist wearing a white lab coat. Behind him stand two soldiers—the same tall, laser-eyed species who ambushed the Emergents back on Heathen.

"Welcome," the scientist says to us. "I'm Dr. Gaddis. I'm pleased you're able to join us today. Tamsin and Tarquin don't have visitors often. To have all the Betas together in one room will be an excellent data-mining opportunity for us."

"Awesome," says Tahir dryly. Tahir has mastered *sarcasm*! I kind of love his Awful as much as I fear its consequences.

Dr. Gaddis leads us to a mobile glider cart and gestures

for us to sit in the back. The cart begins moving. As we are transported, Dr. Gaddis says, "The Betas are in late-stage Awfuls. It could be any day now. You may find their behavior more pronounced than your previous visit, Tahir."

"Are they truly terrible?" I ask Tahir.

"Define terrible," says Tahir.

I can't define it, I realize. *Terrible* or *Awful*—these seem like subjective judgments. I committed murder. That is terrible. But the humans create clones to essentially be their slaves. And yet the world economy seems to benefit from their terrible. Is there an actual dividing line between good and evil, and if so, how could anyone possibly arbitrate that distinction?

"I don't feel qualified to judge," I say.

"Fascinating," says Dr. Gaddis, eyes gleaming. I want to kick him. "The team is excited for this interaction. From your previous encounters, Tahir, we know that Beta hormone levels fluctuate dramatically when you interact with your own kind. We'll be monitoring your conversation and biochemistry closely today."

"You don't need to inform us of that," says Tahir, sounding *haughty*. "We understand that you adults give us no privacy."

"Excellent," says Dr. Gaddis.

The mobile glider stops. We step out and stand in front of a set of gray doors in a long, nondescript hallway. "Entry: Gaddis," says Dr. Gaddis. Tahir and I step inside, and the doors close behind us.

"This is where the Terrible Ts live," Tahir tells me. He takes my hand.

The "dormitory" looks like an empty FantaSphere room, cubelike with whitewashed walls. Suddenly, the back wall drops, revealing another room, with floor-to-ceiling glass comprising the back wall, offering an expansive view over Io—and the steep vertical drop down to the sea. The room is simple and bright, the only furnishings being two violet-colored chairs and a deep purple velvet love seat centered against the back window wall, where a set of teenager love-birds are splayed, the male on top of the female, making out.

"I'll leave you to interact," says Dr. Gaddis, and he exits the room.

Tahir and I approach the Terrible Ts, who stop kissing but do not otherwise disentangle their bodies. The female, Tamsin, turns her face sideways to us and says, "Oh, hello." She is pale-skinned, with long, unkempt flame-red hair and a freckled face.

"Tahir. What's up?" says Tarquin, the male, as he bla-tantly inspects me head to toe, his face looking *lecherous*. He has a mess of curly black hair down to his shoulders, and the kind of medium-toned skin and generic features of a First blended from many ethnicities.

Both sets of their Beta eyes are fully black. Those eyes must be why Tahir and I were granted an immediate visit. This could be the first and last opportunity to see the Terrible Ts.

Tarquin sits up, removing himself from Tamsin, who sits up also and then rests herself in his lap, nestling her head against his shoulder. Her long red hair drapes across his chest.

Tahir and I sit down on the pair of matching purple chairs opposite Tamsin and Tarquin. "This is Elysia," Tahir tells them. "She's another Beta."

"We've heard," says Tamsin, her voice set to *mocking*. "The superior new model. Blah blah blah."

"Aesthetically perfect," continues Tarquin. "So perfectly awesome she gets to live at the Fortesquieu compound."

"Like a little doll," Tamsin coos.

"I'd like to know more about your background," I tell them.

"Why should we tell you anything?" Tamsin asks.

"Because I'm like you. We should feel a sense of connection." The Terrible Ts regard me with *disgust*. "Shouldn't we?" I ask, confused.

Tarquin and Tamsin shake their heads in sync.

"No," says Tarquin, as Tamsin says, "Not really."

Tahir tells me, "They only understand connection to each other. They've been sequestered here for the last year, since the other three members of the Five clones expired. This room is their isolation chamber, their entire world. They've never left it since being brought to Demesne."

In my curiosity to experience the real world, I've felt wholly trapped being confined to Demesne and Heathen. But at least I was able to move about in each place. The Terrible Ts' jail cells have been much, much smaller than mine. My chip relates that I have been relatively *privileged*, and now I understand their *resentment*.

Tamsin says, "But in my head, I've been all kinds of places! Like, I go shopping in Beijing, dune riding in Biome

City, trekking in the Andes. I party *hard* in the New City of Angels. So long as Tarquin is with me, we can go anywhere, in our minds."

"Should we have a foursome? Not in our minds, but for real?" Tarquin asks, implying he's about to lift his shirt.

"No!" I say hastily.

"He was making a joke," Tahir tells me. "For the dataminers' benefit."

Tamsin shouts to no one in particular, "LET'S GIVE THE ADULTS A REAL SHOW, WHY DON'T WE?! FORNICATE RIGHT HERE IN THE MIDDLE OF THE ROOM? THAT'S WHAT THEY WANT, RIGHT?"

Tarquin sounds *proud* as he informs me, "They want what we have, you know. They're trying to steal our energy. That's why we're lab rats like this." I'm unclear if he's proud to be the lab rat, or proud that he's the one to relay this information to me.

"Do you have a razor?" Tamsin asks me.

"No?" I answer. "Why would I?" These two aren't so much terrible as terribly confusing to me. I have no idea how to process all the information they're giving me. Somewhere, the ReplicaPharm scientists here must be having a party reading all the disjointed signals my body must be sending back to their stupid data machines.

Tamsin says, "I don't know, I just hoped you would. I really want to tear up this fabric. I just hate it. Hate it!" She reaches to her side to violently scratch at the arm of the love seat, but Tarquin pulls it back.

"Don't ruin another piece of furniture, Tamsin baby,"

he tells her. "Every time you do they take away something else."

"Like what?" asks Tahir.

"Not privacy," Tamsin fumes. "That's already gone."

"They reduce our caloric intake. They make the room dark—for days instead of just nights," Tarquin tells Tahir and me.

"The better for us to fornicate," says Tamsin. I'm not sure if she's serious. "They like to watch." She looks up at the ceiling and accuses. "PERVS!"

"I love you so much, baby," says Tarquin. It's like Tahir and I are not even in the same room as Tamsin reclines back into his lap, and he leans down to kiss her again. And kiss her and kiss her and kiss her.

I almost admire their crazy love. They're so open and free about it. But the display feels like equal amounts public show as genuine, private affection.

"For their benefit," says Tahir, pointing to the side walls, referring to the unseen surveillance.

"To what purpose?" I ask.

"Science?" Tahir posits.

"But *what* science?" I ask. I was brought back to Demesne and given clemency for more than just to be Tahir's companion. I know it. These humans are too greedy to give two Betas a second chance just for the sake of love. Certainly the Terrible Ts have not been confined to this space in the interest of their true love.

"I'd like to know the same thing," says Tahir.

Tarquin's mouth removes from Tamsin's to let us in on what he knows. "ReplicaPharm are using *our* raging hormones for a project they call Mimetic. If it's successful, it will become a vaccine given to teenagers around the world."

"To do what?" I ask.

Tamsin hisses, "Make them less like us, of course! Awful!"

"I don't understand," says Tahir.

Tarquin says, "Like a flu shot, a vaccine that injects a dose of flu in order to stave off worse flu. Mimetic would be like that. A dose of our reproduced Awful hormones, injected into teenagers to prevent them from being teens. Wild! Crazy! AWFUL!"

"It would sublimate them until adulthood," I say, suddenly coming to this realization. "Make them passive. Easy to control."

"Exactly!" Tamsin and Tarquin both say.

The Terrible Ts are clearly crazy. They have to be making up this nonsense about Mimetic. It's one thing for the humans to try to control their clones. It's a whole other thing for them to try to control all their own teenagers. I'm beginning to understand that destroying the human infrastructure on Demesne is about so much more than Insurrection. It's about protecting clones—*and* our young human brethren elsewhere in the world.

Tamsin cocks her head to the side and *nonchalantly* says, "Yeah, sicko science." Her gaze returns to Tarquin. "I can't get enough of you, baby." She caresses his chin with her hand. "I just love you so much. It's not even fair how much I love you."

"I love you more," says Tarquin.

I'm obviously not going to have the opportunity to make any real connection with the Terrible Ts. They're too into each other. Is that so terrible?

"Give me a baby, baby," Tamsin whispers to him. "Please? My eyes are blacker than black. I need hope. Someone to love who isn't doomed to death."

"I would if I could," Tarquin tells her. "You know I'm trying."

Suddenly she stands up, in what looks like a rage. "You're not trying hard enough! I never get what I want!"

Matter-of-factly, Tahir says, "Elysia made a baby. It was removed from her."

Her face set to *shocked*, Tamsin runs over to stand before me. "How is that even possible? Clones can't replicate."

"I was the exception, I guess," I say.

Tamsin begins pulling out her hair, screaming, "GET OUT OF HERE! NOW! I HATE YOU! I WILL KILL YOU!"

Tarquin jumps to her side to attempt to soothe her, but she's like an animal that can't be contained. "GET OFF ME! I HATE YOU ALL! I HATE EVERYTHING!"

The entrance doors open and Dr. Gaddis and the two android sentinels come inside the Terrible Ts' cage. "I think this visit is over," Dr. Gaddis says to Tahir and me.

Resolutely, quietly, Tamsin walks toward the sentinels. She offers them her wrists. They cuff her.

"I'm ready to be expired now, Dr. Gaddis," Tamsin announces.

So that's the vision of my future with Tahir. We go so crazy that we demand to be expired.

Or, we flee.

Better to die trying.

28

AS WE RETURN TO THE HALLWAY CORRIDOR OUT-
side the Terrible Ts' prison, Dr. Gaddis tells Tahir, "Your
father requested you stop by to see him before your visit with
Tarquin and Tamsin."

"I don't want to see Tariq right now," says Tahir.

"That's not your choice," says Dr. Gaddis. "When the
boss requests to be seen, he is seen."

We sit in the mobile cart and Dr. Gaddis maneuvers us
to the executive wing of the company headquarters, where
a worker is installing a placard bearing the name "Tariq
Fortesquieu" on the outer glass door to the reception area
leading to the executive offices. Dr. Gaddis holds open the
door for us and ushers us into the reception area.

The Governor is in the area, sitting alone on a couch.

Dr. Gaddis tells him, "You received my message.

Excellent. The expiration orders are being authorized for Tarquin and Tamsin. You may handle it." Dr. Gaddis retrieves a tablet from his coat pocket. "Read this manual before the procedure."

Ivan's father, who once lorded over the island but now is demoted to essentially an errand boy, looks directly at me, taunting. "The procedure will be excellent practice for me."

Dr. Gaddis scoffs at the Governor. "You will observe. You're still in training. You may handle the bureaucratic filings necessary for the Replicant Rights Commission. Anything beyond that . . ." Dr. Gaddis laughs. "I hardly think you're ready for that."

If it's possible to measure the temperature of a room by the level of fuming exhibited by one particular human's presence in it, I'd say the Governor could easily set this reception area on fire. At first I thought the "coincidence" of his presence here just as Tahir and I arrived was meant to intimidate me. Maybe it was. But I'm also sure that Dr. Gaddis arranged this encounter to intimidate the Governor as well. Or humiliate him. Same difference, perhaps.

The Governor shoots me a glare that's both hateful and a promise: *We're not finished.*

I agree, and return the same glare to him.

Insurrection will liberate the clones on Demesne. Seeing the Governor's ruin completed will be my personal little victory.

I'm mad and I want answers.

Dr. Gaddis ushers Tahir and me into Tariq's office. It's an expansive space with clear walls that look like windows with different views over Demesne. The people inside the frames start to move, and I realize the walls are live surveillance views over the island: inside the laboratories at HQ where researchers in white coats are monitoring data machines; construction workers laying a foundation for the new building at Haven; ReplicaPharm employees relaxing on the shore at Nectar Bay; Zhara's room at the Fortesquieu compound, where Bahiyya supervises the chestnut-haired maid looking under Zhara's bed—looking for what, I don't know—but the maid emerges empty-handed.

Tariq stands up from his desk and comes over to greet us. He tries to give Tahir a hug, but Tahir is stiff in Tariq's embrace.

"How was your visit with Tarquin and Tamsin?" Tariq asks us, gesturing for us to sit down at the chairs opposite his desk. He sits down at his executive's desk and nods to Dr. Gaddis, who leaves the room.

Tahir says, "The Ts are at their end. Ready to be expired." He doesn't sound *upset*, but I sense he is. We both are. We just witnessed our future. Tahir must not want to give his father the satisfaction of knowing how unnerved we are. His parents gave us this visit as a cautionary tale to encourage us to cooperate with them, to do as they say in the face of hormonal chaos converging in our bodies.

Tariq says, "I feared as much. But their time here has not been for nothing. We've been able to cull excellent hormonal samples from their Beta chemistry."

"For the Mimetic project?" I ask. "Or were the Ts lying about that?" *Please say they were crazy. Please say they were lying.*

I know they weren't.

Tariq shifts uncomfortably in his chair. He sighs. "I guess I couldn't have prevented them telling you about it. I wanted to tell you myself." He didn't. He wanted us to know, and the Terrible Ts revealing it to us was part of the scare tactic. I know it. "Mimetic is certainly no lie. It's the most important scientific advancement of the last decade. It's a prime reason I agreed to forego retirement and come back to work here. Getting that project to market will be one of my proudest accomplishments."

"It will make you richer than ever," says Tahir dryly.

"Yes," Tariq agrees. "But it's not about the money. We already have more than the combined per capita income of half the world."

So share it, I think.

"Mimetic is the rare pharmaceutical compound that will make the world a better place. Save teenagers from themselves."

"It could have saved First Tahir," says Tahir.

"Exactly," says Tariq. "We're pleased with you, son. Of course. But Mimetic could spare other parents throughout the world from the disastrous consequences of their teenagers' wild behavior."

"It's a terrible idea," says Tahir, who looks to me for affirmation. I nod.

"Nonsense," says Tariq. "You two have no real knowledge of the world." *How could we? You've trapped us here.* "You couldn't possibly understand the need for such a vaccine."

"What did you mean by the hormonal compounds of

Betas?" I ask Tariq. There's no use arguing the ethics of inoculating teens against their basic natures. ReplicaPharm will try to bring Mimetic to market regardless of any "opinions" the two powerless Betas sitting in the chairman's office might have. It's up to us to stop it.

Tariq answers, "Teen Betas, because they've been replicated at the juncture of adolescence into adulthood, have unusual hormones we've been able to use to create Mimetic. And I've just learned that cells extracted from the womb machine incubating Elysia's fetus may hold the key to finally perfecting Mimetic."

That thing doesn't even exist yet, and already they're abusing it. Typical, hateful humans. "Are the Beta hormones why I was able to get pregnant?" I ask Tariq.

"We don't think so," says Tariq. "Ivan, as you know, had experimented with various compounds of 'raxia, including batches laced with potent amounts of testosterone. We believe that's why you got pregnant. Not because of your hormones, but because of his. It was a fluke, but beneficial for our research. Clones created from Firsts have been outlawed, and those in existence will die out naturally. But at least now we know the factors that could allow the Demesne brand of clones to procreate. It's a nonissue, really. Would you like to see the new brand of Betas?" he asks us eagerly.

"More clones?" Tahir says, rising from his chair. "That's an outrage, Father!" Tariq just laughs, and tamps his hand to encourage Tahir to sit back down.

Tariq says, "Flesh-and-blood clones are old wave. Meet the new." He presses a button on his desk, and a new person enters the room.

It's an adult male, dressed in a butler's uniform, only the male is a 4-D holo-composite. Yet it holds a physical tray in its hand, balancing three glasses of water. The butler approaches Tahir and me. "May I?" the new and improved Beta asks us politely. We extend our hands, and he places a glass of water in each hand for us.

"Excellent, Jeeves!" says Tariq. "That's what we've named the new Beta. A bit obvious, of course. But we're very fond of him. Soon all the clones will be just like Jeeves. Better even than android machines. Truly soulless, because he doesn't actually exist. He's just a computer model made to look like flesh and bone."

"Do you require anything else, sir?" asks Jeeves.

"That will be all," says Tariq. "You may leave the tray here." The hologram butler places the tray on Tariq's desk and then vanishes into thin air. Tariq beams at Tahir and me. "Spectacular, right?"

I don't answer because I'm distracted by the surveillance wall behind Tariq's head, where a frame flashes what appears to be a prison cell, with cement walls and laser bars separating the room from the hallway. A lone male figure sits on the floor, being guarded by android soldiers outside the confines of his cell. One of his hands has been amputated. For a moment, he looks up, and I see his olive-skinned, black rose–vined face.

It's Aidan. He's alive.

ZHARA

29

ONCE AGAIN, I HAVE DAD'S MANTRA IN MY EAR: *Hold your friends close and your enemies closer.* Bahiyya Fortesquieu is a strange combination of both. She's gracious and generous. But she clearly wants to either control our every move, or give us genuine privacy. I learned that while I hid in the wardrobe while she was having the maid look under my bed for a ring she said she'd lost that she wanted to give to Elysia. She's just like any typical intrusive parent, I guess—but the stakes feel so much higher, with an Insurrection to pull off. She could be our unlikely ally (because ultimately she wants what's best for Tahir—whatever makes him happiest), or our worst foe (because ultimately she thinks only she can determine what's best for Tahir). The only way to gauge is to get to know her better.

I go looking for her in the garden, which Elysia has told me is Bahiyya's sacred spot. I've gotten so used to being surrounded by hard-bodied, hardworking, too-attractive clones with vined faces and fuchsia eyes that it's surprising to see a gardener in these parts who has long gray hair, a slight pudge around her hips, and human brown eyes over a gently wrinkled face. "You do your own gardening?" I ask Bahiyya. At the periphery of the rows of coral-red torch-flowers that surround the Aviate landing pad at her family's home, she's on her knees, wearing gardening gloves, and holding weed scissors.

She smiles at me. She gives a great mom smile—warm and welcoming. "Indeed," Bahiyya says. "I enjoy gardening. I find it very peaceful and contemplative."

"Be careful those torchflowers don't make you *too* peaceful," I say, instantly regretting my comment. Is it okay to joke with such a fancy and important lady?

Luckily, she laughs. "Don't worry. I won't be making any 'raxia from these seeds. But if I did, you can be assured these flowers would only produce premium-quality opiate. Not like the inferior grade that boy Ivan made, which made him so crazy. These torchflowers are grown with more care than the ones at Governor's House."

"Ivan, the boy who hurt Elysia? He made his own 'raxia?"

"His parents didn't discover it until after his death, but yes. Everyone knew he was mentally disturbed; certainly, his experiments with different grades of homegrown 'raxia didn't help. He was an addict, I believe. Once you become an addict, you lose the peacefulness that 'raxia is supposed to elicit. Instead, you become violent and crazy."

"I know. That's how I died—but didn't. Too much 'raxia and I went crazy. Totally lost any semblance of good judgment."

I want her to feel as comfortable with me as she seems to want me to feel with her. Are we both just being honest, or walking a tightrope?

"You won't make that mistake again, I assume?" she asks.

I shake my head. "No way." I believe it when I say it. But I know: The best I can do is try. Every day. My heart clenches, remembering Aidan, who cared about me so much he tried to ensure that all temptation for me to fall back into addiction was removed from me. Aidan. He deserved so much better than losing his life to a failed Insurrection. He deserved a real mate. I should have been that to him. His lover, and his fighter. His true companion, and not just a bunk mate using him for survival. I don't dare to hope he still lives. Do I?

"Would you be willing to do me a favor?" Bahiyya asks.

"Of course," I say, wanting to appear cooperative and helpful. When my dad used to ask me to do anything for him, the best response from me was a roll of my eyes, a resigned shrug, some choice curse words muttered on the down-low. Now my dad suffers in a Uni-Mil prison—if he's even still alive—while I'm stranded in paradise. I'd give up every breath of this heavenly air if I could just go back to miserable, rotting Cerulea so I could tell my dad: *I know it seemed like I didn't like you, but I appreciated you. And I know that in your overbearing, controlling way, you felt the same for me. Thanks, Dad.*

Bahiyya says, "There's a holdout from one of the original Demesne families still living here. Her name is Demetra Cortez-Olivier. She was always a troublemaker. A delightful one, to be sure, but a wild child."

"I didn't realize there were still families living here."

"Demetra's the only one, and it's just her, not her family. She's bizarrely obsessed with clones and with Demesne. But what can you expect when you abandon your child here to be raised by clones? She refused to leave when the other families sold their stakes on the island to ReplicaPharm."

"So she lives on Demesne alone?"

"She lives with her clones in her family's home. Cut off from the world, by choice. Or so her parents claim. The truth, I'm sorry to say, is that they don't know how to handle her. They'd prefer their own child to be hidden away here so they don't have to deal with her. It's unconscionable parenting, in my opinion. But they were never interested in parenting. They wanted a doll, not a person."

"They wanted an Elysia," I surmise. "Or, at least what Elysia was originally programmed to be."

"I never thought about it that way, but yes, you're right, like that." Proudly, she adds, "Soon, because of Tariq's work with ReplicaPharm, parents will finally have the comfort of having that kind of teenager. They won't have to program a clone anymore."

"How?" I ask.

"Pharmaceutical innovation" is her only explanation. "Tariq will be a hero to the world a second time. Until then . . . the Cortez-Oliviers are stuck with Demetra. Or, I should say, their clones are stuck with her."

"Demetra sounds fun, actually." She sounds different. On this island where the clones were all crafted to look great but essentially be the same, and where the humans now lording over the place are essentially corporate drones, Demetra sounds like a refreshingly toxic whiff amid this place's purified air.

"Fun? Yes, I guess that's one word for her. First Tahir and his friends nicknamed her Dementia. It's a horrible nickname, but I think they meant it lovingly. They were all very fond of her: First Tahir, Farzad, Greer, Ivan, Astrid. I promised Demetra's parents that we would check on her occasionally. But she makes me uncomfortable, to be honest. After the security sweep is finalized, I'm guessing she will choose to leave the island rather than be subjected to surveillance, so I'll be relieved of this obligation to her parents. I thought you and Alexander might visit her for me. Perhaps you're eager to see more of the island. If you'd do me this favor, I could authorize the Aviate for you."

"Sure," I say, reminded that Xander and I are unacknowledged prisoners here, and can travel off the Fortesquieu compound only by the good graces of our "hosts." And our window of opportunity to act is rapidly closing.

30

I'M EAGER TO MEET THIS DEMENTIA, AND SET off to retrieve Xander so we can go. The locator screen outside his quarters tells me he's in the FantaSphere. I walk to the FantaSphere corridor of the compound, but the door is closed and the red illuminated sign says IN USE. I request entry to the room. Xander's voice answers from the other side. "Go away, Zhara. I want to be alone."

What happens in the FantaSphere should stay in the FantaSphere, I know. But I don't feel like respecting Xander's privacy. He's been in there for hours, according to the time display on the console, which is very unlike him. FantaSpheres are indulgences, not habitats. An Aquine might have occasional use for one but would never linger there for so long. Something is wrong with Xander in there.

"Enter FantaSphere," I tell the command console again.

No answer this time from Xander. "Pass code," says the console.

"August twenty-sixth," I say. Xander's birthday.

"Denied," says the console.

"Isidra," I guess. His home place.

"Denied," says the console.

I only have one try left, or the system will lock me out and deny me trying again for another hour, unless I break the security perimeter, which I shouldn't do because I don't want Bahiyya alerted to any security infraction, and because this isn't an actual emergency. It just feels like one: my sudden need to find out why Xander is hanging out there for so long, and to get him out of there so we can escape this compound and Aviate toward somewhere else, already, while we still have the permission from Bahiyya.

Impulsively, I blurt out, "Jingjing?" The FantaSphere door opens. I'm stunned. Not by the entry, but that the sentimental pass code causes my heart to ache and not swell. It just makes me miss Aidan more. It's like, when I see Xander in all his beautiful glory, my knees still buckle, but that's muscle memory, a habit. A true romantic gesture without the vision of Xander to blindside me? I think of Aidan.

I step inside the FantaSphere, and immediately I'm standing on a beach. I see Xander in the distance, surfing, although not his preferred big-wave surfing. Instead, he's lying on his stomach on a surfboard, paddle boarding over dark waves—the rough kind like off the coast of Isidra. The sky is overcast and the air chilly. There are empty beer bottles nestled in the sand. That's weird. Aquines don't consume alcohol. Then I hear a loud, uncharacteristic belch coming from the man in the water.

No way! "Are you drunk?" I call to Xander.

"Mildly tipsy. Enjoying my alone time, if you don't mind."

"I mind," I say. "I'm coming in." Immediately, I am wearing a wet suit and have a longboard set down for me on the suddenly cold, damp sand my feet are sinking into.

I pick up the surfboard and step into the rough and tumble water that's the opposite of Demesne's tranquil sea. I paddle out to a spot near Xander's. The water is heavy and thick, and I can't imagine why anyone would want to surf here, until it occurs to me that maybe this homing beacon of sorts is to Xander what gardening is to Bahiyya. Peaceful. Contemplative. He's not even really trying to surf. He's just bobbing up and down, coasting over waves.

"What's going on?" I ask him. "You drink beer now?"

"Apparently."

"Pretty unlike you to do something like that."

"Exactly. That's what I want. To be everything unlike me."

"Why? You're engineered for perfection."

"But I'm a failure. I hurt you, the person I care about the most. Twice. Elysia doesn't want or need me anymore. I'm a lousy commando. My first mission was a covert Uni-Mil op organized by clone rights' supporters. I went AWOL to look for Elysia, and probably exposed the whole team in doing so. Your dad's in a military prison right now, probably because of me."

I search for the right words. I've never seen Xander in this state before. He's supposed to be rallying the cause, not accepting defeat of it. I say, "First of all, you don't know that. Second, you probably saved Elysia's life. That's meeting the mission, isn't it? And you know that Dad never takes on a mission he's not prepared to face the consequences of. If he recruited you into it, he understood the risk—for you, and for himself. He would never blame you." This may be the first time in my life I have defended my father. For all his harsh ways, my dad was always there for me, for my mom, for Xander, for anyone he considered family. He's flawed like all of us. That didn't mean he loved us less. That didn't mean I didn't love him.

Xander reaches his arms toward me, like he wants to touch me. "We need to figure out a way out of here. To find your dad and help him."

"I agree, but I don't see how right now. We have more immediate issues here to sort out, if you remember?"

"It's hopeless," says Xander.

"You're sure that's not the beer talking? Just yesterday you were all fired up and ready to act. What happened?"

"I had a sleepless night, thinking too hard on all the messes I've made. I'm not up to the task of leading. Want to know the dirty truth about me? I trained to be a commando, but I was always better with technology than action. Programming a battle rather than fighting it."

I look at his hulking biceps and laugh. Out of nowhere, I lean over and place an affectionate kiss on his arm. "So, you're a closet nerd. That's kind of beautiful."

He takes the opportunity to pull my surfboard closer to his so that our faces are almost touching. He closes his eyes and turns his neck just so, expecting a kiss on the lips. I give him one—just a peck, for encouragement. I'm amazed by the relief I feel. My lips don't want or need more in return.

I command the FantaSphere to summon the reaction Xander was hoping to receive from me. "Lightning strikes!"

Bolts of lightning light up the sky in the distance.

"What's that for?" Xander asks.

"A wake-up call. Time to sober up and get out of here, buddy. We've got a Dementia to call on."

Xander's turquoise eyes brighten in recognition. "Demetra Cortez-Olivier?" I nod, startled by his positive reaction to the name of the girl that Bahiyya told me was basically a lunatic. "I met with her when I was stationed in Demesne for the Replicant Rights Commission. She's still here?"

"Yes," I say. "Why, are you already looking for a new girlfriend?" One step forward, two steps back, I guess. For every mature moment of self-actualization I experience, I can devolve just as easily back into jealousy and bitchiness. I don't know whether to be disappointed in myself or applaud the acknowledgement of these instincts, and try to do better.

"No," says Xander. "But I have an idea for how we can make the Insurrection happen through her."

Twilight sets over Demesne as Xander and I Aviate over the island to pay a visit to Demetra. The sky has turned a perfect pink as the orange sun sets over Io's lulling violet waves. "Isn't this supposed to be your meditation time?" I ask Xander. Obviously we have more pressing concerns, but I'm surprised he hasn't made a token effort to abide by his daily ritual.

"Meditation's a lost cause for me right now," says Xander. "My mind is elsewhere. I can't focus." He looks me straight in the eyes. "I have a question for you."

"Ask me." Once, I so ardently pined he'd ask me to be his forever mate. Rather than wait for him to ask, I jumped the gun and assumed it. I'll never make that mistake again. I'm probably being egotistical. That's not even what he wants to discuss.

His leg nervously twitches. "Just before I went into the FantaSphere, I found out my extradition back to Isidra has been authorized. Will you go back there with me, when it's time?" He takes a deep breath, and then blurts out, "You know I will always love you, don't you?"

Pat yourself on the shoulder, Zhara's ego.

A year ago I would have cried tears of joy and thrown myself into his arms for saying these words to me. Now, his words mean nothing to me other than relief. I wasn't crazy. What Xander and I shared together was real, at least on that day we gave ourselves to each other. It was so real he took up with my clone after he thought I'd died.

I can't pretend to return the sentiment when I don't feel it. "You're in no shape to make that pronouncement."

"You're right." His leg twitches harder, and I place my hand on it to settle him, but he pushes my hand away. "Our lives are a mess right now."

"*Yours* is a mess," I clarify. "Mine has confusing circumstances, but for the first time, I feel pretty clear, actually."

I'm going to see this Insurrection through, and I'm going to steal back Elysia's baby and raise it as my own. I'm going to send Elysia off to the best possible future she could have, despite its uncertainty.

I've already survived death once, so why shouldn't I dream big and impossible? Back in Cerulea, my big, impossible dream was to make the Aquine my mate. Now I know better than to attach my ambitions to a guy. My dreams should be about what I can accomplish for me and the people in my life first. Those dreams may or may not include a guy. They should always come from a place of love.

31

I UNDERSTOOD, CONCEPTUALLY, THAT THE Fortesquieu compound is considered to be the jewel in the crown of Demesne's architecture, but I see now that the critics called it wrong. The true architectural masterpiece on Demesne is clearly Demetra Cortez-Olivier's home, which is straight-up bonkers.

Xander and I step out of the Aviate and onto the landing pad, where we have a view of two homes. On one end of the property, facing the bluff, is a stately home that looks like a smaller-scale version of the limestone Fortesquieu palace. Gaudy, opulent, whatever. On the other end of the property is, literally, a spaceship lifted into the sky on stilts.

"Demetra calls her house 'the Zeppelin,'" Xander informs me, pointing at the catamaran-shaped spaceship that sits on top of two clear stilts, which also serve as lifts. "Her parents built it for her as a playroom when she was a child. Eventually she just started living there, instead of in the grand house."

"How do you know all this?"

"I had some bizarre visits with her when I was interviewing residents about their clones for the report to the Replicant Rights Commission. She's not like anyone you've ever met. You'll see."

Since no butler has come to greet us, we walk over to one of the elevator shafts inside the stilts and press an intercom button. "Yay!" a female voice squeals to us. "Humans! Come on up!"

The elevator door opens and we step in. We are lifted up into the base of the house-ship. The elevator door opens again and there stands Demetra. I don't know what I expected from all the hype in advance, but at first she looks pretty normal. She has long, smooth, raven hair, highlighted with strands of gold and violet that fall in front of her face, and she wears a simple, short white tank dress over her olive-toned skin. Then she sweeps her hair back from her face, and I start to get it. She has a deep scar at her temple, where she appears to have once tried to razor-cut a fleur-de-lis design onto her face, like the ones all her Demesne servants must have. And like them, her eyes are fuchsia-colored. She points to her eyes and tells Xander, "New contacts! Do you like them?"

"Sure," he tells her. He turns to me. "Zhara, this is Demetra. Demetra, this is Zhara."

"Call me Dementia!" she tells me. "Everyone does. I don't mind. That name feels more like home to me than the one my bios gave me."

"Your bios?" I ask.

"Biological parents." She pulls me to her for a nearly suffocating hug. "I can't believe you're a First who's alive. But I'm freaking touching you and it's so freaking true. And that other miracle, our little murderess Elysia, is still alive too! When do I get to see her?"

Dementia lets me loose. I say, "Elysia's pretty attached to Tahir. Good luck scheduling time in between their make-out sessions."

Dementia sighs. "Lucky lucky lucky Betas! I *knew* Tahir was a Beta, by the way. I totally sensed it. Like, his pheromones were off or something. So sad that First Tahir had to die to make Beta Tahir, but let's be real here. Beta Tahir is so much nicer. First Tahir was a total dawg. He'd make a girl feel like she was the center of his universe just so he could get inside her panties, but once he did, he'd dump her and move on. I know. First Tahir was *my* first. Ha-ha, get it? I'm telling a First about my first with a dead First. Hilarious!"

"Ha-ha," I say, not laughing, even though it is kind of funny.

She leads us into the main room, which is a living room with plush, purple velvet sofas and chairs, floor-to-ceiling glass walls, and a glass ceiling. With the view out to violet-rippled Io from all sides, the effect is like being suspended midair in a sky dome over the sea. As dusk falls into night, the ceiling twinkles with stars in the sky overhead. Dementia pauses a moment to appraise Xander. "I so wanted to jump your bones last time you were here. You are a fine specimen of a man. It's unholy how beautiful you are."

"Thank you?" Xander says, blushing. I don't know if I've ever witnessed him being so blatantly objectified, or seen his chiseled cheeks redden from anything other than a workout. I'm enjoying the show! "I can't take credit for my Aquine genes; my looks were not my choice."

"So you're saying you'd prefer to be ugly, if given the choice?" Dementia asks him.

"I'd prefer to be plain. Unremarkable," says Xander.

"Maybe your good looks give you unremarkable character," Dementia says, as if she's trying to comfort him. "Like, you're so beautiful, you're boring. Your physical looks swallow your soul's potential."

"Thank you, again," Xander says, laughing now. "That's the most backhanded compliment I've ever gotten." His turquoise eyes appear to shine. It's the first time I've ever seen him completely disarmed—relaxed, even. Maybe what he's needed all along was a truly crazy girl to call him like he is: beautiful, but boring. Unremarkable, but with potential.

Maybe he'd like to be someone different than the steadfast Aquine. He tells Dementia, "I like to think I'm not all predictably boring. I did try to subvert your clones into rebelling, you know. I tried to enlist them in the Insurrection."

"I know," Dementia tells him affably. "But they're my family. We stick together. If they went, I would have had to go with them. They knew my presence would ruin your little Insurrection because then my parents would come looking for me out of the bios' misplaced sense of obligation—or ownership—of me. Like, they don't want to deal with me, but if I'm kidnapped, they'd have to put on a show of concern. But their show would have been hiring the Uni-Mil to privately annihilate the Defects trying to have an Insurrection. It would have been cool to go along for the ride with my clones, though."

"Would you like to be part of the Insurrection still?" Xander asks Dementia.

"The Insurrection is dead," she says.

"It doesn't have to be," says Xander. He points to the ceiling. "This ceiling also serves as a planetarium, yes? Because I have an idea for how we can use it to take control back from ReplicaPharm."

Dementia claps her hands gleefully. "Dazzle!" she screams. When there is no immediate response to her call, she shrieks again. "DAZZLE! Please come in here. NOW!"

An elegant male clone enters the room and walks to Dementia's side. He has a medium-height body with narrow hips, a thin face with meticulously arched black eyebrows, and neck-length black hair styled in the manner of a female bob cut. He's vined on his left temple in blue dahlia, but his blue dahlia has been enhanced with cosmetics to heighten its stark beauty, its outline deepened by a black pencil, and sparkle glitter added to the flower petals. His eyelids are colored in a blue shadow that accentuates the blue dahlia at his left temple, and his thin lips are defined in a berry-colored gloss.

"Claude?" Xander asks him. "Good to see you again."

"Claude was *their* name for me," Dazzle says. "*I* prefer Dazzle. Are you here to try to enlist me for a lost cause again, Aquine?" He turns to Dementia. "Don't purse your lips like that or you'll develop worry lines like your mother." He tenderly rubs an ointment around her mouth.

"What took you so long?" she pouts.

"I was here in less than a minute. I was rearranging Nanny Adeline's hair as you requested."

I raise an eyebrow at Xander. He leans over and mutters in my ear. "In her playroom, Dementia has a taxidermy collection of her favorite household staff who were expired once they reached human equivalent of age forty."

Xander was right. Dementia is definitely like no one else I've ever met.

"I changed my mind," Dementia tells Dazzle. "Leave Nanny's hair in the long braid."

"I already loosened it—"

"PUT IT BACK!"

"As you wish," says Dazzle. "Is that why you called me in here?"

"No," says Dementia. "I want to know if the clones here still want Insurrection."

"Of course they do." Dazzle gives a nod of acknowledgment to Xander.

Dementia says, "The Aquine thinks he has a way to use my planetarium to incite the Insurrection for real this time. Help him." She turns to Xander. "If it works, I need you to promise me something in exchange."

"What?" Xander asks her.

"ReplicaPharm is doing a security sweep here this week, and I'm sure they're going to install surveillance all over the place. I wasn't given the option of refusing. This place is so ruined! I have no interest in returning to the world, but I would like to go to Aquine territory, to Isidra. The bios tried to buy me a place there once, but Isidra wouldn't have me. Your people believe land belongs to all and isn't for sale. Crazy! But I could go with you, right?"

"I suppose," says Xander. "If we're successful." He doesn't sound at all repulsed by the idea. In fact, for someone who was mortally depressed just hours ago, he appears majorly rejuvenated.

"Awesome," says Dementia. "I feel like I'm due for a master cleanse, and Isidra would be the ultimate place for that. No one I know has been there, so it's special. Not ruined like every other place. If you can make this Insurrection happen for real, I think I could finally leave Demesne. If I knew my clones here were truly free." She addresses Dazzle. "Promise you'll take extra good care of Nanny Adeline and Chef Ringo if I leave Demesne."

Dazzle crosses his heart with his dark-purple-painted index finger. "Promise. The Emergents and I will take excellent care of them and of the whole island, if we ever successfully rid it of humans." He places a tender kiss on her cheek. "No offense, darling."

She returns a soft kiss to his cheek. "None taken, darling. We're a toxic species. I totally get that and applaud you for wanting to be free of us." She turns to Xander. "How do you intend to pull this off?"

Xander waves his hand in the air, and his pinkie finger suddenly lights up blue. "I've got some technological advantages embedded here."

Dementia laughs. "How cute. But seriously. How are you going to do this?"

Xander looks to me. "I'm going to assist with navigation. Zhara will lead."

"I will?" I ask.

Dementia shakes her head at me. "You're not inspiring much confidence."

"That's because you haven't seen her in action yet," Xander says. "Let's give her some inspiration to work with. Could you please call up the projector, Dazzle?"

Dazzle walks to the wall by the elevator and presses his finger against it. I wonder if he's calling the elevator back, but at his touch, the wall lights up to reveal a console. "Step away from the center of the room, please," Dazzle requests of us.

We step to the sides of the room, and then the middle of the floor opens up in a circular shape, and a projector rises from beneath. I realize the telescope must have been shrouded between the elevator stilts on the ground below, constructed to look like scenery.

The living room goes dark and the sky ceiling reveals itself as a spherical planetarium with all the universe's known planets and constellations lit up in orbit.

I totally get it now!

"Excellent," I say, looking at Xander's blue finger. "Now we can play some real war games with ReplicaPharm."

32

LET'S DIVE RIGHT IN. THE TIME FOR INSUR-rection is now.

We could wait, to make sure Elysia and Tahir are ready to act, but my instinct says they'll know the sign when it comes. We can't risk communicating our intent when their every move is so monitored.

Xander has Aidan's geological programming code embedded in his body. Streaming those capabilities through the planetarium will amplify their power exponentially. "We'll do a test run first," I instruct Xander. "Low-level earthquake, enough to cause the power grid on Demesne to flicker, but not big enough to incite panic. Yet."

"Got it," says Xander. "I've copied the code into the planetarium's console. Ready at your command, General Z."

"Go." I look toward Dementia and Dazzle. "Hang on tight, kids."

The floors and walls of the Zeppelin shake hard, as if hostile. Glass figurines on the tables in the living room fall down, shattering, as the room's chairs rumble and move. "I love it!" Dementia squeals, hanging on to the arm of Dazzle, who looks abjectly *terrified*.

It's a small tremor, what we called a "bounce" back in Cerulea, offering a sweet and scary ride—but not nearly enough to be let out of school over. "Intensify until the power goes out," I tell Xander. "Can you tap into the island's power grid once as it resets?"

"Won't know until we try," says Xander. "We'll have maybe a one- or two-second opportunity to get in there. Not enough delay to—"

"One second is all we need. Is the house attached to a backup generator when the power goes out?" I ask Dementia.

Insulted, she cries out, "Of course it is! Everything here is state-of-the art. The best—"

"Harder," I tell Xander. "Duck!" I instruct Dementia and Dazzle, as a sculpture from the corner of the room comes flying at them. They drop to the ground as the tremor reaches its peak and then, yes! The overhead lights flicker.

"Once the power goes out, send one word to the clones' feed," I tell Xander. "*Insurrection.*"

The lights go out. "Insurrection announced," Xander says. The lights go back on. The tremor dies out and the Zeppelin sways back into solid position.

From beneath a table, Dementia remarks, "That was almost better than sex. Did it work?"

Xander and I look at Dazzle, whose eyeliner is smeared from the sweat of his fear. He wipes the smudge he senses on his face and says, "The word 'insurrection' just flashed across my eyes."

If it worked on him, then all the clones should know: The time is now. If they fall in line, we have a chance to succeed. If they don't . . . we're as good as dead.

Out of nowhere and completely unannounced, a holo-beam of a man appears beside Xander's station at the planetarium console. He looks bewildered, and as surprised by the communication as we are.

"Aidan!" I cry out.

He's bruised and battered, with burn marks on his cheeks and swollen lips. I can only imagine the scars beneath his prison uniform. I want to reach through the empty space and touch him, hold him, comfort him, love him. I have to settle for a holo-beam, for now. My heart surges in gratitude. Aidan is alive!

"Where are you, Zhara?" asks Aidan.

"On Demesne," I say. "Where are you?"

"In a jail cell at ReplicaPharm headquarters. That was an excellent earthquake. A test run, correct?" He looks to Xander, who nods. Aidan holds up his arm. "I'd give you a thumbs-up, but I'm missing some parts." There's a stub where his right hand used to be. I can't even cry, because there's a small smile at my lips. He's been tortured, there's crisis all around us, but he made a joke. There is so very much hope for him. For us.

Unseen in the holo-beam but audible from outside Aidan's cell are signs of chaos: feet trampling. Sirens blaring. Voices shouting.

We don't have the luxury of a reunion right now. We'll have to save that for in person, if we live that long.

"How's this communication possible?" Xander asks Aidan.

Two android soldiers join Aidan's holo-beam. Aidan says, "My prison guards. Our new benefactors. They're new Emergent recruits. They want the humans gone as much as the Emergents do. They're resetting all the androids' feeds now to join the Insurrection."

This is better than I hoped for. Despite all he's been through, Aidan never stopped working toward the goal. I say, "The next wave will come in about half an hour. You know what to do."

"We'll secure this facility as soon as the androids complete the programming," Aidan says. The androids disappear from the holo-beam, soldiers on missions.

I say, "I need you to do one extra thing. Elysia's unborn baby is an incubation machine somewhere in the compound. Find the incubator and bring it to the bunker. I'll find you there."

Aidan's swollen lips attempt to curl up in a pained smile. "Any more impossible tasks for me to carry out on such a deadly deadline?"

When and if I find him after this is all over, I am going

to love that clone man like he's never known it was possible to be loved.

I can't answer his question, because the Governor appears in the holo-beam, charging toward a surprised Aidan, grabbing him from behind and holding a dagger to his neck. To me, the Governor says, "If you want this Defect to live, you bring me Elysia."

The holo-beam disappears.

33

I'M HELPLESS TO HELP AIDAN. I HAVE TO trust he can handle the situation himself. The Governor has no idea what kind of hostage he just tried to take. Brutal. Wily. Fearless. Mine.

Between Aidan and the android soldiers, I have no doubt the Governor is as good as dead already.

"Figure out your transportation off the island," I tell Dementia. "If I can retrieve them, you'll have Elysia and Tahir as cargo."

"How long do I have?" Dementia sputters. "I don't know how to arrange transportation! My clones make those arrangements! And I need to pack my bags, say my good-byes—"

"You have about an hour. Right, Xander?"

He nods. "I'll figure out the transportation. You go

retrieve Elysia and Tahir. The big one will commence in exactly thirty minutes." He pauses. "Do you want the bonus follow-up?"

"I sure do," I say. "There can be no peace here until everything built by the Emergents' suffering is destroyed. Throw in some fireworks, to make it pretty. Give us a new landscape to start over with."

"Epic destruction it is," Xander says.

I run into the open elevator. As the door closes, I remember one last thing. "As soon as you've wrested control of the island mainframe, message the clones to move to bunkers or to higher ground!"

"Done," says Xander. He salutes me. The elevator door closes.

I'm on my own now to finish off the job.

I never had the privilege of riding in an Aviate before I came to Demesne. They were just luxurious vehicles in the distant sky, accessible only to the wealthy. Now, I've just relayed coordinates to an Aviate belonging to one of the wealthiest families in the world, and navigated it to return me to their home, which I plan to destroy.

As the Aviate speeds over the island, the air isn't so soft and sweet any longer. It's smoky and bitter. Across the landscape, I see houses burning, and I smile. Insurrection is alive and on fire.

The Emergents have taken control of their residences.

The Aviate descends in darkness over the Fortesquieu compound, which is alight, but no signs of fire. Instead, Elysia stands at the cuvécs by the landing pad, waving to me from down below. Where's Tahir? If only they were together right now, I could load them onto the Aviate and return them to Dementia's immediately. The Aviate lands and Elysia opens the door to help me step out.

"Where's Tahir?" I ask her. "There's not much time left. We need to leave on the Aviate before the next strike."

"Hurry!" she says, grabbing me by the arm so we can run toward the house. "Tahir is having a terrible fight with his father. Not even the tremor could break it up."

"Did you get the Insurrection message?" She nods. "We need Tahir. NOW."

"I can't leave, because I can't tear him away. He's in full Awful."

We enter the house, where the servants have gathered awaiting instructions. I tell them, "Find a bunker or higher ground. Take provisions for a few days. Quickly!" They don't move, but look to Elysia.

"NOW!" Elysia orders them.

The staff immediately disperses.

Elysia turns to me. "Tahir is with his parents in the FantaSphere."

"Now's the time they play?" I ask, astonished.

She leads and I follow. The house is so big; it feels like forever that we have to run. "Hardly," Elysia says as we sprint. "We had just returned from ReplicaPharm and were about to have dinner when the tremor happened. Tariq went to the FantaSphere because he said it was the only place where he could securely manage the ReplicaPharm compound from a remote location, but Tahir followed. As they were running, Tariq was barking orders to ReplicaPharm about how they had to secure the cell samples, which caused Tahir to strike him. I didn't know what to do, so I went to the landing pad to wait for you. I had the instinct that's where I'd find you. If you came back."

She actually thought there was a possibility I wouldn't return for her. I'm glad to have proved her wrong. "Which cell samples?" I ask her between quick breaths. "The baby's?"

"The baby's. And mine, and Tahir's, and the Terrible Ts'. ReplicaPharm are using teen Beta hormones to create a pharmaceutical compound that's supposedly going to inoculate teenagers against wild behavior."

I let out a scream. "These adults will stop at nothing!" I wail. "That's why we're going to give them our best display of wild behavior tonight. And destroy those cell samples while we're at it."

There's a huge urgency to our run, but Elysia stops long enough to implore me. "But not the baby?" Elysia begs. "Please don't let her be destroyed."

I feel huge relief. Elysia cares. "Aidan's taking care of it." She places a hasty kiss on my cheek. "Earlier today, I found out that Aidan's alive. I was so excited to come here and tell you. Then all hell broke loose."

We resume running. "Almost there!" Elysia cries out. But just as we reach the wing where the FantaSphere is situated, an explosion rips across the FantaSphere walls.

The FantaSphere room is obliterated. The room's white walls are cracked, the ceiling is caved in, and debris smolders around the periphery. The hole in the ceiling exposes an open view to the clear solar panel roof on the next level.

Outside the roof, magenta-purple swirl clouds are forming in the sky.

This seems like an emergency to acknowledge, but Tahir and Tariq remain in heated conversation, acting like there's no need to evacuate the scene, because they have more immediate concerns to discuss.

"I won't take it!" Tahir yells at Tariq.

Bahiyya begs of him, "Tahir, let go of your father!"

Tahir's black eyes are fully dilated. He reaches his hands around Tariq's neck and strangles his father. "You can *never* make Elysia and me take Mimetic! EVER!"

Tariq sputters, "It could be the cure for your Awfuls!"

"We won't be manipulated by you any longer! I HATE you, Father! Everything you stand for. Profit for suffering. I won't be part of it any longer!"

Tariq fights for breath as Tahir's hands squeeze harder. Elysia makes no attempt to stop Tahir. Her eyes, too, have gone black. I start to lunge toward Tahir to stop this madness, but Bahiyya lunges ahead of me, trying to insert herself between her husband and her cloned son. "Have mercy, Tahir! Please, I beg you! Let him go!"

"Let *us* go!" Tahir sneers at Tariq.

"Go!" Tariq manages to gasp. "I'll authorize the cargo plane evacuating the ReplicaPharm personnel to allow you and Elysia on board."

Tahir releases his grip. Tariq falls to the ground, struggling to regain his breath. Bahiyya runs to Tariq, dropping to the ground to cradle and kiss her husband's head. "What have you done, Tahir?" she exclaims, tears running down her face. "You are like that monster Ivan!"

This is the worst name to invoke to Tahir. "I could never be like Ivan, Maman! NEVER!"

How does one delicately step into a heated family melt-down? One doesn't do it delicately. "We need to leave!" I command. "NOW!"

But the family is not listening, too consumed by their own drama. Bahiyya weeps, telling Tahir, "You can't leave. You can't survive on your own."

Elysia says it. "We can. We will." She tries to grab Tahir away. "Let's GO!"

A lightning bolt from the magenta-pink cloud in the sky strikes the solar panel in the Fortesquieu compound, a direct hit. Before we have a chance to react, the walls and floors rumble. Too late.

This is the real earthquake. The big one.

34

"TAKE COVER!" I SCREAM, AND I RUSH BENEATH
a piece of wall that had fallen down from the FantaSphere.
The house shakes furiously. It sounds as if a giant freight
train is rumbling across the compound, ripping it apart. The
floor lifts and then cracks in dozens of pieces as the ceiling
caves in.

I see Tahir and Elysia running for cover, but a wall
falls behind them, and I can't see where they're going, or if
they've fallen beneath the debris.

I've experienced death on the high seas, and it was not
nearly as terrifying as this. The shaking goes on for a minute that feels like ten, protracted and agonizing.

When it's over, I emerge from beneath the crushed wall
that had given me cover and see that the ceiling crumbled
directly over Tariq and Bahiyya, trapping them. I hear her

screams and try to lift the rubble covering her body. "Tariq is dead," she moans. "I can feel him against me."

"I'm trying to get you out," I say.

"Save yourself," says Bahiyya. "I can't go on any longer. Everything precious to me is gone. Let me die here."

Bahiyya closes her eyes. She's not dead yet. But she will be any minute. This is her peace. This is how she wants to go, cradling her beloved.

I allow her that choice, and make my own escape.

Breathless, bloodied, and bruised, I navigate my way out of the ruined house and find my way back into the open air. The smoke of fires across the island billows overhead as the night sky broadcasts the next message. In case there are still any remaining humans left who are deciding whether to evacuate or fight, a bright visual display beams across the dark sky, showcasing a live aerial feed of the island perimeter. From miles outside Io's ring, a tsunami is forming. A countdown clock appears next to the feed, giving a ten-minute warning of the tsunami's approach to Demesne. The tsunami will wipe out whatever structures haven't already been destroyed by the earthquake. This land will go back to what it was once. Raw. Wild.

I reach the landing pad. The Aviate is on its side, tipped and crushed by the impact of the quake. Tahir and Elysia emerge from behind the cuvées. They run to me, grabbing me in a group hug. "You lived!" Elysia cries.

I separate from their embrace. "There's that. Unfortunately, we've lost our escape transport."

As if the feed of the tsunami in the sky isn't bizarre

enough, an even stranger sight appears: Dementia's Zeppelin spaceship house. Flying low, it passes over the strip of fallen cuvée torchflowers, scattering coral-red petals across the air, then lands at the cliff's edge of the Fortesquieu property.

"Except for the flying house," Tahir says.

We run to the Zeppelin, a hatch opens, and a rope ladder drops down. Xander climbs down from it, and then at the doorway, two android soldiers appear, flanking the Governor on either side. They throw him to the ground.

Xander tells us, "I promised the Governor he could kill Elysia."

ELYSIA
35

I SHOULD BE USED TO DEATH AND DESTRUCTION on Demesne by now. Is this how the rest of the world is?

We just barely survived a monster earthquake—and now the Aquine is handing me over to the Governor for execution?

"How could you?" I scream at Xander. To be so betrayed when freedom finally, miraculously, looms is an Aquine's most unexpected, cruel revenge.

"You said you didn't want my protection," says Xander. The Governor stands up from his fall and immediately charges toward me, blinded to anything or anyone else in his line of fire. Xander adds, "But I'm not worried. This one's my parting gift for you, Elysia."

Wild winds from the approaching tsunami blow so hard I can barely stand my ground. Zhara screams, but mighty

Xander holds her back. "Let Elysia have this one," he says. "Let her be so Awful, she is cured."

I'm not Awful. I'm a coward. I bolt, running away toward the cliff's edge, while Tahir tries to follow but falls on a piece of debris. "You ruined me," the Governor fumes, following me. "Now I will ruin you, once and for all."

I stop at the cliff's edge, with nowhere left to hide, taking a last look out over the cliff, trapped. Once, from the cliff at Governor's House, I dove for freedom, only to find that leap was just a temporary escape from Demesne. Whatever happens now, I know this is the last time I will have this view over Demesne. I can't wait for it to be over.

The Governor lunges toward me, and I realize the last gift Xander has given me: equal opportunity. Just as the Governor is about to push me, I step aside. The Governor falls over the edge, delivering him to the same end he gave Xanthe, his Defect clone. I look over the cliff, just to be sure, watching his body roll down the jagged surfaces, relishing the sound of his screams, until he lands in the water and his mutilated body floats in the sea. I doubt Io's soothing waters feel so great when you're dead.

I'm not *proud*, but my chip does register *satisfaction*.

"Thank you, Xander," I say.

The sky has turned a dark gray as mighty storm clouds billow in deep purples above, a few shades darker than Io's violet ripples ringing the island below the cliff as the Governor's corpse bobs over its once-soothing waters. Orange fires and black smoke rise across the island. The entire vista is colored in a bruised palette, broken by the broadcast of a giant, dark blue wall of water moving toward Demesne from deep at sea, miles beyond Io's ring but moving fast, and rising. It's like the *gigantes* have formed together and built a super-wave of terror.

Tahir steps up into the Zeppelin as Dementia stands at the door hatch alongside Xander. "Amazing show my future Aquine husband put on tonight, right?" Dementia asks Tahir as she grins over at Xander.

"That's one way of looking at it," says Tahir.

Zhara stands on the ground next to me and offers me a hand to help me up the rope ladder.

"Are you coming?" I ask her.

"I'm staying," Zhara says. "As soon as you lift off, I'm going with the androids to the bunker below the Fortesquieu house. There's a tunnel linking it to Lusardi's old compound. I'll find Aidan there."

I feel weirdly *giddy*. Within minutes, all the properties on this island will likely be washed away. Good riddance. Within hours, hopefully, Zhara will be reunited with her other clone. The good man whom she loves.

She smiles—my smile, but so much brighter in this moment. "You'll take care of her?" I ask Zhara. She nods and in these last precious seconds together, our eyes share an understanding connected directly to our hearts.

"Hurry!" Tahir pleads as the night sky clock rolls to the two-minute tsunami warning.

Zhara makes me one last promise. "Her name will be Xanthe."

I hug her, and then I climb up the ladder into the strange flying house. Tahir and Xander hastily close the hatch door as Dementia welcomes me. "The Zeppelin wasn't built for long-distance travel. We'll be lucky to make it farther up the archipelago. Don't worry! We'll find some pirates to give us passage back to the world. Adventure, Elysia. It's yours now!" The Zeppelin lifts off the ground, shaking wildly as I look down through a window to wave good-bye to Zhara.

But Zhara's already gone, en route with the androids to Aidan and the Emergents and whatever will become of them.

While the Zeppelin flies away, my heart feels *content* and, for the first time, *whole*. I try to steal one last look at Demesne as our vessel bumpily ascends into the storm clouds. A layer of purple mist quickly shrouds the island, as if protecting our eyes from the Insurrection's final catastrophe about to happen.

My daughter is down there.

I don't know what will become of her Beta mother. Maybe I will survive my Awfuls, maybe Tahir and I will find a cure, and maybe we will live long, rich lives in the outside world that my daughter's First mother once told me was desolate and tarnished. I don't know what will become of Xanthe, what she will look like, or what kind of hybrid person she will be. I only know the one thing I could hope for her, she will have. She will emerge free.

ACKNOWLEDGMENTS

With love and unending thanks to all the amazing and dedicated people at Hyperion, particularly Emily Meehan, Suzanne Murphy, Stephanie Lurie, Simon Tasker, Dina Sherman, Andrew Sansone, Laura Schreiber, Jessica Harriton. Huge gratitude to the team at WME: Jennifer Rudolph Walsh, Laura Bonner, Alicia Gordon, Erin Conroy, Kathleen Nishimoto, Maggie Shapiro, Caitlin Moore, Matt Hudson; and to everyone at Depth of Field: Chris Weitz, Andrew Miano, Brenda Vogel, Lindsay Devlin. Thank you so much to all the international publishers for these books. Thank you, wonderful friends and family, for all the love and support: Patricia McCormick and Paul Critchlow, Norma and Gary Byrne, Jaclyn Moriarty, Melissa Kantor, Megan McCafferty, Melissa de la Cruz, Mara Cooper, Margie Strohecker and Mike Shaw, Leslie Margolis, Morgan Matson, Jordan Roter, Eva Vives and Pete Sollett, Andi Gitow, Megan Sanders, Anna Orchard, Martha Orchard. Lastly, thank you thank you thank you, dear readers. I love you all.